"You're a Beautiful Woman, Mara. . . ."

Mara felt a confusing mixture of pleasure and embarrassment. "I don't understand why you're here."

"Don't you really, Mara?" He laughed quietly.

"I'm leaving tomorrow," she reminded him, reminded herself. The earth was slipping out from beneath her.

"We're here now," Alex said, as he stepped across the threshold and in a single fluid motion scooped her into his arms. His mouth brushed against her lips, her neck, her collarbone, his breath urgent. Mara's thoughts came in scattered waves.

Wanting him was so easy. But to forget him would be torture.

JENNIFER WEST

spent half her life as a singer and dancer in the musical theater before turning her hand to writing. Between books, she takes time out to travel and later turns her real-life adventures into stories. She lives in Irvine, California, with her husband, son and two Akita dogs.

Dear Reader:

There is an electricity between two people in love that makes everything they do magic, larger than life. This is what we bring you in SILHOUETTE INTIMATE MOMENTS.

SILHOUETTE INTIMATE MOMENTS are longer, more sensuous romance novels filled with adventure, suspense, glamor or melodrama. These books have an element no one else has tapped: excitement.

We are proud to present the very best romance has to offer from the very best romance writers. In the coming months look for some of your favorite authors such as Elizabeth Lowell, Nora Roberts, Erin St. Claire and Brooke Hastings.

SILHOUETTE INTIMATE MOMENTS are for the woman who wants more than she has ever had before. These books are for you.

Karen Solem
Editor-in-Chief
Silhouette Books

Main Chance

Jennifer West

Silhouette Intimate Moments

Published by Silhouette Books New York

America's Publisher of Contemporary Romance

Silhouette Books by Jennifer West

Season of Rainbows (IM #10)
Star Spangled Days (IM #31)
Edge of Venus (IM #71)
Main Chance (IM #99)

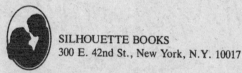

SILHOUETTE BOOKS
300 E. 42nd St., New York, N.Y. 10017

Copyright © 1985 by Jennifer West

Distributed by Pocket Books

ISBN: 0-373-07099-3

First Silhouette Books printing June, 1985

10 9 8 7 6 5 4 3 2 1

All of the characters in this book are fictitious. Any resemblance to actual persons, living or dead, is purely coincidental.

America's Publisher of Contemporary Romance

Printed in the U.S.A.

For my son, John . . .
to remind him
that every moment of his life
contains a new main chance.

Chapter 1

IT WAS MIDAFTERNOON AND PRACTICALLY DESERTED ON
St. Charles Avenue when the streetcar came to a stop. The
few passengers aboard watched listlessly as a single
woman in skirt and heels, carrying a battered old suitcase,
stepped down to the pavement.

She was young and slender, with a delicate face made
even smaller by the thick mass of pale hair falling loose to
her shoulders. For a moment she looked around her, the
deep blue eyes unsure.

The sun found her at once. It hurled down a ray of
blasting heat, as if warning her, a newcomer, of its
supremacy. Dragging the suitcase along, she took shelter
in the shade beneath a gnarled oak.

It had been front-page news: For ten days straight, the
sun had blistered the city of New Orleans, causing
sensible people to put off all but the most necessary of
errands. Even social engagements were surrendered to the
night, when the heat was less punishing to bodies and

temperaments, and after erratic power brown-outs had crippled air-conditioning systems, many workers were not bothering to leave home. No one could predict when the hellish weather would end.

Fishing into her skirt pocket, Mara Kozinski felt for the small white square of paper she had brought with her from Ohio. The address on it was already committed to memory. During the train ride, she must have looked at it two hundred times, at least. Other than the address and the letter she had received two weeks before, there was no other tangible aspect to her improbable journey.

She thrust the paper back into her pocket and lifted her suitcase. A block down St. Charles Avenue, the streetcar was already gliding away. Momentarily hypnotized by the phenomenon, she watched it dissolve into a shimmering fluid apparition. For an instant it was no more than a waving line of light, and then, seeming to disappear into itself, it vanished.

She started forward in the same direction. The weight of the suitcase made her list slightly to the right. Periodically she would have to set the suitcase down and steady herself. A dog barked, a bird hopped from a motionless branch. Other than that, all was quiet as she continued on her way again.

Looking up at the large houses, she imagined secret eyes watching her from windows and forced herself to stare back. A gesture of defiance was always an effective antidote to fear.

She knew what they would see, those curious phantom observers. They'd see a young woman in an inexpensive blue skirt and sleeveless print blouse; a young woman out in the stunning heat with the same shoulder bag used during the dead of an Ohio winter, the purse flapping counterpoint to her uneven stride, which in turn was caused by an old suitcase whose sides were held together more by hope than by material substance.

But it was a nice walk anyway, and in a while she paid more attention to her surroundings, the imaginary onlookers and the heat fading from her mind.

Her path was a double avenue where stately live oaks fanned over the properties they shaded. The homes were all enormous, spaced in polite distance from each other, and to Mara they appeared both forbidding and mysteriously inviting in their aloof serenity. There was a scent to the air, that of flowers and timelessness, a pervading impression that this enchanted place existed unconnected to any other reality but its own.

She stopped, at last at her destination. The address, in her mind for days on end, was suddenly transposed into solid, engraved numerals on an iron plaque. The sign itself was lodged in the center of a wrought-iron gate, beyond which a brick walk led to an imposing home, pristine white, with Grecian columns and a wide porch fronted with flowerbeds.

Gautier. Her tongue traced silently over the scrolled letters etched above the numbers of the address. She had puzzled over the correct pronunciation of the name since the day the letter had arrived.

"Mr. Gautier," she stated at the door, skating quickly over the name.

The woman in the black-and-white uniform did not bother to correct her. Nevertheless, Mara had seen through the woman's veiled expression: her version of "Gautier" was not the proper one.

After stating her business, Mara was left to wait in the silence of the expansive hall.

"Good afternoon."

The words came floating to her from above. Mara cast

her eyes to the top of the stairway. Following the graceful
curve of the banister down from the second-story landing
was a man so handsome he took her breath away.

He was dressed in white—white shirt, white pants—
against which the sparkle of black eyes danced all the
more dramatically.

"Alex Gautier," he said, holding out a tanned hand in
introduction. She took it awkwardly, felt his touch burn
between her fingers, and somehow found hers empty
again.

But her ears clung to the sound of his name. For a
moment it rang through her head like music. *Gaw-tee-ay,
Gautier,* she practiced silently.

"Did you have a good flight?"

"I took the train," she answered. He looked surprised.
"I could see more." It was also cheaper.

"I'm glad you decided to come," he went on easily,
and as he did she found each succeeding word entrancing,
so that whatever he was saying filtered through her
consciousness in the same way that the scent of unseen
flowers had invaded her senses. "It's always been my
feeling there's more grace to these types of legal matters
when they can be handled personally."

He took a short breath as he looked beyond to a room
off the main hall, and raising his eyebrows, said, "Shall
we have at it? The papers are all ready. Signing should
only take a few minutes of your time."

He started forward. She left her suitcase and went along
after him.

"The heat's made the city a dead zone. Damned
sorry," he muttered emphatically, but even that expression was cushioned by the soft inflection of his accent.
"Generally it's a great place to visit. Are you staying
long?"

Mara followed him into the room.

"Only tomorrow and part of the next day. Before the train leaves," she added.

"Too bad. It's a fascinating city."

"There's work," she explained, leaving out that she had barely enough money to stay the two nights. "It's hard to get away."

"I know how that can be," he said, and when he didn't ask what she did, she was relieved.

In her mind she could hear her friends' laughter, their voices strident and harsh as they sat around the lunchroom table crunching on chips and intermittently complaining about their weight. She saw herself among them, no better, no worse in reality, but suddenly, in her present surroundings, the connection to them made her embarrassed and somehow resentful of her origins. It was a snobbish thought and she was not a snob—she detested snobbery. And yet . . . Well, here in these surroundings, here with this man, she somehow did wish she were more.

"Please," he said, and she accepted his invitation to take an upholstered leather chair opposite his desk.

The room's furnishings, she saw, were a mixture of old things, polished antiques and Oriental carpets, and also of new modern pieces, like the chair in which she now sat. There was a framed certificate on the wall near the desk. Juris Doctorate. Georgetown University. A large potted palm was beneath, its dark green fronds tickling the bottom of the tortoiseshell frame. Around her, the air smelled wonderful—rich, of fine aromatic pipe tobacco, of expensive perfume left over from previous visitors.

Unexpectedly, just as the embarrassment had surprised her, a fierce wave of anger arose. She did not know from where it came, nor even why it had arisen, but she felt it intensely.

The inexplicable emotion must have registered outwardly as some physical distress. Alex Gautier rose urgently from his seat.

"The heat," he said. "And the humidity. When you're not used to it, it's like drowning in air. Let's get you something." His eyes, as softly black and serene as a calm midnight sky, had filled with sympathetic understanding.

She could drift in that sky forever. "I'm all right, really," she insisted.

He considered her statement and then shook his head. "Nope. I don't believe in taking chances." He made his way around the desk. Stopping beside her, and looking down to where she sat looking up at him, he said with exaggerated gravity, "The sad fact is, my life's already been severely scarred by fainting ladies. It seems like only yesterday," he mused. "I was eight and she was ten."

Mara smiled, and went along with the humor. "The heat?"

"A worm," he said, and laughed as if seeing it happen again. "I dangled it in front of her nose. An action, I'm afraid, that held grave consequences for everyone concerned. The young lady fainted. I almost had a heart attack, thinking I had done her in. For a moment the worm's life was held in the balance, but in the end it escaped unscathed. Therefore, I insist upon . . . water? No, something else," he amended, answering himself, and went immediately to the hall.

She heard him call out, "Anna?", listened as his footsteps faded into another region of the house, and then it was quiet except for the low whoosh of the cooling system pushing air through the vents. A grandfather clock ticked complacently in the corner.

She tried to relax, but couldn't. Her mind raced in

circles, trying to drag her along with it. But she wouldn't go. It was important that she stay firmly rooted in the present.

There were moments in life that were special; this was one of them. The moment she had seen him, seen Alex Gautier, she had known that a time like this was at hand.

When she had been young, many of those times had occurred in her life, unnoticed, unappreciated. Later, when she would think back upon them, it was with a sad longing to be able to return to that split second when the candles on her cake had been lit, or when her puppy first wriggled out of its cardboard box and into her arms. She wanted to capture those moments and keep them like pictures in the scrapbook of her heart.

So she breathed in deeply, looking around at everything, her mind imprinting the sights, the smells, the feel of the leather chair. Everything here was special, she thought, and accepted the fact that part of the reason was that everything here was a part of him. Later, for all its foolishness, she would want to remember exactly the way it had been.

Idly she wondered if he would ever think of her again. What would he have seen? What would he remember if . . . if . . . he had seen her at all?

She touched her fingers to her hair. It was still clinging to her neck and remained pasted to the sides of her face, with new, flyaway growths lying flatly defeated against her temple. The moist strands felt clammy against her skin. She lifted her hair, twining it into a ponytail, then thought better of it and let it fall loose again to just above her shoulders. When freshly washed, her hair was light, practically pure blond in color with very few brownish streaks; but at the moment her hair was darker, heavier. She had never considered herself a dramatic type in appearance, but on those relatively few occasions when she had experimented with makeup—wild makeup, not the pale, discreet, almost invisible colors she herself applied, but the kind fashion models wore in *Vogue*—a different face than the one she knew as her own had peered back at her from the mirror. The woman she had seen during these abandoned moments had frightened her. The deep eyes framed by powdered shadow appeared too blue, too knowledgeable, and seemingly contained secrets she herself did not know. And the mouth, parted and moist, had glistened provocatively under its coating of Tropic Red or Flame Spirit, the bold colors transforming whatever shape her lips took into a suggestive invitation.

Her attention returned to the present as Alex Gautier reappeared with two tall glasses.

"Anna was repotting a plant, so I took the liberty of preparing us both iced teas. In one woman, I've found a botanist, a chef, a housekeeper, and when I work at home, she's my receptionist, too."

He caught Mara's look.

"And nothing more." He smiled, handing her the iced tea. "You aren't the first to wonder."

He looked down at her a beat longer than the transfer of the glass required. It was a curious look, one that posed a question that seemed in the next instant to be resolved.

"Basically," he said, going back to his desk, "what we've got here is a fairly straightforward transaction. As explained in my letter, your uncle left his entire estate to you. The house and its contents, plus forty thousand dollars."

"I never even knew him," she interrupted. "It seems so strange to have him leave everything to me. There must have been someone else he cared about." It was a question. "Someone here in New Orleans."

Alex studied the papers. Without looking up, he offered, "Maybe they were gone."

"But he wasn't that old," Mara countered, thinking that the mood in the room had suddenly altered. "So you'd think there would have been someone. Usually there is."

"Usually, yes." Alex paused, as if he were going to add something, but he didn't. Instead he continued to explain what he referred to as stipulations of the will as applied to the contract.

Mara tried to pay attention. But she found the gentle cadence of his voice hypnotic in its appeal. It was a voice without hard edges or sudden detours of inflection, his tones flowing easily one into the other like the classical music she had studied in school . . . Debussy . . . Ravel. Her high-school class had been urged to listen beneath a piece's surface calm for the undercurrents of telling emotion as conveyed by the pulse of a cello or the droning, almost inaudible insistence of a bass guitar.

There, she had caught it, a quality of hard masculinity kept veiled by his outside charm; and another strain, too, that of fierce determination. Undetected, she had glimpsed into his soul. She felt as if she had stolen into a locked room holding forbidden treasures.

"The back taxes have been satisfied," he was saying, "and the property is free and clear of any liens."

Mara nodded. He continued on, explaining a clause here, what he called an "addendum" there, and at each questioning glance from him, she again nodded or gave a small sound of agreement without really having heard.

He was tall—she guessed six feet, two inches—and his shoulders were broad and square, but not like those of a muscle-bound oaf straining with weights all day long. Instead, his chest seemed to taper down to a slender waist, and although she tried not to think any further, an image of a hard flat stomach, of taut, powerful thighs, intruded into her thoughts.

A thin thread of desire shot up her back, and, surprised, she closed her eyes, drawing in a quick breath.

"Is anything the matter?" he asked.

Her eyes shot open. "What?"

"Are you all right?"

"Fine, yes," she said, and took a quick sip of her iced tea.

His head was tilted slightly to the side, the dark midnight eyes quizzical.

Under his scrutiny, her desire dissolved into embarrassment. If he were able to guess her thoughts . . . "The taxes and the . . . ?"

"Sorry," Alex said. "This is a bore, isn't it?"

"No. No, not at all."

"You should never try to lie," he said, smiling. "You're not very good at it. Since it's the bottom line that counts, and as you already know how much money you're getting, this formality was all a waste of time."

"It's why I came," she said, "to have things explained. So I'd know the exact situation, and there wouldn't be any questions later. As you said in your letter."

That wasn't it at all, and she hoped he was wrong when he said she shouldn't try to lie. She had come because she wanted to leave Ohio, to escape, at least for a brief time.

And as for the money, of course she wanted the money. Who wouldn't? But if she had to choose between the practicality of money and the sense of life she felt flowing through her every pore as she sat opposite Alex Gautier, she would not take money.

"Tad Engle was a fine man—what I knew of him," Alex said suddenly, disconnectedly. "I just thought you'd like to know," he added quickly in explanation. "So," Alex said, making a big point of gathering the papers together, "I think we can skip all the rest of the legal jargon."

Mara leaned forward. "What was he like?"

The barest frown creased Alex's forehead. He looked down to his papers briefly. When he brought his eyes up, he was calm, saying only, "To be totally honest, we weren't all that well acquainted personally."

"But you did know him, at least slightly?" Mara pressed.

"Only slightly."

"But you'd rather not discuss him. For some mysterious reason . . ." She didn't mean to be offensive. Only she couldn't help fishing for more information. She felt cheated. It was like receiving a wonderful present and not knowing from whom it came.

With seeming effort, Alex looked across to her. "My father had been your uncle's attorney. It was only when my father passed on that I took over on his behalf. I really wasn't all that well acquainted with him personally."

"There was a scandal or something, wasn't there? Something a long time ago?"

A flicker of light passed swiftly behind Alex's black eyes. "Umm," he said, the response too casual, Mara thought. "There was some ancient business, I recall."

"What was it?" she asked. "The ancient business?"

Alex hesitated. He was leaning slightly over his papers, but when she persisted, he relaxed contemplatively into his chair, like a storyteller about to begin. But instead, an unfocused expression of sadness passed through his eyes as he looked about the room. When the direction of his glance shifted to her, she did not feel that he was seeing her, but that she had become someone else in his mind.

A thought appeared in his eyes like a bright flame, and she shivered slightly, certain that in some way her presence was the catalyst for his troubled vision.

Alex's eyes refocused, and he was back with her. "History," he said, "belongs to the past."

"But we learn from history."

They understood each other. He was trying to be polite, telling her to back off because whatever she wanted to know, he wasn't going to tell her. And she was being as nervy as a person could be who was no match for his educated intellect, but who wanted to find out information that had been kept from her all during her childhood.

"History is relevant when it has application to the present. Otherwise, it's superfluous," Alex said. Sensing correctly that she was about to object, he quickly turned his attention back to the papers. "As you agreed in your letter, the house should be placed on the market for sale. It needs some renovating, but it's still a valuable piece of property." He looked up again. "I don't mean to sound negative, but I may as well be honest. It could take a while to unload it. Homes aren't that easy to market lately. As in your part of the country, New Orleans has seen greener days."

"My part of the country has never been green. It's always been gray." Her answer was stated with such vehemence that Alex looked at her in surprise. Even she was startled by the declamation.

"You really hate it there."

"Yes." And that too was emphatic. The single word rang in her consciousness true and clear. It was as if she had been carrying a weight around but had never known it. With the admission out, she felt lighter, unburdened. She even laughed as she freely admitted, "I despise it."

"But you stay anyway?"

The laughter faded. "Umm . . . yes," she said. "Yes, I

stay." *Like everyone there stays*, she thought, and the weighted feeling was back again.

She had never even considered leaving. To actually carve out some other alternative to her present life had never occurred to her in a concrete sense. The alien thought was frightening, but also vaguely exciting.

"But why?" he asked. "If you don't like it . . ."

"It's the way things are where I come from. People settle."

"Some people don't. Your uncle. He got out."

Alex looked regretful at having volunteered the statement. But Mara took the slip as an opening.

"He did," she said wondrously, a kind of pride at his accomplishment filling her. "And believe me, they didn't like it, either."

"I don't think that mattered to him," Alex said quietly.

They were looking at each other then, truly looking, as if both of them had found the same thought at the same time. This time Alex Gautier did not back off from her unvoiced question.

"Yes," he said, "you're like him. You remind me of him."

"How?" she asked, breathless, realizing that this was what she had wanted to know all along. Was there some magical psychic link, through genes or personality, between that romantic, daring rogue of a man who had escaped his destiny, and herself, a prisoner locked within a cage?

Alex studied her. "The eyes," he concluded almost dismissively, as if he didn't want to look beyond the superficial.

"But he had brown eyes, like my mother's. She had an old picture from when they were young."

Alex shook his head. "No, it's not in the color. It's not even in the shape," he said softly, as if picturing

Thadeous Engle a long time ago. Reluctantly he said,
"There's a restlessness . . . a rebelliousness."

"Me, restless? Rebellious!" She laughed, but beneath
the disclaimer, she was pleased. She was also nervous,
upset in the way of a person who finds out something has
been going on behind his back for a long time without his
knowing it. She was going on behind her own back.

She *was* restless. A part of her was screaming to get
out, not just physically to leave Ohio, but her soul needed
to fly free. "You aren't wrong," Mara said softly. "At
least not about wanting to . . . to do something."

He smiled, at first only a bit. Then, as if he were
watching something amusing or something beautiful un-
fold before his eyes, he smiled totally.

For an instant, although she knew she had not moved
but was sitting erect, even rigid, in the chair, she felt
herself falling into an other-worldly space. The house was
forgotten, her uncle unimportant. She danced in that
smile, tumbled in the light from that radiant smile. It was a
perfect mouth, the lips finely delineated, yet generous,
over teeth that shone with the same white brilliance of his
shirt.

And suddenly he was speaking again. . . . She tumbled
out of the smile.

"If you'd care to sign . . . Wherever there's an X." He
was handing her the papers, along with a fountain pen.

His manner was professional. She was both relieved
and disappointed. The fantasy had been very nice. A little
dangerous, but still nice.

Standing, he said, "I'll call Anna to witness the
signature."

Appraising him as he moved across the room, she
guessed his age to be mid-thirties. His hair, which was
almost blue-black, was free of gray. The sharp jawline
contained a hint of a cleft at the chin, and the nose was

straight and narrow. It was a face of finely etched elegance, masculine, but without the harsh crudeness that characterized so many of the men she had known and at one time or another considered attractive.

It hurt her to look at him. He was so impossibly out of her reach.

Turning her head away, she stared at the grandfather clock as it struck four, the papers she was to sign lying forgotten in her lap. Each separate chime seemed to summon forth a scene from the recent past.

It was only two weeks ago that she had received the letter from Alex Gautier that had prompted her trip from Ohio to New Orleans. It was her letter, addressed to her, meant for her; yet, like everything else, her entire family took the matter up as if she and they were a single entity.

"We'll get Anthony Russo to look it over. You can close the deal from here. Tony can send a letter," said her father, putting Alex Gautier's letter down beside his dinner plate. Tony had gone all through school with her father and mother. He was an attorney and was perceived, at least on her parents' side, as practically a member of the family. Maybe once a year he'd come for dinner, that was really all.

"No," Mara had replied, and everyone—her father, her mother, her younger brother and two older brothers (one home on leave from the service, the other married but visiting while his wife was in the hospital, having given birth to their third child)—had stared at her as if she had spoken a profanity.

"I want to go to New Orleans," Mara said. She looked down at her plate.

"Your father said Tony Russo can handle it."

"I want to go, Momma. The letter said that it would be good for me to see the property myself. It said—"

Her father's beefy steelworker fist had come down hard

on the table. "I know what it said. Didn't I just read it?
But what I said is, no. No. Pass the cabbage here."

"There's no good reason for me not to go," Mara
persisted.

"You'll lose work. You want to lose out on work?
You've got overtime coming, and—"

Mara's chair made a squealing noise on the kitchen
linoleum as she pushed herself up. Time stopped. Standing, trembling, she faced the circle her family made
around the table. "I don't care about overtime. I'm sick of
that job. It's miserable and boring and dumb, and I don't
want to spend my life that way."

Her father raised his bulky mass out of his chair. His
expression was dark. "What are you, a movie star? Some
people are glad to have a job. They thank the good Lord
for work."

She was on the verge of tears. She felt not that she was
battling for a trip, but for her very life. She couldn't back
down. Her voice was someone else's. Thin, it nevertheless came out in a determined rush. "I spend all day on
the line, all day doing one thing. I wipe the right-front
fender of cars that come off the assembly track. One after
the other they come, all looking alike. You think that's so
great? This is my life . . . *my life*. I don't want to spend it
like that. I want something more."

"It's good enough for your friends," her mother said
nervously. "Michelle and Loretta and—"

"But it's not what I want, it's not good enough for
me." Her mother never took her side. She had always
hovered in the larger shadow cast by Mara's father, and
always before, Mara had accepted that state of their
relationship as being an immutable fact of life. But now,
suddenly, she resented not having any support from this
single other female in a family of men.

"I want more out of life," Mara said. "Can't you

understand?'' Pleadingly she looked at her mother, whose fingers fidgeted nervously with her napkin. Mara swept her gaze around to the other sullen and stunned faces. "Didn't anyone here ever want more than this?'' she asked in a tense whisper. ''Want more than what you've got here? Didn't you ever just want to—''

"You can go to your room,'' her father said. He was still standing.

"—to live . . . to feel?'' she went on.

"I said to your room.''

"I'm twenty-five.''

"You live in my house.'' His tone was threatening and prideful.

For a split instant they faced each other, father and daughter. A white anger born of injustice filled her. It radiated outward from her eyes to his, which were round and dark with fury; not at her, she understood, but with rage and dismay at the familiar world which had shifted beneath his feet, her defiance symptomatic of his helplessness.

Certainly, she now lived under his roof. But there was more to it, more apparently than he wanted to remember. She had moved out when she was twenty-one, had lived in her own apartment since then, and had only returned to live under her parents' roof five months ago at her mother's request. Her father had been off work for the past six months from the Youngstown steel plant which had employed him for twenty-eight years. Half the town was out of work. No one knew if those on layoff would be recalled, ever. It had been at her mother's confidential request that Mara returned to board with them. The two hundred and fifty dollars Mara contributed each month, ostensibly for her living expenses, actually allowed for meat at every meal. Most important, the supplemental income protected her father from the cultural shock rocking the tender egos of other men who were unable to provide for the accustomed necessities and small luxuries making up their otherwise bleak existence.

The anger faded from her as she saw past her father's impossibly self-righteous facade, saw through to his frightened desperation. Leaving his pride intact, Mara had backed away then, allowing the past, with its tenuous status quo, to survive at least another day.

On the way up the stairs, she had stopped. Looking down at them through the open doorway, she saw them as a small company of actors with whom she had spent many seasons doing the same play. A part of her being stayed with them, playing out the continuing melodrama that had been her life, and that would continue to be her life unless she broke free.

They were her family. But at that moment, seeing them there, knit so tightly together in their smug prejudice, she broke from her detachment and for an instant hated them as much as she loved them, with equal and passionate intensity.

So she had left home on a Saturday morning.

Although it was summer, the day had been gray and forlorn. Michelle drove her to the train station. Her father had left home early that morning to help a friend repair a travel trailer; it meant he didn't have to face her defection. But her mother had ridden along. At the station, they hugged each other.

"You have a good time," her mother said, and there were tears in her eyes.

"Come along!" Mara said impulsively, gripping her mother's hands.

A brief light came into her mother's eyes, then faded away behind a wall of complacency. "You have a good time," she said again.

"I'm just going for a few days. It's not like I'm leaving home."

Her mother had looked at her strangely then. "We want the best for you."

"I know you do, Mama."

"And your father, he does, too."

Mara had nodded in mute acceptance of the statement, knowing there were qualifiers to that goodwill.

Her father was jealous of anyone who wanted out of the gray existence he led. The sooty drabness of the steel town clung to the buildings and speckled the line-hung wash, but most of all it contaminated the human spirit.

In the whole known history of Mara's family, it was only Tad Engle, her mother's brother, who had dared to escape. He had never looked back, either, except to write Mara's mother during the years he sailed around the world as a merchant seaman. He had settled in New Orleans, establishing an import-export business, and that, too, had thrived. From the little Mara had heard of him, he was a romantic, daring figure, as unlike her father as a diamond was to a piece of coal. Tad Engle had elected to leave her what remained of his estate. She didn't know why, really. Perhaps it was because she was the only female child in the family; perhaps it was because it was too late for Mara's mother, and by proxy Mara would be expected to fulfill some unresolved familial destiny as seen through her uncle's eyes.

As the train pulled out from the station, Mara watched her mother's form become a speck. But instead of the anticipated sense of loss or fear or guilt, Mara experienced a rush of exhilaration. Just for an instant she felt a sense of kinship to her uncle that went beyond the property he had left her. She was getting out, going somewhere, if only for a few days. . . .

The fourth and last chime of the grandfather clock was just fading as Alex returned with Anna.

Mara placed the papers on the desk. She found the first X, and raised the pen to sign. Alex was seated again; Anna stood off to her right.

"No," Mara said. She put the pen down.

Alex looked disturbed, as if his worst fears had just manifested. "You came all this way to sign, and now you say 'No'?"

She looked at him. "I want to see my uncle's house first. I want to see my house," she amended.

"Mara . . ." Alex almost sighed. "It's an old place. It needs a lot of work."

"I didn't say I was going to move in. All I want to do is see it."

"Why?" he asked, and he sounded almost angry.

"I don't know," she answered truthfully. "But why don't you want me to see it?" she asked him, sounding almost angry herself.

And when he said, "I don't know," she knew that Alex Gautier wasn't speaking honestly.

Chapter 2

THE ROOM WAS FIFTY-SIX DOLLARS A NIGHT AND IT didn't even have air conditioning. When Mara registered surprise, actually dismay, at the room's cost, the manager, a woman of about fifty with flame-red hair and puffy lids over watery brown eyes, rasped that there was a convention in town and if Mara didn't want the room, it was no skin off her back. A hundred other people would be glad to fork over the money to stay in the Quarter.

"It ain't old, honey, it's charm."

So Mara paid in advance for one night, convinced that the room would no doubt go quickly to someone else agreeable to overlooking the truth, the truth being that the place was a ramshackle dump devoid of any quality even remotely resembling charm.

Clearly the hotel had once been a single-family residence. Situated at the farthest reaches of the French Quarter, it was a narrow stucco building with only a door and a single window facing the street on the ground level. Mara's room was located on the second floor, at the end of a narrow, dark corridor smelling faintly of fish and onions and tomatoes.

But she didn't really care. In fact, given her present state of mind, the alley, seen from her window, was as good as a flowering garden. Her life had changed, all in one miraculous afternoon.

There were things to look forward to, places she had not seen and events that were not predictable. Tomorrow she would not be punching a time clock, but seeing a house—her house. And closely linked to that house was another new element in her life: the man who would be showing it to her. Alex. Alex Gautier.

The sound of his name was beautiful, masculine and lyrical, the combination of letters magically capturing his elegance, his strength, his mystery. Alex Gautier. She whispered the name aloud, and a tiny thrill traveled through her as his image became more solid in her mind. Hugging herself, she imagined the feel of his hands on her bare arms. "Alex," she whispered again. She closed her eyes to keep in the sweet happiness filling her. It was Christmas morning again and she was a child just before arising to open her presents. It was the afternoon of her first real date when she was sixteen years old, jittery and euphoric with anticipation. It was this day, a few hours before, and she was seeing Alex Gautier for the first time as he came down the stairs with his eyes laughing, his smile so dazzling that to think of that image even now, after the fact, made her faint with longing to . . .

To make love.

The moment she thought it, she flushed with embarrassment.

She was nuts, that's what. It was stupid. To even think

of having a real relationship with him was preposterous. The man was a god. Or might just as well be one. He was a handsome, charming, well-to-do attorney. Probably a leading citizen, to boot. He'd have a thousand women after him. If he hadn't married yet, it was because his choices were limitless.

He had even been too busy that evening to show her the property she had inherited. But she couldn't necessarily blame his reluctance on other women. It was clear he hadn't wanted to take her at all, no matter what the date or time of day.

But the bottom line, using Alex's term, was that he was in fact taking her to see the home tomorrow morning. Their appointment was scheduled for ten o'clock.

And that, she told herself, would be that—the tour, the accompanying suggestion that she should sign the papers authorizing the property's sale, the signing of the papers, the brief handshake between them. Then he would fade from her life as surely as the streetcar had dissolved into the mist of St. Charles Avenue.

In three more days she would be back in Ohio, standing before the time clock, punching in. Alleys would look like alleys and not like gardens. And the men she would date would take her bowling and talk about football or who was on tap for rehire or layoff. And knowing all this, she suddenly wished that she had never received Alex Gautier's letter in the mail, and maybe in a way she wished that she had never even been born, if this was to be her life.

In keeping with her mood, the sun had dipped lower. From her place at the window she watched the shadows shift against the roofs of nearby buildings, noticed the gradations of color as the waning light shimmered against brick and stucco walls, some painted pink or light green, gold and blue, along with colors too original for her to name with authority. It was a strangely quiet time, and she could feel the transition of day into evening. Suddenly, almost magically, Mara sensed an imperceptible change to the atmosphere.

Night. Like a splendid, mysterious being, it had entered the French Quarter. She would shower and change, and then she would see what it had brought her.

After all, she was not yet home . . . she was still in paradise, where anything might happen.

His name was Roland LaPierre, but he was called "King" by the press and by those whose condition of social privilege brought them into contact with the ruling force of the Crescent City. King LaPierre wore his name well, just as he wore his diamond studs well and his silk suit costing eight hundred dollars, made last year in Hong Kong to conform to his 280-pound girth and six-foot frame. For years he had ruled the city in one way or the other, either under the table or aboveboard through more conventional legal channels. But, whichever way, it was King who presided over every major decision that was to affect the city's economic or cultural or political base.

"We have need for a good man as D.A.," King said, his voice soft as silk, a trail of smoke following on his words, as if, thought Alex Gautier, who listened at his side, a dragon had issued a decree. In his hand, brandished now and then for effect, was a five-dollar cigar.

"Fresh blood," added one of the other listeners, an oil man whose company had been the beneficiary of King's clout in helping to lift some annoying ecological restraints imposed by the state government some years before. When he became one of the richest men in America, he was happy to return favors, especially as King LaPierre might at any moment choose to rescind his political largess.

"A new face is always welcome with the public," King said, sweeping the cigar in an arc to include the three hundred guests attending his party that evening. "When the political arena becomes stale, we have a bored public. A disinterested public is a dangerous public, gentlemen. Our fellow citizens become unruly and unpredictable. Better to shape our friends' opinions than to let scraggly ideas and half-baked notions of how things are or could be or will be, formulate and ferment in untidy minds."

Alex and the other four men standing in the circle understood. It was the King's way to announce his intentions casually. It was a clever strategy, one which Alex had noted some years earlier when he had first been introduced to King. King always spoke in the softest of tones, and his greatest pronouncements were filtered through the most seemingly banal of conversations. His method, therefore, had the effect of making listeners cling to his every syllable, for in a single throwaway utterance their demise or fortune could be sealed.

Alex took a swallow of his Scotch and water. He was too wise to show emotion at King's announcement that he had been chosen to be the city's next district attorney.

The talk shifted easily to other topics. King proposed construction of a new levee to thwart the Mississippi from claiming the city; one of the men present owned a construction firm. The cigar was waved through the air once again, a diamond ring on King's small finger winking like a shiny conspiratorial eye beneath the lights.

An hour later, Alex faced LaPierre across a sound-proofed study that New Orleans' foremost citizen had swept weekly for traces of electronic bugs.

"We can talk freely," said LaPierre, his voice less soft

now that there was no need for dramatic artifice. "What do you think of my proposal?"

"It's no secret I've been planning on running for D.A.," Alex replied evenly.

LaPierre rocked back on his heels. "They call me the King Maker."

"Yes," Alex said. "I'm aware of that."

"Title's justified, son."

"I don't want to be owned," Alex said bluntly.

King LaPierre's eyes narrowed to slits, became lost in the folds of his fleshy face. "I am aware of your family's history, son. So I know what this position would mean to you. The Gautier name could rise again out of the ashes created by your father's foolishness. He lost everything, your father. The man was a giant in this state. Why, anyone knows he could have been governor of Louisiana. Easily. And who knows, from there, where he could have gone. But he swam against the tide, defending that man and woman. He went against his own class. A grave, grave error of judgment. High principles are for children in school to read about. Men who are going to run things, who can effect real changes and not blow rhetoric into the wind, can't afford such ideological luxuries. You think about it, son. You're tough and you're good. You've got the face I want to see on my fliers and billboards. You've got yourself a good name already. You can finish what your father abandoned to idealism. You're my man, no doubt about it. What you have to decide is, am I going to be your friend or your foe. I have need of a man of my own in that spot. If not you, then . . ." He broke off, the unfinished sentence meant to be completed by Alex, who of course understood perfectly.

"There's one other thing," LaPierre said abruptly. "My daughter. Christina's a beautiful young woman. She's twenty-eight. Good Eastern school education. An intelligent girl, as you already know. Fine horsewoman. Excellent hostess.''

''Christina's all of those things, yes,'' Alex said, understanding where the topic was heading and not wanting it to go any further.

''And my daughter's in love with you. You didn't know that, did you?''

Alex had been uneasy before, but that was nothing compared with his current discomfort. ''We're friends.''

''Friends! You've seen each other for five years.''

''As friends.''

''Umm.'' LaPierre stared reflectively at Alex. ''Well, don't answer now. Take your time, let your mind chew on it.'' The audience was over. The King stubbed out a barely smoked cigar, took another one from a humidor on a table, lit that one, and moved past Alex without another glance.

For an instant, Alex almost gave in to the urge to call LaPierre back. He would tell him to take his offer and smoke it along with his cigar. Both smelled foul. But he didn't, because King was also right in some of the things he said. Idealism was like a mighty sword having the power to cut and slash for the common good. But a man strong enough to wield that sword was necessary. Alex needed the position of D.A. to accomplish the most good for the most people. His father had forfeited that same chance in order to defend the honor of one woman. As far as the issue of Christina LaPierre was concerned, that was an open-and-shut case. She was, indeed, all of the things LaPierre claimed. But he, too, had spoken truthfully. From his side, at least, they were only friends. He had never slept with her, although the option had clearly been there for him; why he had never exercised it, he couldn't say. Maybe a premonition.

Ten minutes later, as the valet brought his car to the

front of King LaPierre's house, Alex still had not decided if the price of one man's personal honor was worth sacrificing for the good he could do a thousand men.

At the foot of the drive he passed an old magnolia, its branches twisted, partially rotting from the looks of it. But the flowers were white and full in the moonlight. Beauty had thrived. Only, he was not a tree.

Mara had never before seen such activity at one o'clock in the morning. Bourbon Street teemed with people taking up the street, the sidewalks, hanging over balconies of private dwellings above public establishments, and from the verandas of hotels.

Several times that night she had caught herself foolishly turning to see if a tall man in a white suit might have been Alex. It was soon evident that there were many tall men in the French Quarter, and that many of them wore white suits. But even so, her mind did not for long leave her reflections on Alex Gautier. The high cheekbones of one man, the laughing dark eyes of another, the graceful swing of a masculine arm—all were reminders of the one incomparable Alex Gautier.

A man would accidentally brush against her, jostled by the crowd, and she would burn for minutes after, letting her mind run with the fantasy that it had been Alex's touch. She would pretend as she walked alone among the couples who passed by, laughing and talking, that Alex was there by her side. If he were not with her physically, then mentally, emotionally, she had captured his essence.

A brightly lit tourist shop selling garish T-shirts and Western hats displayed mass-produced voodoo dolls guaranteeing satisfaction in love and wealth and health, and also on the darker side, recommended an application for vengeance. For fun, Mara purchased a doll for $2.50. She did not believe in magic. She was not superstitious. But then again, she often wished upon the first star she saw on any clear, silent night. She tucked the doll inside her purse, silently ordering it to "Bring me Alex Gautier."

Earlier in the evening she had stopped at a sidewalk café to try what the menu listed as barbecued crab fingers, along with warm French bread and two glasses of white wine to wash down the hot sauce. It was impossible that she could be drunk, yet her head reeled in pleasant sensation from the stimulus of music and lights, from the mingling smells of perfume and fish and praline candy, and from the crush of raucous humanity carrying her along in their stream of levity. Some of the bars where jazz groups played Dixieland or blues boasted they had never closed down in over fifty-four years, remaining open night and day.

As for Mara, her soul might have been willing to carry on until dawn, but her feet argued otherwise. Half-limping, she took what she assumed would be shortcuts down less populated side streets, aiming in the direction of her hotel.

She was blocks from the boisterous crowds of Bourbon Street, and had grown accustomed to the quiet. The only sounds were her heels on the pavement and now and then the agitated yap of a dog from a window as she passed by. Spaced at farther distances than those on the major commercial thoroughfares, streetlamps glowed serenely, their light becoming more diffused as patches of fog collected.

A lone contralto voice, plaintive and intimate, drifted through the night toward Mara.

Mara stopped, listening, not so much to the music as to the emotion filling each succeeding note as it rose and fell, building a haunting pattern of melody and human pathos.

Following the sound, she stopped on the opposite side of the street, where in a squat frame building whose single sign over the open door proclaimed "Beer, Oysters, Wine" in hand lettering, the singer could be seen. Mara stood motionless in the dark, fascinated. Through the open door she saw the woman's lank, slender form braced against the back of an upright piano being played by a young bearded man. Her elbows rested against the piano's top, and her head was bent as she sang. Now and then, as if remembering something, the woman would raise her head to stare into the distance, as if seeing backward into time.

Her face was beautiful, classic and ageless, but the exquisite eyes were ancient green tidepools reflecting an eternity of grief.

Mara was fascinated. She forgot her aching feet. She forgot the time, and even where it was that she stood, as she listened. The woman finished another song, and with a gesture asked for a cigarette from her accompanist. He lit it from his own, and handed it to her. She took a long drag from it, then a drink from the glass on the piano's top, and drifted out of Mara's view, the amazing performance concluded.

By the time Mara returned to her hotel, the fog had dissipated. It was now still and hot outside, the humidity suffocatingly close.

She lay unclothed on the bed, the room's single window open wide.

Closing her eyes did nothing to still the restless wanderings of her mind, nor did shifting her position from side to side, to her back, to her stomach—anything to quiet the stirrings of her body.

She sat up, and in the moonlight which seemed to come and go at short intervals, she saw her reflection in the dresser's oval mirror. In shadow her breasts were full and high, pushing out from her small rib cage, which tapered to a slender waist and the graceful flare of rounded hips.

How would she appear to Alex? she wondered, and instinctively touched herself, as if he had answered her. Her hand traced up from the undercurve of her breast to the full roundness peaked by her nipple. A hot rush sped through her, and she shuddered both from pleasure and from agitation. Finally unable to stand her mind's wanderings, she gave a small moan and caved inward, crossing her arms across her chest and hugging herself.

If this night he had been with her, if he had said to her that afternoon, "Spend the evening with me," would she now be with him in his bed?

She looked down at the empty place beside her and stroked the sheet as if it were his back. Even in the steaming night air, she knew his skin would be cool and silken. She could imagine the muscular curve of his body lying languorously beside hers. If she were to bend to him, her breasts would rest against his skin, and feeling her, he would turn and take her.

How would it be? she wondered. How would it feel to be beneath him? She wanted him to be gentle, and also to be fierce. She wanted him to see her as she was now, not as an unsophisticated young woman come to call one day and gone from his life the next, but as a beautiful woman whose passion was an equal match for his own. Passion, passion, hot desire, the ache of wanting what was close enough to imagine having, but just out of reach, making the misery all that more acute.

Her body ignited. What was she doing? Empty thoughts, feelings with no outlet. Senseless torture.

She left the bed and without turning on the light in the bathroom pulled the shower curtain closed. The cold spray hit her like a harsh reprimand from a wise counselor to wake up to clear reason. But it made no difference, the need would not go away. Helpless to her cravings, she closed her eyes, letting her imagination take its own free course. Her hair streamed against her neck, touched her shoulders like the kisses she craved. Soaping herself, she writhed at the pleasure she took in pretending the fingers that coursed over her were those of a man whose dark laughing eyes had burned into her soul, and whose very memory now inflamed her body.

She did not dry herself, but returned coolly damp to the bedroom.

It was dark, the moon hidden by clouds. Unexpectedly, as she passed the dresser, a welcome breeze entered, lifting the sheer white curtains at the window's edge. Outside, a silver shaft of lightning flashed and held for a long second, illuminating her reflection in the mirror. The woman she saw looking back at her startled her. It was as if for the first time, she was truly seeing herself, not as she had been in the daylight, sitting meekly in her cotton skirt and blouse before the desk of Alex Gautier, but as the whole, complete woman that she was, who had a moment before thrown back her head in abandonment, gasping, as a flood of passion enveloped her.

"Alex," she whispered to the night, "want me tomorrow, want me. . . ."

Lying awake, she watched the lightning blaze across the heavens. It was silent and bright and brief. A brilliant explosion in time and space. There, and then gone. As if it had never been.

If he wants me, she asked herself, *even though it would be just for one time, one perfect, magnificent time, would I?*

And she answered herself, *Yes. Yes*, she said resignedly, and turning on her stomach, tried to stifle, in the cool linen of her pillow, the hot fantasies that spread like a blaze from her mind to her body.

Sometime, when there were no longer any sounds from the streets, and when she had drifted off to sleep, the rain began.

A rolling crash of thunder traveled like a train through her dim consciousness. Drowsy, she opened her eyes to a burst of white light filling the room. It could have been the sound of the mighty, trundling forces; it could have been the current in the air. But something larger than herself, yet a part of herself, connected with her soul.

She sat up. Her whole being was awake, charged with a sense of life. She would not call it destiny, but as she stared beyond the small space she occupied on the bed, to the city lying beyond the window of her room, she knew that in this town she would find her chance.

It had been agreed that she would call Alex Gautier at ten o'clock A.M. to arrange for him to pick her up at whichever hotel she had chosen to spend her night in New Orleans.

The hotel had a single pay telephone in what served as its lobby. She dialed and waited, her heart thumping more loudly than the phone's ring. When Alex himself answered, it came as a surprise.

"This is Mara Kozinski," she said, her mouth cottony from nerves.

"Yes . . . Mara," he said, to Mara the two words sounding importantly preoccupied.

"We were supposed to—"

"Of course, see the Engle house. Where are you staying?"

"At the . . . in the French Quarter." The place was a

humiliation. Concerned for what image she had, she didn't want him to pick her up there.

"Good, that's where the house is."

"Then I'll just meet you," she said quickly.

"No bother to pick you up."

"I love walking, it's good to walk," she exclaimed too enthusiastically. She thought he laughed. At any rate, he gave her the address and she agreed to be there in a half-hour.

The night's storm had done nothing to relieve the heat that had begun at daybreak. Vapor was already rising from the damp pavement. The special pains she had gone to in arranging her hair, back-combing it, smoothing it, then fluffing it more naturally around her face, were all for nothing. Within five blocks the carefully engineered coiffure was wilting like the vegetation growing along the way.

She was almost ready to cross the street when she saw it. The picture on the front page of the newspaper was fuzzy, the image blurred by the plastic case of the coin-operated vending machine. But once having seen that face, one could never forget the large haunted eyes, nor deny them attention. Mara stopped, putting in the correct amount of change to release the paper.

Dominique Moreau was her name. The woman whose singing Mara had listened to the previous night had been arrested two hours later for having withheld crucial information from the police which would have led to the arrest of a well-known confidence man. The woman was a Cajun, the paper explained, brought up in the outlying bayou country. She had once been married to Charles Moreau, also of Cajun descent, a man who had left the area and was reputedly involved in international importation and distribution of illegal contraband. Dominique had worked in Paris as a singer and dancer, and also as a showgirl in Las Vegas.

"I have done nothing wrong," the paper quoted Dominique. "I only want to be left alone. To lead my life in peace."

Mara had the newspaper in her hand when she arrived in front of her uncle's house—*her* house now. At the sight of Alex Gautier, Dominique and her troubles were instantly forgotten.

He was on the sidewalk staring up at the second-story balcony. He had on a suit of the palest blue material, a white dress shirt, and a patterned silk tie. The fit of the suit was perfect, draped to the exact proportion of his body's contours. All the fantasies of the night came rushing back.

Whatever erotic thoughts she might have been entertaining, his mind was obviously on more mundane matters. Still unaware of her, he turned. The vibrant dark eyes were reflective, even troubled, Mara thought. He glanced up again at the balcony, then looked down the street in her direction.

Mara waved. He raised his arm and started forward to meet her.

"Sorry I'm late," she said, assuming that she was. "I took a couple of wrong turns."

"You're on time, I was early."

"Oh," she said. "Good. I'm usually always on time. It's maybe my best quality, being on time. At work, I haven't been late once, although there was a . . . oh, well . . . it's not like I deserve a medal."

She was babbling, or at least saying too much about too little. Even knowing it, she could not stop herself.

Gratefully she became a mute as he began to comment on a building across the street.

He was so beautiful. Was that the word? Beautiful? Yes. He was a man, and he had the power of a man, but there was elegant refinement along with the underlying strength he exuded in his every gesture, in his most casual glance.

". . . very old, of course." Alex paused, his mouth curved into a vague smile of understanding. "You haven't heard one word."

"Oh, I was—"

"Daydreaming, an affliction caused by the air here. Our atmosphere is infamous for it. It reduces men of hard practicality to creatures of dreamy indulgence." Reaching forward, he moved a strand of hair off her forehead. It had been the most inconsequential of gestures, the barest of touches, yet her whole being felt alive from the contact. She veritably tingled with pleasure.

"Anyway," Alex went on, his attention blessedly off her and concentrated on the building before which they stood, "as you can see, it bears the same typical decrepit appearance as most of the places in the Quarter. Only worse," he added. "Of course, there's a strong community-preservation league, and any outside cosmetic improvements have to be approved. But what an owner chooses to do inside is his own affair."

As Alex spoke, Mara took in the two tiers of black, extravagantly laced iron balconies fronting the house. The salmon-pink stuccoed facade had faded to a sickly gray flesh color. Closed shutters with peeling paint boarded all the street-level windows, and upper windows and doors as well. The house had no property surrounding it, but like the others in the area, it had been built flush against neighboring structures, with front boundaries directly against the sidewalk.

Inside, the home was much larger than she had imagined. Alex's mood was also different than she had expected it to be. She had thought he would be in a rush, or that his mood would be black, since he had been subtly coerced into giving her the tour. True, he did seem pensive, but there was some other quality to his mood, as well. It was indefinable, between sadness and anger and satisfaction.

While Alex turned lights on, she looked about.

Through the dank muskiness she could smell the history, as well as visualize it through the furnishings.

"It must have been beautiful," Mara said.

"It was."

"You were here? When they lived here?"

Alex looked uncomfortable. "I was young."

Mara's attention was on the sofa. One of its puffy, down-stuffed pillows had a deep indentation, as if someone had just gotten up. There was even an open book on the round end table. Except for the fact that everything was covered in a thick blanket of dust, there was the feeling that whoever had left the room would be back at any moment.

Absorbed in discovery, Mara momentarily forgot about Alex.

A magnificently carved grandfather clock stood locked away in the back shadows, its pendulum frozen motionless. She didn't think, but acted, impulsively opening the glass case and setting about rewinding life back into the clock, as if it had been a forgotten duty, just remembered.

Alex's hand came down on her shoulder. "Why don't we see the rest of the house."

Mara turned, surprised at the seriousness of his tone. "I just wanted to—"

"Why?" he asked, and gently closed the glass door she had just opened. "Why bother? What's the use?"

Mara stared at him, feeling that something was troubling him, but not understanding what. He moved quickly away.

"The house had two parlors, actually. This one, and a more formal one, across the hall," Alex said, leading the way.

Mara followed along. Alex opened another door on the opposite side of the hall. This room was more ornate, the furniture period French.

"They didn't use this room, did they?" Mara asked, not going in. She stayed at the door. There was no feeling to the room. It was beautiful, but its personality was stiff.

"No, no, they didn't." Alex closed the door.

"Why have two living rooms?"

"It was customary among people of a certain social and financial standing."

"But they never used their room," Mara said, the question implied but not asked outright. She already knew his reluctance to discuss anything personal concerning her uncle and his wife.

"Back here was the dining room," Alex explained, taking her to view a large room with a table that could easily seat twenty-five.

From there, he opened another door and this led into an inner courtyard, surrounded on all sides by the rooms of the house. It was surprisingly cool there. Towering banana trees grew unrestrained in pockets of earth not covered by a dark gray slate floor. A tangle of vegetation, whose identities Mara could only guess at, clung to the walls of the house, draped off balconies, and carpeted much of the patio floor. The green stain of moss and lichen was on everything. One wall was intersected by a high arch with an iron gate leading to a tunnel beyond.

"Once coaches were brought through there," Alex explained.

Mara made no comments. She followed along, listening, seeing, feeling curiously drunk. It was an almost pleasant feeling, but at the same time vaguely disturbing.

She was acutely aware of Alex, who smelled of some wonderful cologne. Beside him, she felt fragile, almost extravagantly feminine. He had guided her into rooms twice, his hand lightly placed on her waist. With pleasure rushing through her, she had nodded politely at the account of how in the original kitchen the food had been prepared in back and brought across the courtyard into the main house. That had been a hundred years before.

At times, there was no speech between them. Alex's mind seemed given over again to his pensive ruminations, and the only sound was of their steps accompanied by the peculiar silence that overtakes people on a pilgrimage.

"This floor contained the master bedrooms and best guest rooms. Then, up above—"

"I'd like to see," Mara interjected, and tried the nearest door. The wood was swollen from the humidity.

"There's nothing exceptional about the rooms . . ." He touched her elbow, making to guide her away.

But too late. Mara leaned hard against the door, which finally gave way.

The room she entered was striking for its femininity. The wallpaper was of faded yellow-and-white-striped damask and velvet, the bedspread white satin, flounced at the borders, and with piles of delicate pillows thrown up against the headboard. There was a kidney-shaped vanity table, dressed in the same material as the bed, the mirrors above it tarnished. On the table's top was a tray with tiny glass and ceramic perfume bottles, and beside them, an ivory-handled comb-and-brush set. Everything was touched by a hazy light, the sun filtering through the warped slats of closed shutters. It was hot in the room, stifling.

With apparent misgivings, Alex had entered after her. Now he stood by a tall dresser. He was lost in contemplation, one hand holding a photograph encased behind glass in an ornate silver frame.

He did not hear Mara as she came up beside him.

The photograph was of a man and a woman.

For a moment Mara held back her question, content to experience Alex's presence in the twilight of the room. From the moment she had entered the house, whatever her eyes touched upon, whatever feelings she had, seemed filtered through a mist of another time, long gone by.

Abruptly, as if hearing her thoughts, Alex turned to her. "Your uncle."

As Alex handed her the silver frame, mostly black from time's neglect, Mara could think of no explanation for the sadness and outrage and the fierce pride she recognized in his dark eyes.

It was a formal picture, yet one look at the couple in it, and anyone could tell that a bond of love had existed between them. The man was handsome in a rugged, individualistic way, with a clean, strong face, light hair, much like Mara's own, and a body that was powerfully built with broad, square shoulders. The woman was beautiful with an air of purity to her expression. In the slightly round eyes, one could almost feel the compassion and wisdom radiating outward.

Mara looked up. Her eyes took in the room with new knowledge of its owner, everything suddenly more personal, more compelling. "What was her name?" she asked Alex.

"Salina. Her name was Salina."

He said nothing more. Mara squinted, thinking hard as she tried to piece together the vague whispered comments made by her parents about someone named Salina when she was a child. Now, even Alex Gautier's behavior was strangely illusive whenever she questioned him about her uncle and his wife.

"What was wrong with her?" Mara asked.

Alex let out a sigh. "Mara, the past is past. Let's just forget—"

"Well, did she have a disease? Was she a criminal? I can't understand what the problem could be that no one wants to talk about this woman. It was the same at home."

"It doesn't matter about Salina," Alex answered sharply.

The silence rang with his rebuke.

"Look, I'm . . . I'm sorry," he apologized, lowering his voice. "No, Salina Engle was not diseased, and no, she was not a criminal. She was . . ." He paused. His face took on a look of softness, even reverence. "A woman of valor."

Then, at the words, a sadness swept over his face. He turned away. Mara respected his contemplative retreat.

"All right. You want the story, you can have the story," Alex said, facing her as he would an opponent in a long-dreaded contest.

He walked slowly back, as if still deliberating on the wisdom of his hastily made decision.

Taking the picture from her hand, he held it as he spoke. "This was Salina's room," he said softly, looking about him. There was reverence to his expression, and once again that look of infinite sadness that for some reason wrenched her insides whenever it appeared. Mara ached for him, wanting to touch his face, to kiss his eyes, to erase whatever turmoil was churning behind the black eyes that now looked directly at her. "She was beautiful and intelligent and kind. A gentle, gentle woman. She was

also a rebel.'' At that he smiled, but the happiness was lost
when he said, "Salina was an outcast."

Slowly, as if he were reliving the events as they
happened, Alex began to relate the events of his father's
life, and those of the lives of Thadeous and Salina Engle,
as he had partially witnessed them himself, and had been
told them by others.

Chapter 3

MARA SAT ON THE DRESSING TABLE'S DAINTY BACKLESS seat. She found the story of her uncle's life fascinating, Alex's description vivid. But being there in Salina's room, it was easy to relive the events of those times. A part of her soul rode along on each word Alex spoke. The ghostly relatives she had never known shot up full-blown in her mind, alive again, becoming to Mara beloved friends. She could feel them, sense them as they had been in those brief halcyon days, a man and woman ablaze with a love that had darkened into tragedy.

As he told the story, Alex moved slowly through the room. Now and then he would pause, perhaps to pick up a book, maybe taking time to fondle a ceramic figurine. Unseeingly he would hold it and then go on to touch the top of a table or brush his fingers against the rippled edges of a lamp shade. Even though she listened attentively, a part of Mara could not help but consider the storyteller.

She studied his elegance and wondered at the source of

his self-possession. She had never known any man like him. This moment with him was precious, it would never come again. She tried to hold it all in, each gesture, every nuance: the way he held his head erect, then sometimes gracefully bent to the side as he looked at her to make a point, the rippling effect of light in his dark brown hair that sometimes became a deep chestnut, and at other times was tinged with the soft glow of gold that seemed to pervade the room's entire atmosphere. At the same time, she listened attentively to each word and its inflection, almost desperate to capture in her memory for all time the words he was saying and the silences between the words.

Where she came from in Ohio, she had known men considered to be handsome, and men considered wealthy, but there was something special about Alex Gautier. Was that specialness inborn? Was his polish the result of a combination of genetic factors? Maybe it was nothing so exceptional. The origin of his refinement might be nothing more than the result of a pampered childhood.

Her mind suddenly became a rambunctious monkey, hopping from question to question. But as she drifted deeper into the past with Alex, the answers she sought came one at a time, wrapped as gifts in the spidery cobwebs of time.

Thadeous—or Tad—Engle had sailed the world as a merchant seaman. Eventually he had settled in the port of New Orleans, where he gambled his savings on establishing an import business. The company thrived, and Tad Engle became wealthy, rich enough to afford one of the old, grand mansions in the Vieux Carré.

Her uncle had been a handsome, virile man, with a natural charm and an instinct for business. Soon those attributes, coupled with his monetary wealth, opened the doors to polite upper-crust New Orleans society.

In an aside, Alex explained how New Orleans had been,

and still was, an American city whose roots remained firmly planted in European tradition. The city's original Spanish and French settlers had devised their own social caste system. A person born of either nationality, or a mixture of both, before the purchase of Louisiana in 1803, was known as Creole. Thereafter, the term Creole became synonymous with the best, be it food or fashion or language, Creole signifying that which pertained to the white aristocracy of the South.

Into this elite society, her uncle was grudgingly admitted as a probationary member. But eventually, as his wealth increased, the reservations against his origins were overlooked, and he was accepted as one of their own.

Then, in the barest flicker of time, the empire he had spent his life building disintegrated. The friends with whom he had shared wine and laughter over elaborate meals turned cold backs to him.

It was all because of his one sin. He had fallen in love.

Passionately, hopelessly, and recklessly, Thadeous Engle fell in love with a beautiful Cajun woman. It was during the thirties. She had come to New Orleans from the back country. Her home had been the swampland where "civilized" men, unfamiliar with the twists and turns of the meandering waterways called bayous, would become lost, sometimes never to return.

It was said that if the gators didn't get you, the Cajuns would. They were a mysterious and fierce people, Alex said. Originally they had been French colonists living in Acadia, the land now known as Nova Scotia. Exiled by the English in 1755, it was natural that they should resettle in Louisiana, then a French and Spanish province.

But they found themselves ill-suited to life in New Orleans. They were a basic, simple people, trappers and fishermen. Their occupations were not suitable for the sophistication of New Orleans, already a teeming metropolis. To earn their livelihood, they took to the outlying areas in the parish, where they built rude shacks for homes on watery banks. Their geographical isolation created a closed society in which their customs and speech developed independently. They spoke their own dialect. It was part French Canadian, part slang, totally their own and incomprehensible to outsiders.

Salina had fled the bayou country for the anonymity of New Orleans. Otherwise, it would have been her destiny to marry a brute of a man whose two former wives had perished mysteriously in the backwater.

When Thadeous first met her, she had come to his import house on an errand for a friend of his who employed her as part of his household staff.

He saw her lovely face, heard her gentle voice with its lightly accented English, and from that first meeting, Tad Engle, a man who had sailed the world over and who had known a hundred women intimately, could not forget this one.

Against all judgment, against the thinly veiled warnings from his Creole friends, he courted her and eventually they were wed.

But in doing so, he had betrayed his privileged status. He had mocked and sullied the tenets of the society which had accepted him as one of their own. It was a subtle hatred at first. Doors were closed to him. There was an end to the frequent invitations for dinners and lavish parties. There were verbal slurs delivered in undertones as he passed through the streets. Finally the snide ugliness escalated to vandalism.

Rocks were thrown through the windows of his home, and one night, when Tad was gone on business, Salina bodily defended their property from being torched by a drunken band of society's finest. She was pushed, shoved, her robe snatched from her body. The gun she brandished as a threat, but was by nature too gentle to use, was wrenched from her. Accidentally it fired. The bullet pierced the heart of a man, a leading citizen of New Orleans.

The papers rang with "Cajun Woman Murders Leading Citizen."

In the entire state of Louisiana, Tad Engle could not find private, non-court-appointed representation for his jailed wife. Then, one night, the most esteemed of all attorneys in the city, perhaps in the entire state, pulled the laughing-headed-gargoyle knocker back and forth against Tad's door. Drawn-faced and spiritually depleted, Tad listened to the man standing in the glow of an iron streetlamp say in a casual but loud enough voice for anyone who might have been around to hear, that he would ". . . be honored to defend an innocent, wronged human being, no matter her heritage."

"That man was my father," Alex said.

In the story's telling, Alex's face had grown pale. To Mara, he seemed to have taken on the gravity of his father's decision to defend Salina. But thoughtfully, as if it were necessary to reexamine what had happened, he continued.

Louis Gautier, who was himself a Creole, persevered against threats to his life and stoically accepted the loss of his previously flourishing law practice. His long-held political aspirations were likewise sacrificed before the altar of justice. Then, on a September morning, he presented his case before a jury.

"Against all odds, he won," Alex said, looking to where Mara sat on the small stool. In contrast to the pallor, his black eyes were bright with pride.

Mara's spirits, too, rose up in gladness for the three warriors. It was a short-lived happiness.

"But," Alex went on, "in his triumph, my father lost

everything. Everything but his self-esteem. He died a poor man." More to himself than to her, he added, "The only thing he left me was a record of his personal honor as a man and a human being."

"That's so much," Mara said. "More than money."

Alex returned a look disputing her opinion.

"My father should have reaped all the rewards of this world—the financial rewards, the rewards of fame. Most of all, he was entitled to respect. But instead, the worst men—worms, in my estimation—ended up with the best of life's fruit."

The injustice Alex railed against was clearly for his father's sake. It had nothing to do with bitterness over his own paltry legacy. The strength she had felt in Alex was his own; he was a self-made man, as independent of character as his father had been. Mara admired him for that, for that and for a thousand other great and small things that she had noted about him so far. She wanted to tell him so, too, but was afraid to cross that line separating the professional from the personal.

Whatever personal relationship they had was purely in her mind. A careless look from him, a word of clear disinterest, and her light and airy balloon filled with hopes and wishes and silly romantic dreams would burst. They were all she had, and even though of little substance, the fantasy was what she clung to as she said only, "But at least Salina and my uncle were happy in the end."

Alex's jaw pulled tight. Shaking his head, he said, "No, no . . . unfortunately that wasn't the case."

He explained.

The ordeal of the trial over, Tad and Salina attempted to reconstruct their lives as best they could. Tad did not want much, mostly that they live their lives with each other's love. He wanted them to have enough to eat and to have clothes on their backs. He wanted them to be able to hold their heads upright as they walked down the streets of New Orleans. But the trial, with its accompanying degradation, had finally broken Salina's spirit. Remorseful and guilt-ridden over ruining the careers, the very lives of two good men, Salina took her own life.

"No, oh no . . ." Mara's voice came out as no more than a dry sob.

Alex went on, but more softly, as if to speak otherwise would bring more pain to the sleeping spirits.

"So your uncle spent the remainder of his years as a lonely, lost man. Oh, the war and its demands made his business flourish again. And time and human avarice worked to diminish his crime against polite New Orleans society. But his heart was gone. He never paid much attention to his business after Salina's death. The company pretty much ran itself on the momentum of the times and through the labors of the employees he had trained. If he had cared even the slightest, you would be getting millions instead of this wreck of a place and a mere forty thousand dollars. It was my job to examine his will when he died." Alex paused. He faced her directly, and she thought of his father, Louis Gautier, as he must have stood before Salina's jury. "Now you know why I didn't want to tell you. It's not a happy tale." He turned away, and his voice was unexpectedly cold when he said, "It's pointless, really."

"How can you say that? Salina's death pointless?"

He glanced sideways to her, the former friendly humor in his eyes gone. "It was. It was totally pointless."

He seemed affronted that she had disagreed, and she shrank back a little in the face of his righteous assurance.

"If you'd like to look around," he said, "the top floor has extra guest rooms, a sewing room, and a . . . There was a nursery there. Never used," he said quickly. "I'll make sure the doors are locked downstairs, turn off the lights. Come down when you're ready."

He gave his speech all in one breath, allowing Mara no chance to protest or comment. He was almost out the door when he suddenly turned back and said, "My father sacrificed his career. For what? For a woman to give up her life? He lost everything that ever meant anything to him, so that she could win."

He wasn't waiting for her response; his was the correct viewpoint, there was no other side to the issue. He picked up a vase from the table beside him and looked at it distractedly while his mind mulled over past hurts.

It wasn't so much that she wanted to be right that Mara found the courage to speak her mind. It was for them, for Salina and Tad, and Louis Gautier, too, that she stood and said in defense, "What your father did, he did because he loved. And what Salina did was because she loved. To say that their love was nothing, well, it's cruel. It makes their lives nothing."

A tear splashed on her cheek. She was crying, and hadn't even noticed.

But Alex had. Like a man who was being torn in two parts, he looked to Mara both as if he wanted to flee from the room and as if he wished, at the same time, to lose himself in the emotion she saw behind his eyes. There was such fierceness, such tenderness. But mixed in with that was anger and resentment, and the harsh won over the gentle.

"I'll wait for you downstairs," he said, his politeness intact but strained.

He left the room without a second glance her way.

"Sure," she said, but only to the air. She heard his steps on the stairs.

Her challenge had put them on different sides. For all her romantic notions about Alex Gautier, and for New Orleans itself, she was in fact no more than an interloper whose presence was irrelevant. Like her uncle and Salina, she was an outsider. Apparently owning property did not necessarily give a person title to respectability. Her uncle had found that out, hadn't he?

The sense of injustice caused her to refuse to give in to self-pity. If she felt anything, it was determination. She picked up the photograph from the dresser. Holding it out, she studied the images captured behind the glass. The woman smiled sweetly out at her. The man at her side was handsome, his features closely resembling those of her mother. Only paper likenesses now; once they had been real people who had laughed and cried and fought for what they believed in.

Setting the picture down, she looked about her and tried to place Salina and Tad in the room as once, long ago, they must have been. From each possession, emotions seemed to be revealed to her—laughter and love, fear and pride, desperation and hope, and futility.

"Salina, why did you stop fighting? You could have won. You could have won, Salina." Her brave words seemed to collide against the silence. She heard them shatter.

Depressed by her own gloom, she went quickly to a window. It was actually a glass-paned double door on the inside, whose outside was boarded by latticed shutters. It took her a minute to release the door's lock and undo the latch on the shutters. She shoved open the door.

Sunlight burst against her and filled the room. Stepping onto the balcony, she took in the slanted forms of rooftops. They were flat and stark in the bold wash of sunlight. She saw scraggly palms and banana plants; she saw French-style streetlamps and an antique hitching post in the shape of a horse's head. But all of this was not through her own eyes, it was through Salina's.

The brilliant sunshine of the day dimmed in Mara's mind. Below, the street became cloaked in dark shadows, out of which had once come cruel jeers, sounds of splintering glass against the downstairs windows, and rising up to where a lone woman stood, the terrifying lick of hand-held fire, which made all else inconsequential.

Mara did not close the shutters when she left the room to go downstairs. She wanted the sunlight to fill every inch of Salina's room, as it should have filled her life.

She found Alex in the drawing room. He was staring up at a painting over the mantel. Hearing her enter, he turned and immediately said, "I'm sorry. My apologies, sincerely. You had every right to express your opinion. Besides which"—and he smiled—"a guest is always right."

"Is that a New Orleans custom?" she asked, but did not smile back.

"Maybe more general, like basic Southern etiquette." His smile was still in place, but not as sure. There was a question in his eyes that had not been there before.

She guessed he was surprised she could speak out, that she actually had thoughts and feelings important enough to defend. Even at home she was not known for taking courageous stances; rarely had she felt strongly enough about anything to bother. Life just went along in its gray steadiness. But this new world she had entered was in Technicolor, and suddenly, so was she. It occurred to her that there were two new realms of geography to explore: the outer; and her own, maybe even more fascinating inner territory.

"But I'm not a guest, am I? I mean," she said, looking around the room, "this is my house, isn't it? Which would make you the guest."

"Technically—"

"Legally," she corrected.

"Legally, then." He looked about. "All of this, cobwebs, dust, stale air. It's all yours," he said, laughing.

"And the memories. I've inherited them, too, haven't I?"

When he saw she was serious, his expression changed accordingly.

"Mara . . ." He seemed at a loss to explain whatever it was that bothered him.

But something certainly did. She had felt it all along. Now that she thought back upon it, even yesterday at his house, there were moments when she had caught him looking at her with a strained intensity, as if he could not resolve whether to draw her closer or banish her from his sight.

His eyes had drifted from her face, as if to search the room for the right expression to his thoughts. When he looked back, the troubled look was still in his eyes, although his voice took on an energetic lightness. "So," he said, "I've locked up. If you think you've seen enough dust, we could take off. I've brought the papers with me. Rather than go all the way back to my place, we can stop at a bank around the corner and have them witnessed and notarized."

As if she had answered affirmatively to every suggestion, he started forward to leave. Mara stayed where she was.

"I'm sorry about what happened to your father," she called after him.

Alex hesitated. She could feel him wanting to go, but his good breeding made it impossible for him to cut her off, especially after he had just admitted she was entitled to her own opinions.

"Well, that's all past," he said, barely looking her way.

"It was an awful thing that happened. To everyone. My uncle. Poor Salina. Your father. But I can't take any of that awfulness back. And I'm not responsible for what happened."

"Of course you aren't." He was looking toward the hall where the exit promised freedom from bad memories; she knew she would be included through association.

"So," he said, "shall we go?"

"A minute," Mara answered. She passed to his right and continued to the far wall where the stately grandfather clock resided in the shadows. She had just opened the glass case when she felt a hand on her arm.

"Let's go," Alex said in a tone somewhere between a warning and a pleading.

He lifted his hand quickly, as if he too had felt the electrical connection between them.

She couldn't look at him, she didn't dare. What if her eyes were a screen holding her dreams of last night? She forced her attention back to the clock.

Her grandmother's clock had been almost identical to it. Perhaps, she thought, that was why Tad had bought it. With her years of previous experience it was easy to set, and when she was done she closed the glass case and stood silently watching the brass pendulum swing back and forth.

"Why bother?" Alex wanted to know, speaking to the clock rather than to her.

She, too, responded with her attention directed to the clock's face. "I like to know what time it is," she said simply.

There was a beat, during which time she was certain Alex considered what she might have meant. But all he said was, "Well, it's time to go."

"I'm staying here," Mara answered in soft contrast. "I'm not going to leave."

There was another term of silence. Then, "Do you know what you're doing?"

"I like this house. I like New Orleans. I feel I belong here."

"Look," Alex said, his arms falling to his sides with exasperation, "why don't you think about it before deciding. The heat—it makes people do strange things."

"Well, possibly. But it shouldn't matter to you what I do." Mara left his side and collected her purse from where she had tossed it on a chair. Clearly he didn't want her to stay. She turned cool, protecting herself from further disappointment.

At his side, she said, "You're just doing your job—a dirty job, it seems. And I'm sorry about that, having to open old wounds, as you put it."

"You're right, of course. Your decision to stay has no particular bearing on my life." Alex went after her into the hall. "It's just that this would be a mistake for you."

"And why? Why is that?" Mara asked, turning around abruptly. They were close enough to touch. He backed off, widening the distance between them. It was then that Mara first sensed that the man whose slightest smile seemed woven in sunbeams, whose dark eyes drew out her heart, might be in some way affected by her presence, as well. It was a startling notion.

"Look at this place," Alex exclaimed, and shook his head disparagingly. "It's a mausoleum."

"It wasn't always this way. I can clean it up. Just opening windows makes a difference."

"You've considered the repairs? They cost money."

"I've forty thousand dollars."

Alex shook his head. "A spit in the ocean. You could drown in the expense."

"I belong here," she said seriously. "I belong in this house, and I belong in this city, and I'm going to stay."

"I see," he said, as if taken aback that she had not bowed to his view of reality. He dug into his pants pocket. "Your key, then." He slapped it into her hand.

"Do you always bully your clients when they don't do what you want?" she asked, going on ahead without daring to look at him, afraid he might see the misery in her eyes.

Her hand was on the doorknob, twisting it, when his fingers came over her wrist and he forced her around to him.

"Listen to me. I don't really know how to explain this. In fact, I can't. And even if I could, it wouldn't make any difference to either of us in reality. It's just a . . . ." He relaxed his grip somewhat as he searched for the right word. "Call it a head trip." He looked into her eyes, as if for confirmation of what he had said. "Maybe," he said, "a head trip."

"I don't know what you're talking about," Mara replied truthfully. He had not let go of her wrist. She didn't think he was even aware that he held it, so absorbed was he in trying to put his thoughts together.

"The past is over," he said. "The past is over," he repeated. "But you see, Mara . . ." He sighed now, and finally abandoned his hold on her wrist as he leaned his back against the door. "I've brought some things from the past into my own present. If you can understand what I mean?"

"No."

He raked his fingers through his hair. Looking at her, he said earnestly, "Every molecule in this city is saturated with history. You breathe in, you take in someone else's exhaled sins or joys or whatever. So it's a struggle to be sure of who you are. That's a struggle for people anyway. But here, it's practically an impossibility. I didn't follow in my father's footsteps because I necessarily wanted to avenge his honor, but because I felt I had a calling."

Mara smiled.

He understood, and smiled back. He reached out absently and touched her hair. "Like you wanting to stay here," he allowed.

"Like me wanting to stay here."

"Okay," he relented. "People are entitled to chase their dreams. But in my life, and in my business particularly, you're forced to see a lot. People with everything to live for mess up their lives because they let passion run off with their judgment."

"My uncle. Salina."

"Them, and nine-tenths of the rest of the world. So, a long time ago, I figured out that the only way to realize my calling was to stay clear of the heat, you know?"

"The heat?"

"I mean being swept away by feelings of revenge, feelings of power."

"Feelings. Just feelings in general," Mara said.

"It's not as tragic or as cold as it sounds."

"So you're trying to save me from my passion over this old house?"

He didn't answer her. Instead, he moved suddenly away from the door, and guiding her before him, said, "Let's get out of here."

Chapter 4

WHILE ALEX STOOD OFF TO THE SIDE, SHE TURNED THE key, locking the door to the house.

His attention was averted, and she could sense his disapproval; she had gone against his better judgment.

"Thanks," she said, coming to where he waited on the sidewalk. "Thanks for the tour. And for the key." She almost flipped it into the air, but thought twice—dropping it would kill the effect.

Anyway, she was childishly satisfied to have gotten in her little dig. He had disappointed her and he had made her feel inadequate. A slight twist of the knife wasn't much, but it was something to shore up her deflated self-confidence.

Alex still wouldn't look at her as they started to walk slowly toward the street corner. He kept his gaze focused resolutely forward and in a detached voiced recited the concluding issues of their business transaction.

"You can take the papers to the bank and have them

notarized. The address is on the envelope. After, send them back to me. All the utilities are on—they're being billed to the estate now. You can change things over to your own name without having anything disconnected.'' He stopped, and turning her way, said, ''You're absolutely determined to do this, aren't you? There's nothing I can say that will make you listen to reason.''

He gave her a clear look stating that she had to be either stupid or mad. For all she knew, maybe she was.

''It'll be okay,'' she said.

''It's impulsive.''

''It's my life.''

''Do you have any idea at all what you're getting yourself into?''

''Not entirely, no,'' she admitted, and wondered if they were talking about the same thing. He looked less concerned about her welfare than he appeared angry. ''But if I lose everything—which apparently you're sure I will— then at least I'll have tried.''

''Where angels fear to tread . . .'' he muttered, and started walking again.

''What?''

''The urge to gamble against the odds must run in your family's blood.''

''Hardly,'' she said. ''The rest of them have souls cast in concrete. Caution runs in their veins in place of blood. Uncle Tad was the black sheep of the family, the renegade.''

''And he lost,'' Alex reminded, casting her a sideways glance.

''That depends,'' Mara said thoughtfully. ''Maybe the contest's not over yet. I'd like to think of it as a family relay race. And now he's passed the stick on to me.''

''I hope to God not,'' Alex replied darkly.

They had reached the corner.

"My car's over there." He nodded to a white Mercedes-Benz roadster. "I can drop you off at your hotel."

"Thanks, but I can make it alone," she said with a studied defiance.

He nodded, her implied message understood.

Backing away, he said, "We'll see . . ."

That was it. He turned, and in his elegant, assured stride, headed across the street.

When he was halfway to the other side, she called after him. "Aren't you going to wish me luck?"

If he heard her, he didn't bother to answer.

"Goin' home now?" the frizzle-haired hotel manager asked as Mara turned in her room key.

"Yes," Mara answered, "I am. I'm going home."

"Flyin'?"

"Walking," Mara said over her shoulder, and lifting her old suitcase, left the smell of beans and fish behind her for a life of uncertainty as she stepped into the sunshine.

The door had just closed shut when Anna appeared in the large entry hall. Her eyes were unusually bright, and even in Alex's disconcerted state he took pause to wonder why. His answer came immediately.

"Sir, there were two calls from Mr. LaPierre. Personally made calls."

Without breaking stride, Alex continued toward his office.

"Mr. Gautier?"

"Yes. Yes, I heard, Anna."

"But I . . ." Her voice trailed off. "He said for you to call him. As soon as you arrived back."

Alex paused at the door to his office. "He said that? He didn't ask, he ordered?"

"Sir, it was Mr. LaPierre." Anna emphasized the name with reverence.

It was not hard for Alex to read her thoughts. The name of King LaPierre was bound to make visions of parties and elevated social status dance in the heads of any woman or man who hungered for such of life's vanities. Even for hired help like Anna, the association would bring a certain prestige and afford endless opportunity to gossip among her friends and peers. What annoyed him was that he was not much different. In the final analysis, he could not exclude himself from the ranks of those who had contemplated being a recipient of the King's munificence.

"Oh," said Alex innocently, "LaPierre. I thought you said someone else."

Anna smiled, visibly relieved.

Alex shut the door to his office. He shrugged off his jacket and with uncharacteristic disregard flung it carelessly on the sofa. Sitting down behind his desk, he reached for the phone and pulled it into the middle of his desk. The typed image of LaPierre's telephone number on the Rolodex card file was clearly printed on his brain.

He lifted the receiver and dialed. There was a hollow moment, then the first ring. Before the second electronic purr could sound, his wrist went limp. He dropped the receiver back into its cradle and stared across his desk at the picture of his father.

The steady brown eyes were watching him, trying, Alex thought, to tell him something.

Look, you did things your way and you lost, Alex argued silently. *Now it's my turn. I can win back for both of us what you lost with your strict allegiance to honor. I will be honorable, that above everything. But, I will also be flexible. And realistic.*

But still he did not dial.

Anyway, he found it wasn't necessary; the phone

shrilled, interrupting his inner monologue on morality. At its sound, he tensed, but not from surprise. He had stalled, knowing the phone would eventually ring of its own accord, thereby making him at least a bit less culpable in the deceit against his conscience.

Anna buzzed him on the intercom a second later. His hand was already on the receiver; even before she made the announcement, he had known the caller's identity. The hellos were brief, perfunctory. LaPierre got right to the point.

"I'm having a few people over to my place tonight, son. I'd like it greatly if you could be with us."

Alex paused, weighing his alternatives to LaPierre's summons. Cautiously he said, "We agreed I could think about your offer."

"I know what I said. You chew on it a bit, was what I said. Now I'm saying to you, chew faster. Time's coming to swallow." LaPierre's voice hardened, becoming less folksy. "It's the opposing side, son. They're moving already and I don't have the time to muck around while you cogitate upon sacrificing what you perceive as your honor, like some old-maid virgin who's going to dry up before she's ever asked again. This is not Camelot here. This is real life, modern twentieth-century dirty politics, if you want to call a spade a spade, which I take is your style of doing business. Now, you're a smart fellow or I wouldn't be having this conversation with you to begin with. So you be here tonight, and you come with the answer I want to hear and everyone's going to be happy and everything's going to work out just fine for us. Eight o'clock. Nothing fancy, just us boys, some fine whiskey and good cigars. Later when we've got this train rolling smooth, we'll celebrate the proper way."

The phone went dead, which was LaPierre's way of doing business. He had said what he had to say in his way and on his terms. There wasn't the opportunity for rebuttal, which was why he was so successful.

Alex suddenly felt claustrophobic. The past was closing in on him.

For one thing, he had meant to handle Thadeous Engle's will efficiently and with the minimum amount of emotionalism. He had actually looked forward to making the final disposition of the Engle property. Salina was gone. His father was gone. Tad Engle was gone. During his father's own life, his father's property had been lost to debts. Now, at last, the Engle home would fall from his care, and he had thought he would finally be free from a past made by others and bequeathed to him complete with accompanying trouble and heartache.

But yesterday, waiting for him at the foot of the stairs, was a young woman with pale blond hair—no more than a stranger, dammit. But in her depthless blue eyes seemed to swirl the same seeds of feminine passion that had drawn Thadeous Engle and his father to their respective destructions.

Like an animal whose instincts were fine-tuned for survival, he had sniffed the scent of danger in her presence. The tactics of emotional evasion were second nature to him, yet he was not oblivious of the source of the real threat. He did not play hide-and-seek games with himself. It was not the "other" who threatened from the outside, but rather his own self who feared being swept away by a passion he could not control. He had seen too much lost in the name of love.

For thirty-three years he had scrupulously avoided emotional commitment to the opposite sex. Early on, he had learned his safety lay in numbers. So in the beginning there had been the society debutantes, and later the scores of clever young professional women, and women who were not professional, nor clever, but beautiful and sometimes kind. Perhaps there had been three close calls, times when his heart had felt attached by strings to the lilt of a soft feminine voice; but he had severed those strings abruptly, rather than risk strangulation. What passion he allowed himself, he reserved for his work. He had his mountain to climb, and the path he had charted was narrow, with room only for one woman along the way.

Being a realist, he knew there was no sense in analyzing what had so attracted him to Mara Kozinski above and beyond some of the other women who had come and gone in his life. But she was special, unique, in a combination of ways that could not be categorized.

He smiled, thinking of her streak of stubborn independence, and smiled again as he recalled her impassioned defense of Salina and Tad. The smile faded, however, when he remembered she had also refused to sell the Engle place and return to Ohio. He did not want her in New Orleans. He did not want to want her. But desire her, he did.

At six o'clock that evening, Mara stood in the dimly lit hall of her new home and took stock of her present circumstances. She had an old house, an old suitcase filled with old clothes, sixty-four dollars in cash, and a bad new case of the jitters. What she also had were second thoughts.

She had arrived back that afternoon in high enough spirits. But throwing open windows and assaulting the dust with rags and the energy of ten demons had done little to improve the house's basic disreputable state.

Alex Gautier was right: she had taken on more than she had bargained for. The stove was archaic, even worse than the one her mother coaxed along at home. Rust came out of all the faucets and didn't seem to go away, no matter how long she ran the water. The refrigerator was in good order, but there was something strange in the house's electrical system, with lights flickering off and on for no apparent reason. Short of ghosts, which she did not believe in, the best she could hope for were weak fuses. Rewiring would cost a fortune, that much she knew.

Besides being tired and discouraged and generally worried, she was also hungry. Wearing the jeans she had packed because jeans were like a second skin to her, she locked up and went in search of an open grocery store.

Thirty minutes later she returned home carrying a bag with practically nothing in it and twenty-nine dollars remaining to her name.

What she felt like doing was to slump into a chair and cry, only she was too hungry, and instead went into the kitchen, where she formed a hamburger patty and muttered to herself about how cheap ground round was no longer cheap, and neither, for that matter, was lettuce or bread or milk or eggs.

But purposeful activity and the prospect of a meal at hand elevated her spirits. As she placed the iron pan on the burner, she was even humming.

Then the worst happened—none of the burners on the ancient gas stove would light. Whether with grease or dust or age or stubbornness, they were clogged.

She sat down on a kitchen chair and stared at the faded linoleum. The floor was perfect scenery for her spirits.

Overhead, the lamp flickered, and resignedly she raised her eyes to wait for it, too, to betray her.

But it didn't; it remained on. The warning, however, had been enough.

She allowed herself fifteen minutes of futile, tearful, self-indulgent lamentation; then, with no further thought, she picked up her purse, locked the door behind her, and for the second time that day set off to alter the course of her life.

Anna opened the door before Mara had time to ring. The housekeeper was holding a large cloth shopping bag and purse; she must have been just ready to leave.

"Oh," she said upon seeing Mara. Automatically her eyes swept up and down, taking in Mara's jeans and the light blue sweatshirt, then returned questioningly to Mara's face, which was still slightly puffy, along with red eyes, from her recent crying jag.

"I'd like to see Mr. Gautier," Mara said.

Anna hesitated. "He's not available at the moment."

"You mean, not home?" Mara prodded, desperate to get things over and done with.

"He's . . . not available right now," Anna insisted, although with less assurance.

"But he *is* home?" Mara persisted.

"His office hours—"

"I know, I know it's late. But I really have to talk to him now. It can't wait," she said, and added "Please" because she didn't want to be the casualty of a feminine power struggle.

With reluctance Anna admitted her to the large reception hall, and then, leaving her to wait, disappeared up the stairs.

A moment later Alex appeared on the top landing.

"Thank you, Anna. I'll see you tomorrow," he said absently, the bulk of his attention on Mara, who was looking up at him.

Anna left, passing Mara a disapproving look on her way through the hall.

"I'm sorry," Mara said when he was almost to her. "I know it's a bad time, but—"

"I'm just going out," Alex said, sounding either

rushed or annoyed that she would have thought to come at all, regardless of the time.

His hair was still damp from a recent shower and he looked cleanly shaven. Even from a distance, she was able to take in the smell of expensive cologne. The sight of him coming toward her in his crisp white shirt and smartly pressed blue slacks made her feel grungy and out of place. Her feeling of general unworthiness was a validation of the decision she had made, and with a kind of masochistic enjoyment, she noted the vast difference that lay between them. For almost two days she had suffered delusions, choosing to believe that she was more than she was, or at the very least, fantasizing that she might someday be more than she was. Well, all of that craziness was over. It was time to be rational and objective.

"I brought these," Mara said, and dug quickly into her purse. She thrust the papers out at him. "The papers to put the house up for sale. You were right, I shouldn't stay here. I didn't know what I was getting into," she said, echoing the same words he had spoken to her that afternoon. "But I've thought about it and . . ." It was too difficult. She had to stop.

Alex accepted the papers from her. Opening them, he flipped to the signature page.

"They're all signed—wherever there was an X."

"Not good enough," he said, folding them back up. He handed them back. "They need to be notarized."

"Oh," she responded, misery swamping her. "Oh, well, I . . . Why? Why aren't they okay?" she asked, seized by desperation.

"Because otherwise they aren't legal. Anyone could have forged them."

"Look," Mara said, "can't you just . . . well, you could take them yourself and have them notarized. I'm leaving tomorrow morning. The first train out of here."

A shadow of regret passed briefly over his face. Checking his watch, he shook his head and looked back up. "Look, I don't mean to be rude, but I can't talk about this now. I have to be somewhere in twenty minutes and—"

"Well, that's okay," she cut in. "What's there to talk about? It's settled. I'm going to sell the house, just like you wanted me to in the first place. If the papers aren't legal now, then I'll take them home with me and I'll sign them and do whatever has to be done to make them okay, and then I'll put them in the mail and . . ." Demonstrating her intent, she stuck them back in her purse. "Sorry to have bothered you for nothing." Ending abruptly, she turned and started for the door.

"What happened to change your mind?" Alex called after her.

Without stopping, she replied, "The heat—it was the heat all along, just like you said. Made me crazy for a while."

Her hand was on the doorknob. A new waterfall of tears had begun to cascade down her face. She swiped at them with her free hand. "But now I'm sane." She swung open the door, just wanting to get out, just wanting to die.

"Mara!"

He was across the room and by her side in an instant. He moved her aside and closed the door.

"Look," he said, "I didn't want things to go wrong for you. But this is the best decision. Really," he said, and added, "the best and the wisest and the . . ." But he stopped there, and realizing his hand was still on her shoulder, quickly drew it away.

"Sure," she said, and tried to smile.

They stood there looking at each other, neither of them speaking.

"So," she said.

And he nodded. "So."

"'Bye."

This time when she pulled open the door he didn't stop her. For a moment she hesitated in the door's frame, taken by the sight before her. The night was a deep blue, balmy and close. A million nocturnal insects had already begun their tunes. They stopped abruptly when she stepped onto the porch.

"It was a nice visit, anyway," she said softly, not knowing if Alex could hear, but needing to say it for her own sake. "I didn't belong, but I enjoyed being a tourist in your world."

Then, while she could still see through the tears, she stepped out of the soft yellow light slanting across her shoulders and disappeared quickly into the thick blue haze.

Alex remained in the doorway, his fists clenched, forcing himself not to go after her. There was a tight knot in his stomach when he closed the door, and he told himself it had nothing to do with her, but with the meeting he was to attend in twenty minutes. Yet halfway up the stairs the knot had expanded to an aching need and there was no way to pretend anymore.

He wanted her in his world. Not as a tourist, as she had said, but as a permanent fixture. Damn. He wanted the woman.

He paused, looking down to where his office door was ajar. The frame holding his father's image was turned away from him, yet the expression of sad resignation had long since been indelibly committed to memory. That time-frozen disillusionment was reminder enough of the pain and destruction that loving someone passionately could wreak.

Reassured, he climbed the rest of the way up the stairs.

It was best that she go back to her own world and leave his empty of heartache. She would never know how he had felt, and for him . . . well, there were things he had to do.

With grim resolve, Mara went through each room of the house and secured the shutters she had opened to what was to have been their new beginning together only that afternoon.

When that was done, she went upstairs and packed her clothes into her disreputable suitcase, leaving out only what she would wear on the train.

And when that was done, she bathed and lay down nude on Salina's bed. Someone across the way stood on a balcony, playing a harmonica. The notes came out slow and sultry as the night air.

She stared into the darkness, waiting for sleep to come, waiting for the daylight to come again, waiting for nothing at all anymore. . . .

The rumpus room swirled with the gray smoke of cigars and cigarettes. In spite of the casual atmosphere, there was not a man at the meeting whose nerves were not at raw ends, except perhaps for King LaPierre, a man used to orchestrating high-stakes drama. Chewing on a cigar, he stood before a long table. On it was an array of food fit for any pasha.

Moving as quietly as shadows, three of LaPierre's kitchen staff collected plates and glasses, while coffee and after-dinner drinks were silently offered by two other employees.

LaPierre continued talking throughout the discreet activity taking place. His eyes swept back and forth over his colleagues assembled around the room, some standing, others seated along the thirty-foot horseshoe-shaped sectional and the rest in armchairs.

Alex was one of those who had chosen a chair. He sat with one leg crossed, his fingers curled around a Scotch and water, listening as LaPierre outlined his future before a gathering of twenty of the city's most powerful men.

Now and then, eyes would turn to him speculatively, but he gave no show of his feelings, remaining merely a passive spectator.

"Promises, gentlemen, are what we are here for tonight. Promises." LaPierre paused, then his eyes fastened upon a man whose family had parlayed ownership of a shipbuilding concern into a multinational transport corporation.

The man rose without hesitation, in deference nodded to LaPierre first, then to the others as a group, saying, "I can bring in my union people, no problem. And I can work some pressure on my competitors. Maybe a problem, but"—and he looked meaningfully at LaPierre— "sometimes for friends, one can solve problems. My promise." He raised his glass in salute, locked eyes with LaPierre once more, and retired to his seat, to be followed in quick succession by every other man in the room.

It took perhaps a half-hour to conclude the pledge of loyalties to LaPierre's cause, that being to support Alex Gautier in his bid for district attorney.

"To our next D.A.," LaPierre said, lifting a full champagne glass in toast to Alex. All the other men there also stood and likewise lifted their own recently filled glasses.

Alex had not left his seat. His own glass was still where it had been placed on the end table beside his chair. With slow deliberation he uncrossed his legs and finally rose.

He found LaPierre's eyes locked with his own. In a low

voice sounding loud in the room's tomblike quiet, he said,
"We need to talk."

He walked across the room and through the double oak
doors without a backward glance.

LaPierre was out after him, slamming both doors shut
in an exclamation of rage.

They were in what LaPierre called his central pavilion,
a large room with checkered squares of black and white
marble for a floor and a skylight overhead. A marble
fountain with Pan as its center piped a liquid melody
throughout the hollow atmosphere. The fronds of giant
palms planted in authentic ancient Roman tubs swayed in
the draft from the air-conditioning system.

"You have a hell of a nerve," said LaPierre, danger
radiating from his eyes, from every pore of his massive
frame.

"No, you have the nerve," returned Alex, his voice
snapping back like the crack of a hard ball against a bat.
"You didn't ask me," he said.

Understanding, LaPierre's eyes narrowed. "Those men
gave their pledges to put you into office. You heard
them."

"But no one heard me. I didn't give my promise."
Alex moved in slowly, closing the distance separating
them. "No one should have the kind of power you have,"
he said. "No one."

"Watch your tongue, son, before you trip on it. You fall
in my presence, you aren't ever going to get up." There
was no kindness to the advice. It was a threat.

"I will not be owned by you or anyone else. I'll be put
into office on my own merit or not at all."

"You're a fool like your father," LaPierre said, visibly
shaken over Alex's defiance.

Alex nodded. "Yes, like my father. And that, for

reasons which you're unable to comprehend, is the highest compliment you could pay me."

"You're done."

"No, I'm not. I'm just beginning."

"You are finished," LaPierre intoned lethally. "I am going to put you in the mud and then I'm going to walk over you to get where I'm going. If a man's not my friend, he's my enemy. Now, get out of here," he said. "You get the hell out of my sight."

Alex turned away and did just that. Oddly, when he closed the front door behind him and walked into the humid air, he was struck by a chill. His mind was in a fever.

Chapter 5

IT BEGAN AS A FILTERED THUD-THUD, THEN ROSE IN HER sleep-sodden mind to a distant but louder boom, until the insistent banging could no longer be ignored. She awoke, fully conscious of the night and the heat and that someone was pounding on her door downstairs.

She felt around for her nightgown lying on the foot of her bed, and having no bathrobe, slipped the sheer cotton material over her as she moved quickly through her bedroom into the hall.

The pounding was still going on intermittently when she arrived downstairs.

She stood by the door, not knowing what to do. There was no peephole, and even to ask who was there seemed a frightening proposition. They—whoever it was—would hear a lone feminine voice on the other side.

She thought of calling the police, then remembered the phones hadn't been connected yet. That left three alternatives: she could stand there trembling, frozen in fear; she could run upstairs and hide under the covers and hope whoever it was would disappear into the night; or she could open the door and deal with the situation.

The jackhammer pounding continued.

Now she was truly angry.

Falling against the door, she placed both hands flat against the wood and yelled to the other side, "What is it!"

"Me," came a muffled voice, "Alex. Something I forgot to say . . ."

Mara opened the door.

Alex stood there, no more than a dark shadow silhouetted against the light from a streetlamp. She could make out the outline of his suit, saw that his tie hung lank, unknotted around his neck. It wasn't necessary to see his face to pick up his troubled state.

"Mara," he began tentatively, seeming to waver slightly on his feet. He broke off, and then, with an expression of wonderment, said, "My apologies. It's late."

She had forgotten; the same streetlight protecting him from clear view illumined her body in the transparent gauze gown. At once she slid back into the dimness of her entrance hall.

As she did, Alex took a step forward and she caught the scent of liquor on his breath. Another clue that something was wrong.

"Alex . . . Mr. Gautier!" she said, his name a rebuke.

He remained just at the door's edge. Softly he said, "You're a beautiful woman, Mara."

With a confusing mixture of pleasure and embarrassment, she realized her body had been visually absorbed and appreciated.

"I don't understand why you're here."

"Don't you really, Mara?" He laughed quietly, almost self-deprecatingly, extending his left arm to the doorjamb for support.

"No," she lied.

"Well, I think you do. I think we both know why." He made a motion for her.

Evasively she stepped farther back into the hall. "It would be wrong," she said.

"No, it would be right," Alex replied emphatically. "It would be the one right thing that's happened between us since the moment we first saw each other."

"I'm leaving tomorrow," she reminded him, reminded herself. The earth was slipping out from beneath her.

"We're here now," he said.

And this time he was too quick for her. He stepped across the threshold and in a single fluid motion scooped her into his arms.

His tongue drove through her parted lips, sending a rush of tingling warmth throughout her body. Instinctively her arm looped around his neck, bringing him closer.

Alex pressed her to him, moving his torso against hers in a driving rotational motion, while his mouth brushed against her neck, her collarbone, and back to her lips again. His breath was as urgent as the rhythm of his pelvis.

She told herself he was drunk. But that wasn't it. He was more wild than high on alcohol. And what was she? Sober. Being reasonable for the first time since she had been in New Orleans. Bad timing. Oh, Mara, bad, bad, timing.

Her thoughts came in scattered waves. Wanting him, it would be so easy, so simple to give herself to him. But to forget him would not be simple. Forgetting him would be torture.

Moving like silk, his hand caressed the small of her back, traveled languidly over the flare of her hips, and all the while he continued to kiss her.

With resolve, she stiffened and turned her face away. She was not willing to unpack and repack her feelings again and again, as she had done her suitcase since she had come to his city.

Releasing his hold, he backed off. There was a moment of awkward silence, and then he cleared his throat. "Inappropriate," he said. "Forgive me." He made an elaborate motion with his hand. "Must be the magic in the air. That old black magic," he parodied. "New Orleans is very big on spells."

"It's more like the alcohol content in your bloodstream."

"I have been drinking. That's very true."

"Then don't blame the heat or your city or voodoo or the night."

"Along with the Scotch I've been drinking, I have also been thinking. Deep thoughts. Heavy contemplative thoughts, Mara. And what I've—"

"Please, Alex, I am going tomorrow. It really is the best thing. I don't want to have any memories. So, please . . . just good night." She stepped forward, meaning to close the door, but he reached out and pulled her back into him, not roughly, but with a sense of male urgency that set off the desire in her.

"Be with me tonight," he said, his breath a soft whisper against the hollow of her neck.

She closed her eyes, fighting her body's needs with her mind's wisdom. "And what about tomorrow? When tomorrow comes, what happens?"

"Mara, now is just beginning. Tomorrow—"

"Is another day," she finished for him, and tried to wriggle out of his hold.

But he held tightly to her, and as if challenged, said, "No. No, tomorrow . . . I want you to stay."

Holding herself apart from him, she studied his face for confirmation going beyond the words he had just uttered in his inebriated state.

"I mean it," he said softly.

She came back against him, and closing her eyes tightly, felt like a child again, an innocent who believed in miracles and fairies and in all things wondrous and impossible by the sensible standards of ordinary mortals.

His hand moved to her face, and tracing its outline with his fingers, he stared intently into her eyes, while she in turn watched with fascination as phantom thoughts, now tortured, now radiant, appeared and dissolved in his.

"There's a whole world in your eyes," he said wonderingly.

"What do you see in my world?"

He looked closely, staring. Then, as if he had seen too much, he closed his eyes and drew in a deep breath.

"It wasn't good?"

Slowly opening his lids, he said, "I see you. And me."

"And?"

"And we're together."

"For a night?" she asked. "And after?"

"I wish I knew that," he said. His gaze drifted past her shoulder, into the house. He seemed more sober. "Mara, if you want me to leave, I'll go now. But I want to stay, I want to be with you tonight. Only I don't read tarot cards or tea leaves like some of the people in the Quarter. I can't give you any guarantees about the future. No matter how much I'd like to, it isn't possible now."

Mara nodded. "Stay," she said.

"Without the guarantees?"

"I'll take my chances."

He kissed her, and this time she did not move away as his hand brushed lightly against the side of her breast. She felt him shiver, while she herself burned.

''Come,'' she invited, and led him across the threshold.

Taking in her body encased in the sheer fabric, he sent her an honest glance electrified with desire. He closed the door and locked it, his eyes never straying from her form.

Mara drifted slowly back into the hall, moving out of a patch of charcoal shadow into a filtered pool of golden light from a wall sconce, and then back into the shadows. The gauze caressed her skin, and in turn his eyes caressed her body, clearly visible beneath the filmy covering.

He came after her, just as slowly. They moved down the hall weaving between shadow and light until at the foot of the stairs he caught her hand. Drawing her into him, he bent her back, kissing her as he brought one hand to cover a breast.

She dissolved in his arms, his mouth never leaving hers even as he began to slowly raise the hem of her gossamer gown.

Helping him, she lifted it over her head. With one hand, he captured her wrists, keeping her arms stretched above her with the wispy material held between her fingers.

The other hand moved with the feel of satin against her skin. She closed her eyes, sucking in her breath as his fingers traced from her face to her collarbone to the rise of her breasts.

His breathing came loud and slightly ragged in the silence of the wide hallway, so that she knew they were both experiencing the same agony, the delay of pleasure becoming more difficult with every passing second and with every new touch.

The fabric fell like a feather to the floor, and bending, Alex sank with her to the stairs.

He supported her in his arms, and his mouth found her lips, then moved to each breast. With a soft moan of encouragement, Mara arched into him, offering herself.

Slowly he slid lower, his mouth urgent against her skin, her fingers wrapped in his hair, twining and twisting the dark thick strands as he increased her pleasure.

She wanted to touch him too, but he wouldn't allow her to move, holding her hands away from his body, and instead continuing on his journey. His tongue was hot fire flicking at her. She began to tremble, her body betraying whatever sense of modesty she had.

His hands slid beneath her. Raising her slightly at an angle, he arched her into the position he wanted.

"Don't" he said when she tried to stop him. "Let me." His breath was like steam against her leg. She was hesitant, but he was insistent, and in the end she relaxed, letting him have his way.

Lightly he grazed the inside of her legs with his mouth, a moan from him accompanying the barest pressure of his teeth on her skin. "Oh," she cried, her head dropping back as he moved to the center.

Her hands were on his shoulders and she felt him tremble, his excitement increase as her hips moved in small upward thrusts, meeting his tongue.

In the back of her mind she heard herself calling his name, but mostly she was aware of nothing but the surge of energy which was growing independent of any lingering scrap of rational judgment.

Then suddenly she felt herself both dissolving and expanding at once, simultaneously finding herself and losing herself, aware of nothing and aware of everything, holding, holding in an explosion of time and space.

When she was finally still, and the room had come back into view, she brought Alex up. His eyes were bright and hungry, his breathing quick.

This time, he let her touch him through the fabric of his slacks, and moaning softly in response, encouraged her to press her fingers against him.

The pulsing beneath her palm sent a shiver through her, sent heat radiating again from a single vital point in her pelvic region through every erogenous channel in her body.

"Let's go upstairs," he said, lifting her easily into his arms.

They ascended the stairs slowly, his mouth never leaving hers.

The room was dark when they entered, darker than the hall had been, with only a faint silvery wash of moonlight illuminating the large bed on which Alex placed her.

"It's all right," he whispered, sensing her shyness. "It's okay to want this. Come on," he said, and with his hand guided her fingers to the first button of his shirt.

She undid the first one, then the second and the third.

The tension in his body radiated outward, capturing her.

She slid the shirt off his shoulders and let the material drop to the floor.

Torturing him, she moved her mouth languidly over the smooth planes of his chest, touching with her hands, tasting the salt of his skin. She brushed her breasts against his bare skin, and caught his hands when he tried to possess them.

But as she continued, brushing and teasing with her upper torso, he moved into her with his pelvis. Iron-hard, he pressed against her.

"Undress me," he said, kissing her.

He made it easy for her to undo his belt.

Fairly, he did not shrink from her gaze, and partly afraid, partly curious, partly excited, and partly out of her mind with desire to have him completely, and to give

herself to him completely, she allowed herself to be bold.
He stood before her, silken skin gleaming in the silvered
light, the graceful flow of muscles melded to hard sinewy
limbs.

They moved together, and gently he laid her back onto
the bed.

Instinctively she touched him, and he shuddered, whispering a gentle expletive at himself to maintain his
control.

"Mara," he said, taking her hand in his and touching
her fingers to his lips, "from the first time I saw you, I felt
like this." He came down, stretching his body over hers.

They were joined, he a part of her, she a part of him.

Moving slowly, at first they savored the discovery of
each other, but it was difficult for him. He stopped and
started several times.

"It's all right," she said, and began moving slowly
beneath him.

He moaned, whispered her name, cursed lightly again
as he began to move with her, then to lead her in his own
accelerating rhythm until she was crying out with him.

"Love me," she said into his ear, as at that moment the
pleasure of her intensified beyond anything she had ever
known in her life, had ever thought possible in her life.
She clung to him, her legs surrounding him, her nails
against his back, her lips seeking his mouth, tongues
entwining.

He knew what he was doing to her, and each time she
cried out to stop, he only moved differently, bringing her
onto another level of pleasure, as if her body were a
musical instrument that he could derive different sounds
from, as if her body were a series of corridors through
which she had never walked before.

Then, suddenly, she was her own master and his, too.
Tumbling over him, and laughing, she began to torment

him with her own body, so that his eyes closed tightly and his breathing quickened and small sounds became words for her to continue and to continue and to continue. . . .

The contraction began with his stomach, and with that simple action, a bolt of white heat filled her body, spreading from her pelvis into her back, radiating through her chest, up her neck, exploding until her entire body was trembling.

He pulled her mouth onto his, moving his tongue with the same slow, driving assurance as his pelvis. Matching him, she gave way to her own natural rhythm, and taking over, she drove him higher until he shuddered. He held his body rigid for a time, before driving harder, relentless in his urge. He cried out at the moment the spasms took over her body, carrying them both into the center of the same heart.

Chapter 6

ALEX STOOD WITH A TOWEL AROUND HIS WAIST. THE sun was streaming in through the open-shuttered doors, a patch of light playing in Mara's hair as she sat up in bed, watching him hunt down his clothes.

"Looks like we were in some hurry," Alex said, laughing as he retreived his trousers from the floor.

Mara laughed too, but when their eyes touched, the laughter faded and the intensity took over again.

He came over to her, and sitting on the edge of the bed, kissed her fervently. It was a realistic good-morning kiss, and she was blessedly glad for the reassurance. While the water had run in the bathroom, doubts had assailed her. Moonlight madness. That sort of thinking.

"Stay," she coaxed.

"Wouldn't I love to," Alex said, his eyes falling to the rise of her breasts modestly obscured by the sheet. He moved a lock of hair from off her shoulder, touched it between his fingers. Then he was suddenly up, and busy, slipping into his slacks, putting on his shirt. "Would love to, but can't. I have a war to win," he said, and a grim look replaced the jovial expression of a moment before.

"A war?"

"An accurate term, yes."

"A legal war," she interpreted. Watching him, she sensed he was more troubled than he wanted to let on.

"In a sense. I'm running for district attorney."

"Alex! That's fantastic!" Modesty forgotten, she rushed over to throw her arms around his neck.

He kissed her, clearly amused by her enthusiasm, then gently drew her away and returned to the business of knotting his tie.

She slipped on her jeans and a T-shirt.

"I hope the rest of New Orleans' citizenship feels the same way about my announcement."

"Of course they will," she replied vehemently. "You've got everything." She was already imagining him in the position, seeing a large office, seeing the press, seeing him on television. Adulation, that's what she saw everywhere.

"Umm . . ." Alex said. "Not quite everything." He borrowed her brush from the dresser and ran it quickly through his hair. It waved easily into place. Facing her, he was a study of casual perfection except that his beard had grown dark during the night. He ran his hand along its roughness, as if following her thoughts. "I think maybe I'll shave before I give any public addresses."

"What besides a shave don't you have?" she wanted to know.

"Nothing," he said easily, dismissing her query. "I've got to go." He walked over and gave her a light kiss.

"What?" she asked, deciding not to settle for his evasiveness. "What don't you have?"

"You don't give up, do you?" he asked, smiling. He stroked her hair, but avoided looking into her eyes.

"Uh-uh. I'm relentless."

"So I'm learning. What I don't have," Alex said, "is the support of one man."

"And one man's that important?"

"More than important. Crucial."

"So, what do you have to do to get his support?" Mara asked, incredulous that anyone could resist Alex's charm.

"Sell my soul." He thought it wise not to mention the bartering of his body along with his soul. Christina LaPierre would have to find some other, more fervent suitor.

"Oh," Mara replied, sensing a deeper concern behind the offhandedness of his manner.

"The auction was last night."

Mara was silent. Her mind worked to put together the disparate pieces of information she had just been given. She looked up, troubled by the finished picture.

"Yes," Alex said, lifting her chin, "what you're thinking is true. Coming here was due in part to my decision to be a free agent. A moment of truth," he said. "What I wanted in life came sharply into focus."

"So what things did you see?"

His gaze remained steady on her as he spoke. "I saw goodness. And I saw fairness. I saw freedom. And I saw it was okay for us." His voice rose passionately. "I wanted you—all along, I wanted you. You had to sense that," he added. "Only I was afraid."

"And now you aren't?" Mara asked.

He took a long time to answer, then, slowly nodding, said, "Yes." He sighed. "I'm still afraid. A little."

"That's natural, isn't it? I mean, doesn't everyone feel that way when they . . . ?" She stopped herself, because suddenly to say the words "fall in love" seemed to be presumptuous. It was better to talk around their feelings. Otherwise it might be too much, too real, too soon. She didn't want to push whatever it was they had, for fear that the little she had would disappear.

"We'll just take it one day at a time," Alex said.

Mara smiled and stroked his cheek. "One day at a time."

"I'm out of here," Alex said, stepping back. "Get the phone hooked up. I'll call later."

Then he was gone.

She listened for the sound of the door closing after him. When it came, it was not laden with ominous symbolism, but instead was friendly and warm. A man going off to work. Her man.

Don't be stupid, Mara. You're getting ahead of yourself. One day at a time, remember? But it was so hard to put those restrictions on herself. Her feelings were flying into the future, Alex at her side, the two of them soaring together for a lifetime.

With her change of attitude, the house seemed altered as well. Each room was again reopened and dust covers were removed and folded to be put away. She was, after all, there to stay.

The entire day was spent in constant motion. There was the visit to the bank to see about clearing the forty-thousand-dollar check. There wouldn't be any problem. "Mr. Gautier called earlier. The money will be available to be drawn upon tomorrow." That was a major relief. Then there were the other administrative matters, like switching over the utilities and having the phones connected. The phones would take a couple more days. That was okay. Everything was okay. No, everything was great.

It was four o'clock by the time Mara returned home. The bouquet of flowers she purchased at a florist shop had cost only five dollars, but at the moment she supposed she was technically broke. An extravagance. But tomorrow would be another day. Tomorrow she would have her inheritance. Of course, nothing as mundane as money made any real impression on her. Alex was all she thought of. His name ran through her mind like a song, and her body was still energized by last night's lovemaking. Alex, Alex, Alex. In the middle of filling the vase with water, she stopped, seeing him as he had been in the moonlight. A moment later the container she held was overflowing. It didn't matter, nothing did, for her heart was likewise spilling with love. The smile on her face was becoming a permanent imprint and so, so natural. Life was wonderful. Love, sweet love, was wonderful.

It was an enormous decision: to risk missing Alex's knock on her door while she bathed, or to be hanging around waiting for him, looking like a limp doll. She decided to risk bathing, all the while keeping one ear trained upon the slightest sound from below. It was a quick, unrestful bath, but at least she emerged clean and fresher than before.

But by seven o'clock she had still not heard from him.

She waited in the parlor, the clock marking her vigil with its chimes every quarter-hour.

At ten o'clock she went upstairs and crawled into bed. She did not cry. She was afraid if she began, she would never be able to stop.

The heat was never going to let up.

She hadn't fallen asleep until early in the morning, and when she finally rose it was going on nine o'clock and ninety degrees.

She stood in the middle of the bedroom and wondered what the hell she was going to do with the day, and for that matter, with the rest of her life. Her suitcase was in the corner of the room. Seeing it, she was seized with the sudden overwhelming urge to throw her clothes in it and take the next train out of town, just as she had originally planned.

When Alex said he couldn't make any promises about the future, he wasn't talking about a month or a year down the line. Apparently he had meant the next morning.

The ache of loss tore at her insides. How could she think of him in those terms, as a cheap user, an exploiter, out for a warm body? Alex was so noble. He was upright and stable. She knew he was.

How did she know he was?

Because she loved him.

That was no reason.

How could love be wrong?

The circuitous rationalizing made her feel momentarily better, good enough anyway to dress and go out for a box of dry cereal and a morning paper. It was as good a way as any to kill time.

She returned from her errand and brought the bowl of cereal to the inner patio, where she wiped off a round glass-topped table and a white wrought-iron chair. Studiously she made a big deal out of it. She was making a big deal out of everything, anything to keep from thinking about why Alex had not come last night.

Picking up the paper, she poked listlessly at her breakfast while making an aimless perusal of the world's latest disasters.

On the first page, it was business as usual: the Russians were hurling insults at the Americans, the Americans were denying the accusations and returning some of their own;

a movie star was divorcing her sixth husband and remarrying her third husband; and farmers were having a record crop of wheat. Mara flicked to the next section.

Her whole being froze.

There in black and white was Alex—or rather a picture of Alex. Three other people were in the photograph, two men and a woman. Her eyes skimmed the accompanying story, written by the society editor. Alex Gautier was the guest of honor at a party given Wednesday night at the home of George and Ethel Preston (pictured). Also in the shot was Jack Purvis, former pro-football quarterback, and now a Hollywood movie star. It was a large party, Mara read, at least by her standards. Supposedly a hundred guests had attended. The article went on to describe the food, some of the designer outfits worn by various women, who it was that had come from where, and where they were going to be next.

Last night. The party had been last night.

While she had been waiting for Alex, expecting him to come knocking on her door, suffering because he had not come knocking on her door . . . all that time he had been at a party.

She let the paper fall into her lap. She didn't know what she felt. Betrayed? Like a fool? Like she had imagined the whole thing? Like maybe she really didn't understand the way things actually were in the world that Alex Gautier moved in?

Shoving the chair away, she stood and looked around her, searching for some sort of psychological exit from her confusion.

She loved him. That much she knew for certain.

She had thought he felt the same way. He hadn't said the words exactly, but they were there in silent expression, in the spaces between his words, in his eyes, in his kisses.

But he hadn't acted like a man in love last night, had he? No, not at all. Carrying her bowl back into the kitchen, she tried to think logically about why he hadn't invited her to the party with him. There was another woman. That had to be it. There was another woman in his life; but that couldn't be so. He had told her he wasn't involved with anyone, and of course it made sense, as he was afraid of becoming emotionally ensnared the way his father and her uncle had become.

She washed the bowl and put it away, then decided she'd pay a visit to the bank to see about withdrawing some money to live on. She had to exist somehow until she could decide if she was staying or would be fleeing with her tail between her legs, just another naive casualty of a handsome, sophisticated man given to fancy turns of speech and practiced moves on sultry moonlit nights.

The knock sounded on the front door when she was coming down the stairs with her purse and keys.

When she opened the door, Alex was on the opposite side. He wore beige slacks and a white polo shirt tucked in. As usual, he looked like a handsome prince, an escapee from the pages of a fairy tale, come suddenly to life in the real world of distressed damsels.

He smiled and made a move to bring her into him for a kiss, but she quickly sidestepped his overture. "Was the party fun last night?"

Rather than look ashamed or surprised that she knew, he said, "Profitable."

"Profitable," she repeated, not ready for the statement's neutrality.

"May I?" Alex asked, looking past her.

Mara stepped dumbly aside, letting Alex pass into the house. This wasn't at all what she had expected. An apology perhaps. An instant rushed explanation of his trespass. But as she closed the door and followed Alex into the parlor, there was no hint that any of those alternatives was on his agenda.

"Have you arranged for the money?" he asked. "I called the bank yesterday morning. The funds should be available."

"Yes," she said, "yes. I went down yesterday. I was just leaving now to go over there. I can have the money today." What she wanted to say was, "Why couldn't you have stopped by early or late yesterday? Why couldn't you have taken me with you to the party? Why have you come into my life and driven me so crazy I can't think of anything but when it is I'm going to see you next?"

Instead, though, she said, "You looked good in the picture. I saw it this morning in the paper."

"Ah," Alex said, "yes. Mirabelle Racine covered the bash. I was glad. She has a lot of clout, knows everyone. Belle's the society editor," he added by way of explanation.

"Really," Mara replied loftily. "Mirabelle Racine. Lovely. How musical. Mirabelle Racine. The very ring of a beautiful young Southern belle."

Alex burst out laughing. Pulling her to him, he gave her a kiss. To Mara's immense dismay, she found her body responding to it, and to the way his hand was running along her back and grazing the side of her breast. It was spoiling her self-satisfied indignation.

Breathing harder than she wanted to, and furious with herself, she pushed herself out of his arms and stood a safe several feet away, trying to assemble what she hoped was a frosty facial expression of emotional distance as well.

"You're jealous," Alex proclaimed, and laughed again, even harder than before.

"A simple question. It's a big deal to ask?" Mara returned, infuriated he had seen through her.

"You're jealous and you're angry," Alex said, coming down from his hilarity. "Okay. For the record, Mirabelle's in her fifties. When in her twenties, it's rumored, she was considered marginally attractive. The most anyone with two eyes in their head and a discerning sense of beauty would give poor old Belle now would be 'holding her own.' But you—you're beautiful . . . desirable . . ." He was moving back to her. She stepped away. He continued to walk forward, the slightest smile playing at the corners of his mouth. "And I want to make love," Alex said, his voice dipping into a sultry register more appropriate to the night. "I didn't come here to fight." He pulled her into his arms.

She was lost again. She would always be lost, regardless of his trespasses, regardless of anything. For the first time, she truly understood Alex's fear of loving. To love could be terrible as well as wonderful. It made one vulnerable. It made one powerless.

They walked up the stairs together, touching now and then, their eyes never leaving the other's. This time, they undressed themselves, and this time the clothes were put neatly into place on one of Salina's dainty chairs. Their deliberateness was for each other, a silent testimony to the reality of their relationship.

Sunlight danced over their bodies as, lying on the bed, they moved in each other's arms. "I missed you so much last night," Alex said, his mouth buried in the hollow of her neck.

Mara wanted to reply. She wanted to ask him why he wasn't with her, then. Instead, she brushed her fingers through his hair, luxuriating in its feel.

"What's wrong?" he asked, turning on his side and raising himself up on one elbow.

"Nothing," she lied, moving her finger up the inside of his thigh.

He stopped her hand, bringing her fingers up to his mouth and kissing them. "Tell me," he demanded gently.

She was suddenly ashamed of her doubts. Here he was, being so sensitive, so caring. Again she tried to divert the topic to the physical, changing her position and pushing her fingers lightly against his chest so that he lay back with his head upon the pillow, where she kissed him long and deeply.

He allowed her this maneuver until he was clearly losing his control, and then, twisting himself quickly from beneath her, he flipped her over, reversing their positions. His black eyes twinkled as he smiled wickedly down at her. "Oh no you don't. Out with it."

Mara sighed. "I'd rather not." She tried to wriggle away, and he grabbed her wrists. Holding her firmly imprisoned, he glowered down at her, waiting for her to tell him what he wanted to know.

"Okay, okay," she said peevishly. "I waited for you all last night. I thought you'd come back to me after work. Then, when you didn't, I started to think I had been wrong about you. That when you said you couldn't make any promises . . . you were just trying to give yourself an out."

"Umm . . ." Alex said, and released his hold on her.

"Umm? Umm? What does that mean?" she said, alarmed and even a bit angry.

"Maybe you were right," he said.

Mara felt a cold weakness fill her. She moved farther away from him on the bed.

"But maybe you weren't," he said, and drew her back to him. "Mara," he said, the evasiveness gone from his manner, "I couldn't come here last night. I couldn't," he emphasized.

"Not for ten minutes, not for—"

"There wasn't time. Attending the party was a last-minute decision. I had previously declined the invitation. In fact, I had every intention of coming straight over here when George Preston called. He had some unsettling news that made it imperative that I attend his party. And I had to attend alone. After the party there was a meeting between some men who are going to be my supporters. Some of them hadn't ever met me before. It was like a very serious fraternity rush. Can you understand?" He lifted up her chin, his eyes pleading and sincere.

"Oh, Alex. I feel so ashamed. Of course I understand."

She cuddled into him, and was about to deliver a confirming kiss of her remorse, when he held her back and said, "But look, Mara. Maybe it's good we face this now. Things could get a little strained in the future. My campaign for D.A. isn't going to be a shoo-in."

"I'm standing by you. All the way," she said, raising her arm like Joan of Arc rushing into the breach.

"I'm serious."

"So am I."

"How can you be? You don't know what I'm talking about."

Mara sat up in bed, clutched her knees to her chest, and tilting her head, said, "Ugly politics?"

Alex nodded. "Not on my side."

"So I wasn't raised in a cocoon, you know? I mean, some of those Ohio union elections get pretty raunchy."

"Things aren't done like that here. This is a gentleman's game. And in a way, it's a lot more deadly than a few broken bones."

"Meaning what happened to your father . . . losing everything."

"Yes. Everything." His eyes darkened, and Mara saw memories of the past move like ghosts across his face.

"I've got to do everything I can to win. But I can't do anything wrong. It's got to be all aboveboard."

"Or it won't be winning," Mara interpreted.

"Yeah." He smiled warmly. "You're a smart lady. Besides being beautiful and extremely . . . desirable."

Mara took his hand and kissed it, turning over his palm and saying, "I can see success here. I can see—"

"Some serious kind of lovemaking here," Alex said, and brought her down on her back.

She made love to him with all her heart and all her body, denying him nothing, giving everything so that he would know with all certainty she was his completely.

The way he made love to her was with a raw passion that left her weak. Beneath his fingers, she was like clay, malleable, softly yielding to his slightest desire. It was strange the feelings he brought out in her, in one moment making her feel like a fragile doll on a pedestal, a woman he worshiped. Then suddenly a fierce hunger would overtake him, and she knew he had to have been with women who were far more experienced and lusty than she. But she would learn. Even now she found herself acting upon the slightest innuendo of what he desired of her—to wrap her legs more tightly around his waist, to lift her pelvis, to withdraw her body at a crucial point, to offer and at the right instant to deny, which was also part of the glorious game they played together.

"I can't get enough," he said, laughing, but his eyes were gleaming with a wild, dark singleness of intent to possess her again.

Their bodies were slick with perspiration, her perfume and his cologne mingling in the moisture-laden air, as if they lay together in a bed of flowers.

Alex would bring her to the edge of frenzy with his knowledgeable touches, able to link every erogenous zone in her body to every other, so that it seemed her entire being was forever poised at the brink of some cataclysmic state of bliss.

Then, when neither of them could withstand the intensity any longer, Mara quickened her movements beneath him, and Alex deepened his spiraling thrusts until they were one entity together.

"Oh," she said softly, quickly, taking a deep, long breath. "Oh . . ." The sigh became a shudder, and her body the same as a rolling wave, autonomous in its urge to flow and flow.

Alex emitted a low growl, desperate and exalted at the same time. For a driving, thrusting instant he was a primal being, hot and demanding, taking and plundering. She was totally his to possess.

"Mara," he asked minutes later, as they lay beside each other, the air even seeming cool compared to their heated bodies, "did I hurt you?"

She turned to him. "No."

"I don't know what came over me," he said. He shook his head. "For a moment, I—"

"Forgot everything but the feeling," she finished.

"Yes. It's never happened before."

"For me, too," she said. "Just for an instant it was just like I wasn't there. It was just the urge, the feeling."

"I'm glad," he said. "It makes it perfect. We're in the same space then because of each other. That doesn't happen very often with people."

He drifted off then, his eyes falling slowly closed. Mara watched him for the longest while, gauging his shallow breath, waiting for it to deepen and level off. Then she rose and bathed, dressed again, and went downstairs to check out something that had just occurred to her.

It was an hour later when Alex found her in the parlor

writing down the room's measurements. She had also written down the sizes of all the other first-level rooms, including the patio, and had taken a sketchy inventory of furnishings.

Alex watched her from the doorway. He had no shirt on, only his slacks. When she looked up, she had to catch her breath. He was so handsome. She wanted him again, and the way his eyes were traveling the length of her body, it wasn't hard to guess he felt the same way.

"How long could it take you to get ready to go out tonight? To a party," he said.

Mara put the pencil behind her ear and considered the question. "A dress-up thing?"

"Everything in New Orleans society is dressy. Especially when it's hot. That way we can be even more miserably uncomfortable."

"I don't have anything to wear," she said in mock lamentation, although beneath the satire her pathos was genuine. Then, hearing herself, she had to laugh. "But I don't—really, I don't, Alex."

"Well, you still have time to get something," he said, glancing at his watch. Mara looked to the grandfather clock. It was going on four o'clock.

She brightened momentarily, and then the shroud of despair descended once again. "Money," she said morosely. "The bank . . . I had meant to go."

"That's okay. You can take this." He reached into his pocket for his wallet.

"No!" She backed away, horrified. He might just as well have reached for a spider or snake.

"You can pay me back," he said, handing her three one-hundred-dollar bills, "since you're obviously one of those hard-nosed females of independent spirit and concrete principles."

"Hey," she said, holding the money uneasily in her hand. "So what is it? You've cornered the market on honor?"

"Okay. Point made. But I want you to go with me tonight."

She looked down at the money. "And I'm supposed to look good."

"It goes without saying you'll be the most beautiful woman there, or anywhere, anytime. But some people are impressed by finishing touches. Something blue," he suggested, appraising her as if he were an artist picturing his masterpiece completed. "Something for your incredible eyes."

He would pick her up at eight that night.

Anna had a secret smile on her lips when she opened the door for Alex, who had his keys out ready to use. She must have been waiting for him.

"You look like a cat who's just swallowed the canary," Alex said, striding past her to the stairs. "Why so pleased, Anna?"

"There was a call for you," she said, her voice light with happy anticipation.

"Only one call?" mocked Alex. "My business must be falling off." He knew of course there had to be many messages, there always were; but only one—the mystery call that Anna was still savoring—was important to his housekeeper.

"Christina LaPierre called," Anna said.

Alex noted her almost breathless excitement.

He continued up the stairs.

"She wanted you to return her call," Anna added with a note of uncertainty.

"Thank you, Anna."

"Shall I get her on the phone? She said she'd like to hear from you as soon as you returned."

"No," Alex replied when he was almost at the top of the winding stairway. At the landing, he turned suddenly and looked down to where Anna was still watching him, a frown of confused disapproval etched on her face. He was torturing the poor woman. His personal life was none of her business, of course. But still, she had always been efficient and loyal, and he supposed it was natural for her or anyone else to identify with an employer's social position.

"Anna," he said patiently, "I will return Christina LaPierre's call. I will. So put your mind at ease." He could see her visibly relax. It was unfortunate, Alex thought, that her peace would be short-lived. "But there's no sense in calling now, because I already know what she wants and I can't—I won't—be able to oblige her."

"Sir?"

"Christina would like me to escort her to a party tonight. That won't be possible." It was all he was obligated to tell her, if that. Yet Anna remained looking expectantly up at him. "Anna, I'm involved in a relationship. A relationship with someone other than Christina."

"Yes, sir." Her eyes swam with dismay as she waited for him to offer further information.

"You don't know her well yet, but you will. Mara Kozinski's—"

"But, sir, you've only just met her. And she's not—" Anna broke off as abruptly as she had begun.

Alex was perfectly still. "She's what, Anna?"

"It was nothing, sir." A frigid look passed over his housekeeper's face. "I was relining the pantry shelves. I'd best get back." She started off in the direction of the kitchen.

"I'd appreciate it if you were to finish what you began to say, Anna," Alex snapped.

Anna stopped, turned slowly and looking up, said with a sense of measured restraint, "I was just surprised. She doesn't seem to be the kind of woman whose background is in the best interest of your career and position. She's very pretty," the housekeeper conceded, as if sensing she had overstepped herself and thought it prudent to temper her opinion.

"No, not pretty, she's beautiful," Alex said. "And I don't care if she's good for my image. She's good for me, the man that I am. Is that clear, Anna?" he ended sternly, but also kindly, knowing Anna's opinion would no doubt be shared by a great many others. He was prepared for that. So even if he detested the small-mindedness of people, it was not fair to penalize Anna for expressing what would undoubtedly be a popularly held belief.

"Yes. Perfectly clear, sir."

Alex gave her a long look, confirming that they both understood each other, then went the rest of the way to his bedroom. He showered and was changing when the phone rang.

It was his private line, and he picked it up himself.

"Yes?"

"Alex, it's Christina." Her voice bubbled over the wire.

Alex took heed of the false lilt in her voice. Beneath the nonchalance he detected pique.

"Yes, Christina. You called earlier. I got the message just a while ago."

"I've been waiting." She spoke with a soft Southern purr, her delivery the female equivalent of her father's— manipulative.

"I hadn't intended on returning the call, Christina. It was not to insult you, you know that."

"Do I, Alex?" The confident timbre of her voice had subtly diminished.

"You know precisely why," he said, his voice losing its hard edge, speaking to her as the friend he had been for years. He regretted that their current positions could not help but make them adversaries in the future.

"Alex, perhaps Father pressed his case without proper consideration of your finer feelings. You know Father. He's so proud. It's difficult for him to beg for something —for someone—he really wants." Her voice caught. She was also speaking for herself.

"That's exactly it. Christina, I'm not a thing, an item to be owned."

"No, of course you aren't. I know that, Alex. I can appreciate your feelings. Let's talk tonight. You'll be at the party. We can slip off after the others are too pie-eyed to realize we've escaped."

"I'm not coming alone." Better he get it over with.

There was a pause. With the hint of coldness he had expected, Christina said, "I see. Well, we can talk anyway."

"There's not much to say, is there? It would be nice if we could remain friends, but you and I both know future circumstances aren't going to allow for that."

"Who is she?" Christina asked abruptly.

"Christina," Alex said into the phone, not bothering to hide his exasperation, "you are making sounds like there was something heavy between us, and there wasn't. Friends, that's what we've always been."

"Well, maybe it's taken me a longer time than it should have to wake up to some of my own finer feelings, Alex. And maybe," Christina said, "you'll wake up to some new feelings of your own, too. I just wouldn't want that to happen too late. I'll see you tonight."

She was off the phone immediately. Just like her father, Alex mused without particularly warm remembrance. She would not give up. Pensively he inserted small onyx-and-diamond studs into the cuffs of a dress shirt. Tonight was not going to be particularly easy for him. Well, it had to be done sooner or later. He'd have to display his colors on the field, if he wanted to have people follow him into battle.

Mara knew immediately she was out of place. Of course, maybe she was just being paranoid. Alex had told her she looked beautiful when he had come for her, and perhaps to him she did. But still, as she looked around at the others in their full-length gowns, she felt dowdy; hers was short and modest, a blue as Alex had suggested, reaching just to her calves. She felt embarrassed. For a while, as they circulated through the crowded home, she tried to keep up a brave front, but the frozen smile she had thus far been able to maintain had slipped, and her eyes stung from more than the cigarette smoke. To make it worse, everyone there seemed immensely interested in who she was.

"What's wrong?" Alex asked, guiding her out of the main room, thronged with beautiful, laughing and drinking guests. They moved down a hallway. Alex opened a door and they stepped into a quiet study richly paneled in cherry wood. Sounds from the party were muted, almost nonexistent once the door was closed.

"I don't fit in here," Mara said flatly. "I feel uncomfortable and unwelcome."

"You're the most beautiful woman at the party," he said.

"Oh, Alex . . ." Mara turned away. "People were looking at me because I'm . . . different." She let it go at that. But he didn't.

"That's garbage. It's because you're—"

"No," Mara said. "Please, Alex. Don't let's lie to each other."

Alex nodded. "Okay, all right. A different dress might have been more appropriate. But it's a lovely dress, and in any other place, in any other situation, it would have been fine." He shook his head, obviously frustrated, obviously wanting to spare her feelings. "Mara, most of these women have dedicated their lives to outdressing each other. They're so competitive they could make an Olympic event out of what they wear to these nonsensical social affairs. If anything, it's my oversight. I should have been wiser, should have helped you prepare."

"It isn't even that," Mara said, and she held her eyes steady. "A lot of people don't like me. It isn't just because of the dress, either. It's because of me. Like I'm not one of them. Not one of the in crowd."

"That, my love, is a plus. It's precisely why I'm with you, not anyone else. They're cookie-cutter people. The same iced heart and identical distorted intellect residing in each of them. Not all, but a lot of them," he revised generously.

Mara smiled. She was thankful for his honesty and touched by his loyalty. It made her feel less alone in a world that had suddenly become populated entirely with strangers. She crossed the few feet separating them, and circling both arms around his neck, kissed him deeply, lovingly. Almost at once she felt him respond, the hardening telltale sign of his desire pulsing against her.

Alex emitted a low, muffled moan and slid his hand over her bodice, making her respond with her own sound of abandoned pleasure.

"Let's go home," Mara said. "Let's leave all of this and just be us, alone . . . together," she whispered into his ear suggestively.

"Not possible," Alex said, his lips playing lightly against her hair. "But later I am going to do such things to you . . . such things," he said. "If those others out there had any idea, they'd be reaching for their smelling salts."

"My word, Alex, you do sound wicked," Mara drawled, feigning her version of a Southern accent.

"I am wicked," he growled, biting an earlobe. "I'm a scoundrel."

"And I love it," Mara returned, looking deeply into his eyes.

There was a click, then a rush of sound as noises from the party replaced the room's quiet. Both Alex and Mara turned together. A young woman, resplendent in a white-and-silver beaded gown, stood in the open doorway.

"Alex," the other woman said, looking from him to Mara and then back to him again. She was slender, with eyes that varied in shade, like opals catching different degrees of light when she moved her head even slightly. Her upswept hair, a warm shade of golden honey, was fastened into place with diamond-and-pearl combs.

Alex's arm squeezed more tightly against Mara's waist, and she felt herself being drawn in closer to him, whether for his well-being or for hers, she could not tell.

"Christina," Alex began, his voice like silk, elegantly refined. "I'd like to introduce Mara Kozinski."

Surprisingly, the other woman's tenseness evaporated. A smile appeared and she came forward, manicured fingers outstretched to Mara.

"A pleasure," she said, or more accurately, she crooned. "Christina LaPierre." The two women touched hands briefly, and then, her serene smile still intact, Christina said, "How is it we've never met before?"

"I've only just moved to New Orleans," Mara replied.

"Oh, how lovely. How very lovely for us." Christina flashed a smile to Alex. "It's a wonderful party, isn't it?

But so crowded," she added pointedly, and then quickly recovered with an overdrawn, "And hot!" She made a fluttering, fanning motion with one hand by her face. "I'm absolutely parched. Alex, would you? A cool something for me? Otherwise, I'll wilt dead away."

Alex nodded, not appearing too pleased with the request to fetch Christina's refreshments. "We'd hate to have you wilt, Christina." He looked to Mara. "Mara? Anything?"

"Nothing, thanks. I'm fine." From the expression in his eyes, she thought he was trying to tell her something. Whatever it was, was lost to her, and remained a mystery as he left her alone with the stunning Christina LaPierre.

Christina had the proper look to suit the evening's occasion. In fact, to Mara she appeared to be the exemplar of whatever was the most elegant, the most refined, and at the same time the most dazzling, in her floor-length dress. Mara had chosen to wear her hair down, softly waved at her shoulders, in contrast to Christina's hair, which was arranged sleekly atop her head. In spite of Christina's statement to the contrary, Mara thought the other woman actually looked cool.

Alex had left the door open after him. Now Christina closed it. This time when she turned back to Mara there was no trace of the former politeness in her speech, no warmth in her eyes, no upward curve to the now tightly drawn lips.

"Well, how are you enjoying the little get-together?" Christina asked.

"A little get-together?" Mara smiled uneasily. "Where I come from a shindig like this would be the event of the year, maybe of the decade."

"Really? Would it really?" Christina asked, and laughed.

"Yes. It would."

"Oh, of course. I'd forgotten you're not—" She stopped abruptly.

Mara was amused. "Go on, say what you were going to."

"Say . . . ?" Christina shrugged. "Oh, all right. If it's honesty you're after, very well. You're not one of us. I must say, it's to your credit that you can at least see it. Some people try to crash our group and truly believe they fit in!" Christina laughed gaily. "Such bores, really. You can't imagine the jokes we all make behind their backs. I know that sounds cruel, but after all, they deserve it. Trying to be more than one really is . . . pushy and cheeky and tacky."

"Maybe it's just being friendly."

"Then they should go where people will be friendly back. It's impossible to force some things. You know?"

"I'm beginning to," Mara replied dryly.

"It isn't, of course, that people are better than other people. It's not a moral thing."

"Of course not," Mara replied. "But perhaps immoral?"

"Oh, I've offended you." Christina looked aghast. "There! You see, that just goes to prove my point. Even in simple discussions, when people aren't on the same footing, that is, when they see life from their own restricted perspectives, there's such grief. Misunderstandings. Confusion. All for nothing. I, for one, was merely expressing a certain truth as seen from my vantage, and you misunderstood. Why, you probably thought I was being intentionally rude."

"I did," Mara said sincerely. "Snide, actually."

"Well, there you are." Christina tsk-ed.

The charade had gone on long enough. Mara's hand veritably itched to wipe the expression of condescending benevolence off Christina LaPierre's face. Instead, re-straining herself, she said, "I'm not ashamed of what I am or where I've come from. So I didn't go to fancy schools. So my family's name has never been on any social register, at least not for long. I'm sure you're aware that my uncle was once a provisional member of your elite group. But he blew it. Married from the wrong side of the tracks. Shameful, wasn't it? But," Mara said, parodying Christina, "there you are."

Christina gave a disinterested shrug. "Bad blood will out. A local expression."

"Where I come from we had a few local expressions, too. Like bad manners will out."

Christina narrowed her eyes. "My family goes back generations in New Orleans. We are the keepers of tradition, of a style that cannot be emulated or learned. You may not believe it, but as cruel as you think I am, I'm actually doing you a big favor by being straight about all of this. This is a big game you've entered into. My father's a powerful man who doesn't like to have his plans messed up. Alex is a necessary part of those plans. King will go to any lengths to get what he wants. If you're foolish enough to stay, you'll find there are a lot of people around here that way."

"Including you?"

"You're really intent on making me out the villain in all this, aren't you? All right, yes, I've been known to take a certain selfish interest in my own welfare. And I'd advise you to do the same for yourself. Look at yourself clearly, at your situation clearly. Otherwise, my friend, you're likely to get that noble heart of yours broken. That, I can absolutely, without any reservation, guarantee. So, we understand each other?"

Mara felt claustrophobic. She felt suddenly as if Christina was filling all the space in the room. She felt as if she was being edged out of her own self, and fleetingly, for an agonizing instant, she began to wonder if Christina might not be right. She had come to the wrong city. She was out of her class and with the wrong man. It was all going to end very sadly.

Wanting to escape, Mara moved quickly past Christina. She opened the door just as Alex arrived with two tall frosted glasses.

"These ought to lower the temperature a little," he said cheerfully.

"Umm, perfect," Mara replied not quite as happily, relieving Alex of both glasses, "just what we were needing. You can't possibly imagine how hot it's gotten in here." Mara strode back to where Christina stood.

The two women were barely noses apart. Christina's eyes traveled nervously to the drinks held in Mara's hand.

"Something nice and wet and icy, Christina?" Mara asked sweetly.

"Don't you dare," Christina warned between clenched teeth, and took a quick step back.

Mara stepped forward. She wore a radiant smile. "Oh, come on, Miss LaPierre. In the tacky neighborhood I come from, we'd never take a drink and pour it on top of someone's head. Not even if they deserved it. But maybe the women where I come from have more class." She thrust the drink at Christina.

Haughtily, Christina turned away.

"Well, if you'd rather wilt," Mara said agreeably, and put the drinks down. Then, turning to Alex, who looked to be desperately trying to follow what was happening, Mara made an enormous point of linking her arm in his, and said, "It was lovely talking, Christina. No doubt we'll meet again."

Christina gave her a cold glance. "Oh, count on it, darling. Count on it."

Chapter 7

"OKAY," ALEX SAID ON THE DRIVE HOME. "SINCE YOU aren't going to talk about it, I will. I got the distinct impression I was witnessing the start of a world war back there. Mind filling me in?"

"You were just overhearing some friendly advice from one of my own gender," Mara dissembled. "And I was just volunteering some of my own. Just light chitchat, girl talk, that sort of thing." This time she found it impossible to keep the darkness out of her voice.

"Ah, and that's why you're shaking—from receiving some friendly advice." He took her hand in his, clasping it lightly to let her know he understood, even if he didn't understand what.

She knew he didn't believe her, and was grateful to him for not pressing the issue. Perhaps, she thought, that was because he respected her right to privacy, or maybe it was for his own sake he didn't want to know the cause of her distress—a definite application of the adage "Ignorance is bliss."

At her door, she gave him a chaste kiss. It was the best she could manage under the circumstances. She felt like a vial of nitroglycerin. A slight bump against her psyche, and boom, a major explosion.

"I take it I'm not invited in?" The question was posed with ironic good humor. Underlying the light sarcasm was their shared and unspoken knowledge that they were both avoiding an important issue in their relationship. It was, Mara felt, as if they were both sharing the same thoughts, feeling the same feelings, and fearing the same fears. If they were to talk about "it," the "problem," the "major issue," it would become tangible and then they would have to deal with it. By not speaking of it, they could at least buy themselves time.

"Would you mind?" Mara asked, tightly reining in her emotions, knowing that of course he minded. It had been perfectly clear the entire night that he had wanted to tear off her clothes and ravish her, and that she would have welcomed and returned his passion in kind. Then she had had her conversation with Christina. Once she had read an article saying it was necessary to feel good about yourself to enjoy making love. She definitely did not feel good about herself now. It was ridiculous that someone else's opinion of her could shake her self-esteem. But it had, maybe because there was more than just a little truth to Christina's observations.

"You're tired," he said, making an excuse to save both their faces.

"A bit, yes."

Alex's nod could just as well have been a sigh. Both of them were speaking in code. They needed to back off, they needed some space.

"I'll see you tomorrow."

"Tomorrow," Mara agreed, trying to put some cheer into her dismissal.

Alex backed off, still looking as if he expected her to change her mind and call him back. Instead, she unlocked her door. Behind her, she heard him start away.

Oh, Alex, she thought. *Just go, stay away from me before I ruin everything you've worked your whole life for.*

She pushed, and the front door swung open. But instead of going in, she turned to catch just one fading glimpse of him, as if he might really disappear out of her life forever.

Alex had also stopped. He was looking back at her. They both smiled, slow smiles, slightly sad smiles of mutual understanding that both damned and acknowledged the underlying reality of their relationship. They had problems, big problems that weren't going to disappear no matter how intensely satisfying their lovemaking might be.

"It's okay," he said, raising his hand to wave. "So I'll take a cold shower. Have a good sleep."

"Alex, I want you so much." Tears were in her eyes. She made no effort to brush them away. "You know?"

"Yeah . . ." he said sadly, "I know."

She pretended to shut the door, but opened it a second later when she knew he would not see her watching him go down the street to his car.

He was like part of the moonlight, a perfect man, a living piece of poetry, a song. Her song.

The following day, she moved like the wind itself through the streets of New Orleans, refusing herself the opportunity to give in to depression. There was so much to do, so much, and by one that afternoon she had done most of what she had set out to accomplish. Or rather, she had put into motion certain events which would either make or break her future with Alex.

Facing up to things was the perfect antidote to her fear. By the time she returned home, she felt positively exuberant as the telephone man went about connecting the phones. She barely had time to bathe and change into some fresh clothes before the man from the used-furniture store arrived.

With Mara traipsing after him, delivering a running spiel on the hidden value behind each and every piece of furniture, the man made more realistic notations as to actual worth on a clipboard. Forty-five minutes later, he presented his opinion neatly delineated on a yellow piece of paper.

"That's all? That can't possibly be all this beautiful furniture is worth," Mara objected, handing him back the paper.

"Look, lady—" the man said.

"No, you just take another look," Mara insisted, and escorted him on a second tour. "I'm sure you'll see new features you missed the first time around. It's deceptive, this furniture. It has a kind of charm that comes through with familiarity." Of course that was utter rubbish, which they both knew. But it allowed him to revise his estimate without looking like a jerk or a crook.

By the time they had gone through the third room, the man had reconsidered. "Ma'am, I'm in a hurry. I'll give you another ten percent for this stuff."

"Twenty."

"Ten."

"You're not the only man in New Orleans who buys furniture, you know."

"Fifteen," the man relented wearily.

"When will you be by to get it," Mara wanted to know as she signed the agreement.

"Tomorrow okay? That soon enough for you?" he asked sarcastically.

Mara smiled. "Sorry, I haven't been here long enough to develop the charm of my Southern sisters."

"No kidding," he commented beneath his breath as Mara saw him out.

The first call she made was to Alex.

"Hi," she said when Anna had put her through. The housekeeper was reluctant to do so, Mara thought, judging by the woman's tone.

"I miss you," he returned, almost urgently.

"Good, then you'll be happy to see me tonight."

"Damn right I will. We'll go to the Commander's Palace."

"No we won't. We'll eat right here. I dipped into my inheritance today. Went wild. Bought totally extravagant treats for us to have for dinner. Alex," she said, finally becoming more serious, "I don't want a lot of people around tonight. Last night was enough. I'd like tonight just for you and me."

"Sure. I'll drink to that," he said.

"Good, so it'll be Scotch and soda at seven. See you later."

"Oh, Mara . . ."

"Yes?"

"Just thought you should know. You're not going to get rid of me so easily tonight. In fact, you aren't going to get rid of me at all."

"What makes you think I want to?" she said, laughing. Her heart beat in wild leaps, and a familiar, tantalizing rush of heat spread its way through her body.

"Just so you know."

He arrived at six-thirty, ahead of schedule, carrying flowers and two bottles of wine. He seemed almost shy, almost a schoolboy, and she was totally captivated by this heretofore unseen side of the dashing, elegant Alex Gautier. There were several times during dinner when the conversation stopped and they would peer into each other's eyes, communicating feelings too strong, too impossibly tender to find a description in words.

"You're beautiful," he said. "There's a light in your eyes. And"—he paused to consider her expression—"excitement. Yes, excitement. I'd like to think it's because of me." Leaning back in his chair, he continued to appraise her. "Only something tells me—"

"You're right." Mara quickly jumped up to clear away the empty plates. "It's being here with you, the candle-light."

He took hold of her wrist as she reached for his plate. "I told you once, you're not good at telling stories. What's going on?"

"A surprise," she said, both pleased and frightened that he knew her so well.

"For me?"

"Yes, for you. For us, too."

He didn't appear entirely satisfied by her response, but relaxed his hold enough that she could escape into the kitchen and avoid further scrutiny. It was absolutely imperative that he not know what she was up to.

Later, Alex was in the kitchen when she returned to the dining room to blow out the candles still flickering on the table.

Alone in the room, Mara recognized it as another one of those important moments, one of those landmark moments that needed to be honored. She took a moment to memorize the dining room as it was then, and as it would never be again. "I'm sorry," she said softly, speaking through her heart, "I'm sorry, furniture . . . I'm sorry, Salina . . . I'm sorry, Uncle. But I've got to do this, just the way you had to do what you did."

When she blew out the candles, there was a feeling that they were with her and approved, or at least understood.

They were present as two ghosts whose passion could never be completely extinguished from the rooms she now occupied.

The whole evening was experienced as if she were conducting a ritual. To her, it was a sacred night. After this night, she thought, while bathing, knowing Alex was already in bed waiting for her, things would never again be the same.

"Make love to me," she said, standing in the doorway with a white towel draped around her. "I don't ever want to forget this night," she said, "not through all of time."

Alex was stretched upon the bed, only a corner of the sheet covering his middle. His eyes burned hot against her skin.

"Glad to oblige," he said. "You don't need that towel." His voice was low, sensual.

The towel slid to the floor. With his eyes on her, her nipples immediately grew taut.

"Turn around for me," Alex said, and she did, slowly, deliberately, knowing exactly how she must appear to him. Only a moment before, she had stood before the mirror, seeing herself through his eyes, wanting to be sure he would be pleased. Although she had never considered herself vain, she knew that she was beautiful, that she was desirable. For that she was glad, because everything she was, she was for him alone.

So, as she turned slowly around, she did so proudly, knowing she was a gift to him. Her legs were long and slender, her thighs and buttocks firm. A small waist separated the graceful flare of her hips from the gentle upsweep of flesh leading to her breasts, which were high and full, reaching forward and up so that they probably appeared larger than they actually were. She moved toward him and brushed her fingers lightly across his body.

Alex leaned forward on the bed, the sheet falling off and exposing his aroused state. He caught her glance, and only smiled, knowing what she must have been thinking.

"We could probably torment each other until we are both mad," Alex said. "You're so beautiful. Do you know how beautiful you are?" he asked.

"It only matters because I want you to see me that way."

She stood before him, only an arm's reach away. But he made no move to touch her; instead he devoured her with his eyes.

"I would kill any man who ever touched you," Alex said, suddenly reaching out and pulling her down to him, as at the same time he swung himself into a sitting position on the edge of the bed.

"No man will," she said as his mouth came upon her stomach, his breath hot, his fingers on her buttocks demanding as he pushed her into his face. "Not ever, not ever . . ." she said, and involuntarily gave in to a series of spasms as his hands cupped the underside of both breasts, the thumbs reaching up to explore her nipples.

His tongue darted lower, and one hand came down to part her legs. Instinctively she made herself accessible to his needs, losing her shyness as the heat in her pelvis grew in exact proportion to the obvious pleasure he was experiencing in having his way.

She felt the wave grow from a tiny swirling eddy of delight to an onrushing torrent of desire that swept her away, leaving only a racking feeling of ecstasy. She was only dimly aware of calling out for him to stop, and that her hands were locked against his head, twined in his hair, and that low, muffled groans of encouragement were coming from him.

At last, she gave in to the pleasure, and cried out once

from a sudden wrenching jolt that changed to a feeling of expansion. She was the entire universe, expanding outward forever.

When she came back, she was in one piece, breathing in short gasps, her body slick with sweat and tears trailing down her face.

"Mara . . . Mara . . ." Alex was saying, his voice so dim, becoming more real as the spasms subsided.

"Thank you," she said, kissing him, letting the tears of happiness fall against his own face turned to her. "I've never, never felt like that before. It's you, you who do this to me, for me."

He never removed his mouth from hers, but laid her upon the bed. Then, still kissing her, his tongue as urgently insistent as the rest of him, he began to move his hands possessively over her body.

The heat began to build in her again. She felt his hardness against her, felt him pulse, knew the effort it was taking to maintain his control when he was fully ready to have his own satisfaction. Her hips began to spiral in counterpoint to his. Both his hands clasped her waist and he moved her to his rhythm.

She forgot they were two, their bodies so smoothly working in unison to each other's needs.

"Now," he said, his voice male and gravelly as he lifted her buttocks off the sheets, "is not the time to be a Southern gentleman. I hope you will forgive me."

And he moved into her with a cry, with a total, possessive command of her flesh. There was no time, no energy to talk anymore, to whisper endearments; he was man and she was woman.

"I love you," he said, the words coming out as a form of release, just as his body suddenly tensed, and closing his eyes, he let out a low moan of satisfaction.

It was perfect, Mara thought as she stroked the side of his face lying against her breast. Making love with him had been perfect. When it had mattered most, he had finally said it: I love you. He had said the words. I love you.

"Alex, my darling. I love you."

She waited for a reply, but he was already asleep.

She could not sleep.

All the activities of the day played through her mind, and when she brushed those aside, the plans for the future intruded.

Leaving Alex to his peaceful sleep, she threw on her nightgown and slipped softly from the room.

The stairs creaked as she made her way down them to the bottom floor. She removed the sketches she had made, along with the detailed lists, from a sideboard in the infrequently used formal parlor. For the next hour she sat in the kitchen sipping coffee, occasionally dreaming, but mostly being absolutely practical. She had to succeed with her plan, she absolutely had to.

Mara looked up, thinking she had heard a sound on the stairs. And she had. Quickly she shoved the papers spread out on the table into a cupboard. Not a moment too soon. A second later, Alex appeared in the kitchen, his eyes blurred from sleep, but still questioning.

"Hi!" Mara said gaily, putting her coffee cup in the sink.

"Why are you so cheerful? It's inhuman and unnatural. And besides that, it's"—he paused to look at his wristwatch—"three o'clock in the morning."

"I couldn't sleep."

He moved over to where she stood and took the cup from the sink. "Umm, I see. So you thought you'd come down here to have a cup of coffee, huh? A strange remedy for sleeplessness, if I've ever heard one."

"Okay," Mara said, "you're right. Now, this is going to sound ridiculous."

"Try me. I'm a lawyer. I hear all kinds of stories."

"Ghosts," she said. "I just have this feeling. Sometimes it's like there are ghosts living here with me."

"Mara . . ."

"See, I told you."

"Well, I'm no ghost and I'm tired." He ran his eyes over her. "And you don't look like a ghost either. Come on," he said, grabbing her by the waist, "I can't sleep without you."

She obeyed, her secret surprise still intact as she climbed the stairs with his arm encircling her waist.

The morning seemed to come almost immediately, and with it the sound of someone pounding on the front door.

Mara sat up in bed, for a moment too disoriented to be alarmed.

Alex stirred beside her. "What? . . . Noise . . . s'terrible."

"Oh, no . . ." she said beneath her breath. Leaping out of bed, she frantically threw on her jeans and T-shirt. "I forgot. How could I have forgotten?" She was out of the room and down the stairs before Alex could ask her anything crucial.

By the time he had joined her downstairs, she had her excuse ready.

"Mara?" Alex said, staring after the two men carrying a sofa out the front door. "Why are these men taking away your furniture?"

"Well," she said, "the thing is . . . I just felt so haunted, you know. Like everything here belonged to Salina and Uncle Tad. So I thought I'd redo things, all new. And," she went on, talking perhaps too quickly, but hoping her speed would pass for excitement, "that's really the surprise. You've ruined it now. I'm redecorating."

"Really?"

"Really."

"The whole place?" Alex's attention was on the two men now carrying away a chair.

"Oh, yes. Absolutely. You won't recognize this place when I'm through. That's why," she said, "after this morning, you aren't allowed back until you get a formal invitation."

"To the unveiling?"

"Umm, something like that," Mara agreed vaguely.

It wasn't five minutes after Alex left that the remodeling contractor appeared on her doorstep.

"No one, absolutely no one, must have any idea of what I'm doing here. Is that perfectly, absolutely clear?" she demanded of the burly tanned man and his two assistants.

"Sounds fair to me," the man drawled, "seeing as how we don't know ourselves." He stared down at the sketches she had spread out on the kitchen table. "So what are you doing, lady?"

"Well," Mara said, "basically I'd say I'm going to open an entertainment club that's going to make New Orleans stand up and take notice." That in itself sounded like an outrageous statement, considering the club was on St. Louis, just a half-block off Bourbon Street, where some of the finest jazz in the world was played as a matter of course.

None of the men looked impressed. "You ever run a club before?"

"No."

Their silence said it all.

"I'm not going to fail," she said defiantly.

Their continued silence wasn't at all encouraging.

"You'll see." And she walked from the room, feeling not at all brave.

Alex called late in the afternoon.

"I've got to make a little trip," he said, sounding both worried and apologetic. "A meeting's been arranged for me to glad-hand a few men who might be enthusiastic to my cause of becoming D.A. I could use an agreeable face or two in my corner."

"Something bad happened today?" Mara probed, sinking down into one of the kitchen chairs, glad for the excuse to take a breather.

"Let's just say I've had moments in my life when I've felt a mite more popular in this city. LaPierre hasn't wasted any time. He's picked out his new boy already. Well, of course, he always has someone waiting in the wings, so I can't exactly give him points for speed. But on the other hand, he's managed to have a story printed in the newspapers about his candidate. A glowing story. I've got to give the King credit. He works magic, all right. He's managed to turn a first-class rat into a white knight."

Mara was up now, pacing back and forth like an enraged lioness over the short distance the telephone's cord reached. "You can have your own publicity," she said. "Your picture, your background. No matter what that other guy is like, you'll wipe him out. The public isn't stupid, Alex. The public can—"

"The public has to be reached first," Alex said.

"Then you'll reach them."

"I contacted the advertising firm I'd spoken to earlier about running billboards for me. Everything had been set up, all the preliminary artwork, the photography, everything. Suddenly they were very sorry, but it seems they can't quite find the space we talked about previously. I then offered them more money to see if they might take another look, might possibly discover there's a little more space there than they thought," Alex said, his voice laced heavily with sarcasm. "It appears I don't have the right tender for them, the popular currency being power."

"There's newspapers and television."

"They're looking for angles. They need hooks to run their stories on, items that'll capture the public's interest. It's show-biz out there. I know that, and so does LaPierre. He's waltzed his candidate into the limelight already. How about this for openers? The press is already jumping up and down because my opposition is hosting a charity gala. A full-coverage event. A nice tame interview with a nice honest man who merely wants to put away rapists and murderers isn't going to play against that kind of razzle-dazzle."

"It's only the beginning," Mara objected.

"Exactly. LaPierre's planning on burying me before I'm out the starting gate. He wants to cripple me now, before I have a chance to run any kind of decent race."

"Are you going to let him?" Mara asked.

There was silence. "Crippled or not, as long as I can crawl, I'm going to be in. Anticipate pain," he said so lightly that she knew how serious he actually was.

"How long will you be gone?" she asked him before they said good-bye.

"Possibly a week," Alex said. "There may be some other meetings at different places. I won't know until I'm along the way."

She almost said "good," it would give her time to carry out her arrangements. But instead managed to say, "I'll miss you." Which was also true.

The place was still a mess when the first auditionee showed up with her flier in hand.

"This the place? Salina's Place?"

The sign painter had not yet finished his work. "Yes."

"I'm a singer."

"I'm looking for great singers," Mara said. "Only the best."

The man holding sheet music looked deprecatingly around him. "For here?"

There was plaster and sawdust and loose beams and fragmented bricks wherever one walked. Walls had been torn down, opening the bottom floor to make one wide room. Workmen hammered and sawed, drilled and slopped fresh plaster against the walls.

In the middle of the commotion was a rented baby-grand piano covered in a paint tarp to protect its finish.

"This place is going to be the only place in this city to be," Mara returned haughtily. She was wearing jeans and a sweatshirt, a kerchief around her hair, and there was white paint on the tip of her nose.

He was the first to come. By the end of three days, she had listened to two hundred additional singers of varying degrees of talent. The accompanist, a man with years of experience behind him, showed her the ropes; so, as a novice entrepreneur, she managed to put on a pretty good show of professionalism herself.

Out of the two hundred auditionees, she settled upon three people: two men and a woman. She was no talent expert of course, but in a way, that was a plus. Or so she told herself. Her taste was representative of the likes of average people, and maybe not just average people, but people with money, sophisticates like Christina LaPierre. The common denominator among all people was their basic feelings of love and joy and sorrow, and that was basically what music was all about. It was a channel for the heart to feel.

The three singers she finally selected were good, but not great. There were a couple of near-greats, according to her rating schedule, but she couldn't afford them. As it was, the deal she offered her new employees was a chance to be heard, or "showcased," as the accompanist put it. In addition, they could share a percentage of the profits. She guessed they took her deal because there wasn't any other one around at the moment.

Mara did not know if she was more depressed or more desperate. Her enterprise was using her forty thousand dollars like sand running through a sieve.

On Thursday, she sat down with her bank balance before her and the itemization of bills to be paid and work that still needed completion. It was definitely serious. Black and white columns jarred her out of whatever idealistic illusions remained concerning her enterprise.

She had wanted everything to be perfect when she opened Salina's Place. She had wanted the best talent performing in terrific-looking surroundings with her as the center of it all. Alex was to marvel at her accomplishments. He was to sweep her into his arms with kisses and exclamations that she was the most clever of the clever. Christina's words would sail out into the cosmos along with all the accompanying insecurities they engendered in her, never to return again.

Only that was now impossible. Money was what she needed. Now.

"We're opening tomorrow night," Mara announced that Thursday morning when her three new singers and the accompanist arrived to rehearse. She had to yell above the sounds of hammering. The small troupe of entertainers looked at her as if she were crazy.

"I'm going to have leaflets printed up this afternoon, announcing the opening, and they'll be distributed tomorrow on the streets. I'll get some kids to do it. We don't have our liquor license, but we can serve tea and I'll get

some stuff from a wholesale bakery to serve for snacks.''
Now they looked at her as if she were totally demented.

"It's all going to work out," she said when no one else
said anything. "You'll see."

"There's nothing here," one of the singers whined.

"A great tree springs from a tiny acorn," Mara
answered.

"Honey, we're not acorns," the accompanist said,
slouching over the keyboard.

"So pretend!"

Mara left them to their pouting. She had other things to
do.

The construction workers were ordered to stop work at
three on Friday. Then the real work began.

"I know you're artists," Mara said, positioning one of
the newly acquired dining chairs at one of the newly
acquired cocktail tables. "But unless you help me get this
place ready, you aren't going to convince anyone else.
Your audience isn't going to have anywhere to place their
backsides while they, too, discover your talent."

Grudgingly, everyone helped with the physical prepara-
tions.

"Next thing, she'll have us bussing tables," said one of
the singers.

Mara smiled brightly. "As a matter of fact . . ."

They were open for business at eight that night. No one
actually showed until nine. The French Quarter had a lot
of interesting establishments, but Mara doubted any had
quite the ambience, quite the decor exhibited by Salina's
Place that night. In a way, however, there was a sort of
original charm to the half-plastered walls and the lack of
matching furniture.

"It's so spontaneous here," said one of the few
customers who arrived before ten o'clock.

The entertainment was good, though; that was for sure. By eleven o'clock Mara counted the evening's receipts and discovered she had broken even on the bakery goods.

Mara was on her way to a table with a tray of iced teas when her attention was caught by a tall, motionless figure standing just inside the doorway.

It was Alex.

Her heart stopped. When he hadn't called her, she assumed he was still tied up with his meetings. This was terrible. This was awful. For him to see her like this was not how it was supposed to have happened.

She finished dispatching the drinks. The love song being crooned took on the mood of a dirge in Mara's mind as she moved across the room to where Alex still remained.

"This is what you call redecorating?"

"It wasn't supposed to be like this," Mara said quickly.

"I like it," Alex announced suddenly and with conviction.

"I know how it seems, but . . . What?"

He pulled her to him, and kissing the tip of her nose, said, "You've got guts. And originality," he added humorously. "I like the touch of the loose plaster. Some just hit me on the head."

"I've got guts, originality and hives," she added. "Especially hives." But she was so relieved over his approval, tears had come to her eyes. "I wanted you to be pleased."

"And I am."

"Yes, but—"

"The way you are is perfect—just the way you are. No changes were necessary, or are necessary." As he spoke, he stroked sticky strands of pale hair from off her forehead and the sides of her cheeks. Even though the shutters were open on the windows and the paddle fans churned around from the ceiling, the room was still close.

"Oh, Alex, I've got to run. Customers," she said, nodding with a smile to a man who was hailing her from across the room, his raised glass empty. "Find a seat, any seat, and I'll be back between making my millions."

But she didn't get back. As the night progressed, the crowd increased. Some people left when they discovered there wasn't any liquor to be had. Others were happy with anything cold, and the music was good enough to hold them for at least one set of songs.

By two o'clock in the morning, two-thirds of the tables were filled with a mixture of conventioneers making all the rounds, and locals who had come to check out the new place.

It was then that the small, noisy group entered. Even through the half-light, and from far across the room, Mara felt the electricity they generated. Power and assurance veritably radiated from them as they moved like a single force into Salina's Place.

Mara glanced quickly around the room, spotted a table large enough to hold the party of three women and four men, then started toward them. But she stopped. She stopped because one of the guests was Christina LaPierre. Both women saw each other at the same time.

Christina's bright smile froze; then, tossing her head, she shared a comment with her group, who also as a single entity turned their attention to Mara.

Alex must have caught the interaction. He rose from his chair and intercepted Mara as she started forward again.

"Don't let her get to you," he said.

"Of course not," Mara replied. Alex didn't follow along behind her, for which she was glad. It was his vote of confidence that she could handle herself among present unpleasant company.

"Well, well," Christina said, "wasn't I right? We do meet again. And so soon, too." To her friends she introduced, "Mara . . . Kozinski, isn't it?" Slight nods and a mumbled "pleased" followed along with what appeared to Mara as a collective attitude of amused curiosity slightly tinged with condescension. "I had to see it for myself," Christina went on. She reached into her purse and drew out one of the small fliers Mara had had distributed earlier in the day announcing the opening of her club. Before they had been duplicated, Mara had signed her name personally on the bottom, the intention being to make the fliers more personal.

Christina's eyes flicked off to the right, beyond Mara's shoulder. The expression of scorn changed to one of uncertainty, and then a mixture of anger and regret.

Mara turned just as Alex came up to join the group.

"Hello, Christina." As he spoke his greeting, he swept his arm around Mara's waist.

Mara understood his action was on her behalf, meant as a protective gesture, but she wished he would have left her to deal with Christina on her own. She did not like the woman, who was obviously spoiled and incapable of any generosity of spirit when she did not get what she wanted. But in all fairness, Mara could understand Christina's disappointment. Christina had dreamed her own dreams, and had Mara not entered the picture, those wishful imaginings might very well have become a reality.

"How are you, Alex?" Christina responded. Her eyes had become suddenly misty, and it was clear to Mara and probably to anyone else watching that Christina was having difficulty keeping control.

"Tired," he said.

"Yes, you would be. I heard you were away to gather support for your campaign." She fidgeted uncomfortably. Alex had not removed his arm from around Mara's waist.

No matter what was being said, that fact seemed to override all else.

Mara broke into the awkwardness with a suggestion. "There's a large table over there," she said. "It has a good view of the stage. The next performer's going on in a moment. Maybe you'd . . ."

Christina was already moving away, going to the table, the social convention of a pleasant good-bye to Alex unobserved. Mara and Alex exchanged looks of mutual comprehension. It was going to be all-out war on all fronts.

Christina sat immobile during half of the singer's set. If she heard anything, if she disliked what she heard or enjoyed what she heard, there was no outward reaction. Her group of friends was more animated, but occasionally, Mara noted surreptitiously as she served other customers, nervous glances would be cast to their social leader for clues as to their behavior.

At one point there was a brief conference between Christina and one of the men, who rose soon after to ask Mara if he might use the phone to make a local call. When he returned, the party rose as if on cue, leaving in the same manner they had arrived, close together and assured.

From the sidelines, Mara watched them, more out of curiosity and a grudging admiration for the aplomb with which they maneuvered life to their purposes, than from jealousy or any overt ill will. Enveloped in a cloud of French perfume, they floated back out into the night, leaving the room slightly darker in the absence of their glittering smiles and the sheen of flowing silk gowns.

"Well," she said, walking over to where Alex sat, his face set into a grim mold, "at least that's over and done with."

He shook his head. "Is that what you think?"

"She came, she saw, and she conquered. I'm sure to

her way of thinking, my enterprise looks like a stupid, ill-conceived folly, destined to fail. Christina should be satisfied.'' Out of a sense of pride, Mara had meant to keep her voice light. Only she couldn't. She was humiliated and frightened and frustrated that she had no real resources with which to defend her position.

"She isn't satisfied," Alex replied.

"Well, what the hell does she want? To have me tarred and feathered and run through the streets of New Orleans?"

"To the contrary. That would only be a reminder to her and everyone else that you humiliated her. What Christina wants is that you leave the picture altogether."

"Well, she's going to be disappointed. I may not have much, but I'm stubborn. I have no intention of giving up what's mine."

"Mara," Alex said, taking her hand, "it's wonderful to shout brave rhetoric into the wind, just don't underestimate the determination of people like the LaPierres to get what they want."

"Isn't that what you're doing?" Mara replied gently, accepting his concern in the manner it was intended—not as a rebuke, and not to dissuade her from putting up a fight, but because he wanted her to deal with reality.

"I don't have any choice," he said.

And she knew what he meant. He might be tilting at windmills with a slightly broken lance, but he did so with his eyes wide open to his chances of failure or success. He had lived through his father's ordeal as a powerless spectator. Now he had to take up the challenge for himself, or not be able to live with himself. Mara's heart swelled with a fierce, overwhelming pride for his true bravery. It was not difficult to march into battle when you had never seen a bloody field, but had only heard the bugles and trumpets and drums. But Alex had seen the fallen bodies, and he was still going back into the fray. So, yes, he was right to warn her.

"But you do have an option," Alex went on. "All of this isn't necessary." His eyes swept around the club. "You're just going to invite trouble you may not be able to deal with."

"Thanks," she said, "for worrying about me."

One of the waiters was signaling. Two more groups had just come in and needed seating.

Before returning to her duties, she touched her hand flat against Alex's cheek. Instantly, reflexively, he turned his mouth against her palm, kissing its hollow. "But I can't change your mind, can I?" he asked, looking up.

"Maybe . . ." Mara said, "maybe I don't have an option, either."

There was a round of applause for the singer as Mara broke away and went to tend to the new arrivals.

He cared about her, even loved her. But he did not see deeply enough into her to know that just as he had his sense of honor and pride of self, she did also. It was something that could not be given to anyone.

"Hello, welcome to Salina's Place," she said, greeting a group of three couples. "You're in luck. A great table right in front just became vacant."

As she passed by the stairway, her eyes flicked to the top landing. A curious warmth filled her. It was as if a friendly smile had been directed her way. Salina, she thought, hesitating slightly as if she might actually see the ghostly, approving image of her relative watching her from above.

There was nothing there, of course. And yet, the warmth persisted as she led the way through the crowded room.

Chapter 8

MARA'S HAND FLEW TO HER MOUTH, CHECKING THE involuntary gasp. The hand holding the newspaper went limp and the paper dropped to the floor.

Tate Crawford retrieved it, glowering at his black-and-white likeness in the entertainment section as he brought himself up.

"It's damned unfair," he said. "I wasn't ready. It was only my first night. I'm a lot better than that. Hell, I don't get it, anyway. Look—five pictures. Five!" he said sulkily. "Sinatra doesn't even get five pictures when he opens a show. I just don't get it," he mumbled.

"I do," Mara said, her voice faint with shock. She looked back up the stairs, and this time a feeling of coldness washed over her as she thought of Alex still sleeping soundly—peacefully—in her bed. He had decided to stay over, and she had convinced him he deserved at least a half-day's holiday from work after being gone for a week. Readily he had agreed, seeming almost grateful for her suggestion. But rest was a luxury she could not afford herself, and dressing quietly, she had tiptoed from her room to let the workers in.

Tate, her youngest and most talented and certainly most ambitious singer, had entered fast on the heels of the carpenters. With him, he carried a paper. He hadn't been looking for anything about himself, he explained defensively. Who would have expected that one of the most prominent reporters in town would cover Salina's Place, a virtual hole-in-the-wall club, the first night it opened its doors to the public? Who would ever have thought that could happen! Tate raged over and over again, while Mara read the article with the accompanying pictures.

Vaguely she remembered flashbulbs going off during the night, but hadn't thought anything of it. Probably two-thirds of the crowd had been tourists; they all toted cameras and thought nothing of shooting anything and everything that took their fancy, no matter what the propriety of the occasion.

But, clearly, one of those camera-toting patrons had been the man who had shot the pictures and written the scathing article on Salina's Place. There was a picture of Mara herself as she served a tray of iced teas to a table of patrons. She looked frazzled and hot, no better than an overworked waitress slinging hash in a truck stop. The pictures showed the crumbling walls to disadvantage. There wasn't any charm; the place just looked crummy and dumpy. If she were some anonymous reader sipping coffee and scanning the morning paper, she'd make a mental note to cross Salina's Place off as a dive.

And there, along with the other four pictures, was one not taken last night. It was a stock photo, apparently held in the newspaper's files, of Alex. He looked wonderful. That was the worst of it, too; surrounded by the other four pictures, juxtaposed against the tired seediness, Alex looked slightly ridiculous. It was the kind of contrast that brought to mind a politician's corruption, that hinted at some unsavory hidden life.

The accompanying article critiqued the talent, which was said to be valiantly mediocre at best. The refreshments were reported to be almost nonexistent. Physically, the establishment was said to be a shambled wreck, devoid of charm and dank of climate. It was "a suitable place for mold." There was an entire paragraph devoted to Mara being from an industrial town in Ohio. Pointed references were made pertaining to other "outsiders" who had failed at other enterprises. The essence of the paragraph was that here was yet another "carpetbagger" come to exploit the citizenry of New Orleans.

Alex was worked into the story under the guise of "notables in attendance." There were, of course, no other luminaries there. Included along with Alex's occupation was a mention of his family's Creole heritage. His father's "well-publicized fight for justice" was touched upon briefly, the thrust of the information hinting that the same social taint, that same flawed propensity to choose alliances on the wrong side of the social tracks, might have been passed on like a germ to Alex.

Of course it was all assembled and stated very subtly, or, as Mara suspected, legally presented, free from the threat of litigation. And the killer of it all was that because it was all stated so nicely, couched as it was in the blandness of reportorial jargon, the article gave the impression of impartiality, and therefore would bear credence with the public.

"You may as well board up the place," Tate whined.

"Why?" Mara snapped back at him. Of course she knew full well why.

"For one thing, no one's going to come here," Tate said. "Unless they're crazy or they can't read. And," he went on as he strode toward the piano at the far side of the room, "because you aren't going to have any entertainment if they do. Of course, I can't speak for the others." Hastily he went through a stack of sheet music and separated his from the scores belonging to the other two entertainers. "Sorry," he said. "There's just no sense in wasting our time over this. It was a nice dream."

"And I'm not ready to wake up quite yet."

"Suit yourself," said Tate, exiting to nerve-jangling background music produced by an electric buzz saw and two hammering carpenters.

He was still lying in bed when she entered the bedroom. His eyes were open, and when he saw her he smiled.

"You're awake. I thought you'd sleep in," Mara commented, unable to return the smile. Her throat was dry and constricted. Her right hand had a death's grip on the folded newspaper.

"That's not exactly a lullaby down there." Alex laughed and rose up on one elbow, watching her intently.

She stood in the middle of the room, afraid to come any closer, afraid not to. But no matter what her geographic position, it had to be faced.

"What's wrong?" Alex asked, suddenly serious.

"I'm sorry," she said, and handed him the paper.

While he read the damning words, she stood by one of the open shuttered doors and stared unseeingly at the street.

When she looked back at him, he had finished reading. He was sitting upright, leaning against the headboard with the paper beside him. He appeared unaware of her presence.

"Say something," she said, coming within a couple of feet of the bed, but not daring to venture any closer.

"What can I say? What would you like me to say?" His fingers curled the edges of the newspaper.

He still was not able to look at her.

"I don't know," she said. "Maybe that you don't blame me?"

He shot her a swift, almost tortured glance. "No, of course I don't. It's just . . ." He broke off.

"It's just that you're thinking to yourself: 'Oh no. Here it goes again, a woman dragging a man down. I'm being sucked into an emotional quagmire.'" Tears stung at her eyes, but she still hadn't given in to them.

"Yes," Alex said wearily. "That is what I was thinking."

"I see." She nodded, a reasonable gesture, she thought, considering she felt as if the earth were shifting beneath her feet. "I see." She had always thought the truth made one feel good; now she knew there were exceptions to that belief. She felt lousy.

One quick, fluid movement, and Alex was out of bed and holding her against him. "Stop it, Mara. Just stop it right now. I told you things were going to get ugly, that you didn't know what the terrain was here. Now you're getting a taste of it. Christina called the paper, of course. The deed bears the LaPierre mark on it. Subtle and lethal. She probably promised the reporter something, some social favor, maybe an economic favor, for all I know."

Now she was crying, sobbing silently against his chest. Everything was falling apart and she was powerless to do a thing about it. She was even incapable of putting on a brave front. Maybe that was the worst of it, that she was making herself small in Alex's eyes. She, who had wanted to be so independent, who had craved the public's admiration to offer up as emotional dowry to their relationship, was in the final analysis only extra baggage to him, in every respect a deadweight.

"It's okay, it's okay. It's not the end of the world," Alex was saying, as if she were a child whom it was his adult duty to comfort. But the ruse was wasted because she wasn't a dumb kid. Beneath the consoling manner she could detect his concern based upon a thoroughly educated perspective of the real situation.

Looking up, she said, "It's the end of the world I tried to build for myself. That's end of the world enough for me." She struggled out of his arms.

"It's not necessary to be so tough," Alex said. "It's not necessary for a person to have to build a whole world just to feel they're successful in life."

"And I've only got to look around me for ample proof of that. Southern womanhood. Soft and yielding. Flowers of femininity. They have only to smile and the world trips at their feet. Well, it isn't really like that. Maybe for the Christina LaPierres it is. But you can only be sweetly soft and wait for things to come your way when you know damn well there's an army in your employ within whistling distance. I'm sorry. Call it sour grapes if you want. But that's really and truly the way it is."

"Look, I would love it if you were some Southern debutante with family ties going back to the first blueblood who ever set foot on these shores. I would love it. Then everything would be easy. But that's not the way it is, so we're just going to have to step around it."

"Even if it means losing your chance to be D.A.?"

There was a long space of excruciatingly painful silence. Whatever answer he might have given, it would have come too late after that extended interval, so she moved away, and without saying anything, handed him his shirt and trousers.

"Mara . . ." he said, and made an attempt to bring her back into him, but she sidestepped the gesture.

"No answer," she said, cutting him off from saying

more. "I don't need an answer. I'd never let that happen," Mara said, "that you would lose your chance because of me."

"I love you," Alex stated slowly, distinctly, as if trying to drive home a point that she might be incapable of recognizing.

"I know you do. But how much could you love me if I'm the cause of you losing everything you've worked for, everything your father worked for?"

"That isn't the point."

"Isn't it? You aren't just in this for yourself. It's for your father, too. I have to face it, Alex. The paper had it right. I'm just an interloper. A new kid on the block. There is such a thing as history, no matter what you say. And loyalties tied to tradition."

"That's why there are revolutions, to break old, outmoded patterns."

"Fact. Not all revolutionaries are successful."

"Some don't deserve to be. But we've got a good cause."

"Okay," Mara said reluctantly, and attempted a dim smile through the remaining tears. "You know, you sure can make a case for anything."

"Having a sympathetic jury helps." He brought her into his arms, hungrily bringing his mouth against hers.

For a moment, encased in his arms, she surrendered to the familiar stirrings of her body. Contentedly she allowed herself to be lifted and placed on the bed. Happily she twined her arms around him as he lay beside her.

"I love you," Alex said, "I love you . . ."

Opening her eyes, she had meant to repeat those same words to him. But there, just past his shoulder, she caught the reflection of their bodies in Salina's mirror over the dressing table. Once two other people had lain entwined together, two other people had vowed their love, had planned their lives, had undoubtedly sworn to triumph in the face of adversity, all within the same frame.

But they had lost. In spite of their love, they had lost materially, and finally they had even lost each other.

"I love you," she whispered with a determined force meant to drive away doubts and knowledge alike. All she wanted was this, moments together in each other's arms, moments lasting forever. She kissed him deeply, with a violence brought on by fear. "I love you so," she repeated even more fiercely as he moved over her, and blessedly she lost the mirror's reflection.

Oh God, she thought, *let us win.*

"You understand the conditions?"

"Yes," Mara said, trying hard not to appear nervous. She had never been in a police department before.

"If the accused does not appear for the court date, you are responsible for the bail. And make no mistake, we'll get it from you."

The bail bondsman was a tall, attractive man, dressed in a business suit. There was nothing at all sinister about him. Yet now, as he gave his warning, a hardness entered the gray eyes that would serve to erase any miscomprehension as to his underlying nature. She didn't know if that look was called at will; if so, it had met its purpose.

"I understand."

"Okay. Wait here. I'll handle things. It'll take a while for the paperwork."

Mara took a seat in a metal folding chair and did as she was told. She waited.

It took forty-five minutes.

A door opened to the sound of a buzzer and Dominique Moreau entered the waiting area. It was two o'clock in the afternoon and the room was almost vacant.

Dominique scanned the faces of the few people there.

When her glance touched Mara, Mara smiled slightly, unsure at that moment if what she had done was wise. She rose from her seat, and considered how to approach the formidable-looking presence.

Dominique nodded, as if she had just put a puzzle together, and the accompanying look in her eyes mirrored contempt for the picture she saw.

The singer started for the exit, but Mara moved quickly into her path.

"I'm Mara Kozinski," she began. She had a small speech rehearsed for the liberation, but there was no opportunity to deliver it.

Dominique gave her a sharp look, and stepping aside, continued out the building.

Mara went swiftly after her, starting to panic.

Abruptly Dominique turned. "I said nothing. I won't say anything. All I want is to be left alone. I want peace. Can't anyone understand that? I just want to live my life in peace."

Mara didn't know what to say, so she began again with her speech. "My name's Mara Kozinski, and I own a club . . . a nightclub. It just opened. Salina's Place, it's called. I heard you sing one night recently, and I thought you were wonderful. Really," she said, feeling as if she were botching the whole spiel. It was inane, standing in front of a police station giving out compliments about musical ability. "I thought you were the most exciting singer I'd ever heard."

Dominique stood with a hand on her hip, one leg bent. She was tall, taller than Mara, and had a lean-boned sleekness that gave her a kind of feline sensuality. Her dress was slightly wrinkled. It was a cotton print, cut low, with a row of buttons down to the wide belt, and a flare at the hip that eventually draped into a circular skirt. Her hair was almost black and she wore it pulled severely back from her face and gathered together by a rubber band into a long, straight ponytail. Even without makeup, Mara thought she was exquisite.

"What the hell are you talking about?" Dominique asked, her speaking voice carrying much of the low, throaty timbre heard in her songs.

"I put up the bail for you because I'd like to have you sing for me."

Dominique responded with a long look of incredulity. Mara had envisioned gratefulness, a kind of "Gee, there really are people who care . . . breaks really do come to people" response. Instead, she was being eyed with scorn by a wild panther of a woman.

Dominique said nothing. She turned with an air of the most elegant hauteur Mara had ever witnessed and proceeded through the parking lot on her way to the street.

Mara had no choice but to go after her.

"Look," she called, coming up beside Dominique and keeping pace with her much longer strides, "I know all about your troubles. I went over to the place where you were singing and I talked to some people there. They told me you got yourself mixed up with someone, a man, who got himself mixed up in some bad kind of stuff, and that he has this kind of obsession over you."

Mara ventured a glance at Dominique. She was getting through. At least Dominique's jaw had tightened.

"Anyway, I guess he's trying to make things very rough for you. He wants you to be beholden to him. Right?" No response. "You get a job somewhere, and he sees that you're canned. And so, we can help each other. You can come and sing in my club and you'll have a means of support, and I'll have an entertainer who'll put my place on the map."

"Look, you," Dominique said, stopping and turning

suddenly, "you're not from around here, are you? Let me tell you, then, there are some things better left alone. I am one of those things. Charles Moreau cannot be dealt with. There is no way. And I don't thank you for taking me out of there." She jerked her head in the direction of the jail. "In there, I was better off. I was safe, just as long as I kept my mouth shut."

"You want to spend the rest of your life like that?" Mara countered.

"The rest of what life?" Dominique shot back. "I don't have a life. Either way. He will never, never give me up. It is his pride that I am his woman and I remain his woman. You don't escape from a man like Charles. He is crazy." She started walking again, but more slowly.

She spoke with a slow, easy cadence, partly drawl, partly French accent. It was, Mara supposed, attributable to her mixed Southern and Cajun background, along with her travels as a showgirl in Europe.

"He can't control you. There are laws—"

"Laws! What good are laws against a man like Charles? He is his own law."

"You can't run forever, Dominique. You can't. That too happens to be a fact, since you seem so fond of facts."

They had reached the corner. Dominique stopped, and while staring across the street, spoke in a monotone. "I didn't ask for your help out of there. But you did it, and I'll show up for the hearing." She stepped off the curb, and walking with a slow, assured gait, almost a sway, made her way to the other side without so much as a formal good-bye, with no thanks to Mara, without even a glance back to hint at some recognition of Mara's kindness.

Oddly, Mara didn't know if she disliked Dominique's attitude or if she admired it.

But it did present her with a problem. One that appeared

to be insurmountable. She had counted on Dominique. She really needed her.

Just how much she needed Dominique was made clear that night.

Almost no one showed up, only a few tourists. But in a way, that was just as well, because two of her three singers had quit. The one who remained was the weakest talent of the original trio hired.

Alex arrived at nine. One look at the deserted club told the whole story. She did not need to make explanations, and there was no chance of bluffing her way out of the situation with a brave smile. She had failed.

"I'm not going to make it, Alex."

The singer's voice filled the long silence.

"It's not the end of the world," he said.

"Isn't it? I have nothing. All I had was this place, and I've sunk just about every cent I inherited into tearing it up and turning it into a"—she swept her eyes through the darkened room—"mausoleum. I can't even sell it as a home now."

"So what? You can come live in my house."

She stared at him as if he were stupid. "I can't, Alex. I can't! Don't you . . . can't you see that?"

"No," he said, going after her as she started to run up the stairs.

He caught her when she had just entered her bedroom. Spinning her around to him, he said, "I didn't fall in love with you because I thought you were some whiz-wonderwoman entrepreneur. I wanted you, and just as you are, whatever you are."

"But that woman is nothing, Alex. And even if you don't see that, other people will. I'll be a burden, an embarrassment to you. It'll be just like my Uncle Tad and Salina, all over again. If I had something, some claim to fame or prestige, something of my own, then I could rise above all that pettiness. But I can't come to you empty-handed, because eventually you'd start to see what all those fine society people you hang out with see. That I really don't belong." She pulled herself away. "And I couldn't bear that."

"False pride?"

"True pride."

"Whatever it is, it could tear us apart."

"It doesn't matter, Alex. We'd be finished anyway."

He fixed her with an endlessly long, endlessly dark look. Then he turned and left her to her virtually empty club and what gave every impression of being an empty life without him.

The carpenters and plasterers came the next morning to finish the work they had begun and had already been paid for. By four o'clock their work was completed and they had all cleared out.

Mara stood alone in the vast downstairs room. Everything was ready at last, but there was nothing to be ready for. There was a sadness to the scene, and she felt horribly responsible for those empty chairs and tables, as if they were people she had roused to some frenzied state of happy anticipation, only to let them down, to drain them of their joy.

The grandfather clock was still against the wall, its ticking comforting to her, like an old friend who understood and sympathized with her predicament.

Someone was at the front door. Mara turned, listening with aggravation as the person tried the handle. She had made it clear to anyone who might show up that Salina's Place was closed. Silence followed, and glad of it, Mara started up the stairs to her room.

She hadn't quite reached the top when someone began a loud knocking that gave no impression of letting up.

It was annoying. It was an aggravation.

Mara stared down at the door, and finally, with nerves jangling, she ran the whole way down the steps and threw open the door, ready to blast whoever it was that couldn't take a hint.

But she never did that. Instead, she stared silently at her caller, who said nothing, but also stared mutely back.

Dominique Moreau slanted a cool look at Mara, and without being invited in, stepped past her into the club. Mara shut the door. When she turned, Dominique was moving through the room with her slow, sensuous walk, looking here and there, taking in the surroundings with her green sloe eyes.

She stopped at the piano and ran her fingers lightly along the keys, then sat down on the chair and began to pick out a few notes, paying no attention to Mara.

The tinkering with the keys changed to a full melody, at first hesitant and then becoming a performance, or of performance caliber. Dominique's eyes were closed, and she hung her head down, slightly tilted to the right, as if she were listening to someone else sing. The notes came out just as Mara had remembered them—rich and fully textured with all the colors of life. She sat down and listened, entranced, captivated, while Dominique went through a medley, never once acknowledging her presence.

When the last note sounded, Mara applauded.

Standing, she said, "You make me cry, Dominique."

Dominique looked at her and shrugged. "I make me cry." Then she sighed. "But I'm tired of crying. I'm tired of a lot of things. When you get this tired, nothing matters anymore. You know? So whether I sing or I don't sing, whether I live or die, it's all the same."

"Don't say that, don't sound so hopeless," Mara admonished, suddenly afraid, maybe even for herself.

"I don't have anything fancy to wear," Dominique said. "I've got this. It's the best I have."

She was wearing a red dress, close to a persimmon color. It was fitted to her body and cut low off her shoulders, with small sleeves. Her jet-black hair was pulled over to one side and fastened with a clip, and with her tawny skin, she looked exotic and intriguing. It did not matter what someone like Dominique wore; her presence, the way in which she carried herself, was more than enough.

"I can't pay you much. But as the crowds grow—which they will," Mara said, beginning to feel a renewed surge of excitement arise, "you'll get a cut."

"How much?"

"Uh . . . fifteen percent?"

"Be serious. I want thirty."

"Okay, thirty," Mara quickly agreed.

"Don't worry," Dominique said, standing, "I'm worth it."

"I know that."

Dominique Moreau was going to pack them in.

This time Mara was very careful. She did not open her doors until she was ready. This time she *was* ready, completely. It took a week and a half. Dominique was a big help—no, she was Mara's savior.

She knew how to arrange for waiters and she knew someone who could pull strings to get a liquor license. When Mara could not afford the liquor, Dominique used her connections to get the alcohol put on a tab for the time being.

"Thirty percent isn't enough," Mara said on the afternoon they were to open.

"I know that," Dominique replied flatly. She was studying the advertisement Mara had run announcing the reopening of Salina's Place. Dominique refused to let her name be mentioned, however. She had guts, but apparently her bravery did not extend that far. The impression Mara got was that there was such a thing as living independently and flaunting one's autonomy in the face of one Charles Moreau. The fine distinction separating the two was apparently the line between one's physical well-being and major trouble.

"I can't give you more now," Mara said.

"I know that, too."

"But maybe someday, somehow . . . more money . . . and, well, whatever my friendship's worth."

Dominique looked up from the advertisement in her hands. There was a flicker of emotion in the eyes. Dominique was touched. Dominique liked her, too. "I've got a friend. A florist. He might have some leftover carnations, something for these tables. People like flowers," Dominique said with uncharacteristic wistfulness as she walked away, going to the telephone.

Mara smiled. She had a friend. It felt good not to be so alone.

Alone. That was the problem. She could not bring herself to confide her arrangements to Alex. For one thing, he was totally involved in his own problems. LaPierre was pushing Alex's competitor for all he was worth.

On a recent night, Mara had sat beside Alex at his home, watching a late-night news program on which Alex's opponent was guesting.

The guy wasn't bad, Alex said, but Mara objected, saying the man looked like a noodle and sounded like warmed-over broccoli.

"I wasn't aware broccoli talked," Alex said.

"Well, if it did, that's the way it would sound." She stared hard at Alex's foe being interviewed on camera.

The other reason she could not share her plans with Alex was that she did not know for certain if she could actually rise from the ashes. She knew Dominique was solid gold. She knew the club was now in proper physical shape to host the guests she hoped to attract in droves. But she didn't know what kind of trouble she could expect from her enemy Christina LaPierre. It was true that she did not understand the terrain on which she had staked her claim. And because Mara now knew this, she was determined to tread lightly, to keep a low profile. To share her excitement, to share her fears with Alex, would draw them even closer together, if that could be possible. If she failed, that closeness would make the ultimate devastation of leaving him, which she would have to do, all the more terrible.

It was there at last, the afternoon preceding the real opening, the true opening that she had originally planned for Salina's Place, with the lighting right and large palms placed attractively throughout, with green cloths on the tables and the walls a dazzling, contrasting white. So with everything she could possibly do for the club already handled, she made a reckless, flamboyant, totally female gesture of pride and self-gratification.

Dominique was practicing the last scheduled song on her set with the accompanist. She had on the red dress she would wear that night. Mara was wearing her usual working uniform, old jeans with a T-shirt and her hair pulled back in a rubber band. She felt dowdy and tired and suddenly everything else began to look that way too, even Dominique.

"Come on," Mara announced, overriding the final

strains of Dominique's song. "We've got something to do."

As she led the way through the narrow streets of the French Quarter, Mara was as mysterious as Dominique herself, who never confided anything to anyone. When they finally came to At Last on the Rue Royal, they were desperate for the blast of frigid air that met them upon stepping inside a shop filled with feathers and sequins and satins and exotic skins and furs.

A slender, dapper man with silver hair was holding court toward the back of the shop in a section given over to shoes. Bent on one knee, he was slipping a pump on a tittering matron responding with obvious pleasure to the thickest line of blarney Mara had ever heard. The woman loved it. Mara herself was not immune to his infectious good humor and flattery when moments later his charm was directed her way.

His name was Morris, but he was called Morrie Baby by the steady stream of customers who buzzed through the racks, coming and going with armloads of theatrically dramatic creations of dramatically priced outfits.

"Don't . . . don't . . ." he admonished Mara, who had selected what she thought was a splendid outfit in aqua. He grabbed it from her hands. "That's trash. I don't know who picked it out. Probably me," he said, and dashed off to a rack to select a black dress. "Now, this ain't trash. This is *très chic*. This is heaven. This, lovely princess, is you."

"You're sure?" Mara looked skeptical.

"Would a prince lie to a princess?" He pushed Mara toward a dressing room, throwing a feather boa to another customer as she went by.

Dominique rolled her eyes, but a moment later seemed every bit as captivated by the silver-haired, silver-tongued devil presiding over his sinful array of goods, as he turned the full force of his salesmanship on her.

A few moments later, Mara and Dominique met each other in the center of the room, Mara in black and Dominique in gold.

It was the only moment the room was silent. Even Morrie Baby was struck speechless.

"Ring it up," he finally managed to say, shouting back to the cashier. "That's a sale!" There was no discussion needed.

Mara swallowed hard as she wrote out the check for the two dresses.

"That is too much," Dominique whispered over her shoulder, sounding every bit as nervous as Mara felt.

"It's a business purchase."

They walked back through the streets of the French Quarter, silently carrying their black and gold extravagances.

Dominique waited until they were in sight of the club to say, "So now you are broke, what?"

"Flat out," Mara said.

Maybe because it was all so horribly, so painfully, so desperately serious, they burst into laughter.

The people arrived that night, at first not in great numbers, but then more came, and by eleven-fifteen, Salina's Place was half-filled.

Up until then, Mara had taken care of the greeting and seating. But at half-past eleven, she put one of her best waiters at the door and excused herself to go upstairs.

Dominique was waiting in Mara's room, already wearing the gold dress. It had been decided she would not sing until midnight. In the Quarter, night did not truly begin until the small hours of the morning.

Her hair was worn long and straight down her back, and facing away from Mara, she stared outside beyond the balcony's railing.

"Starting to pack 'em in down there," Mara called cheerfully, shutting the door behind her.

Dominique turned slowly around. Mara knew even before she saw her face that something was wrong. She could feel it in the air.

The rims of Dominique's eyes were slightly red. The condition was clearly an embarrassment to Mara's generally tough-acting employee, who, as she moved, seemed to hang close to the room's shadows.

"Nerves?" Mara inquired lightly, inviting a discussion of the problem, but leaving the decision up to Dominique. Mara walked over to her bed and began slipping out of the dress she had worn during the early part of the evening. The black dress she was to change into lay on the bed, waiting to make its debut.

Dominique turned her head away. "Nerves, yes."

There was no time for bathing, although Mara would have liked to. She stepped carefully into the black dress. It felt wonderful, like a part of her, as she pulled it up into place.

All the while, Mara had been watching Dominique. Something must have happened to scare her, something having nothing to do with her performance. Singing to Dominique was as natural as breathing.

"What do you think?" Mara asked, the dress now in place.

"You look very good," Dominique said without undue enthusiasm.

"Just very good?"

"I'm going downstairs," Dominique said, casting an eye to a small clock on Mara's vanity table. "It's almost time." When she was at the door, she hesitated. "No, really," she said, "you look very, very good." She attempted what Mara took as a smile, and left the room.

But standing before the mirror, Mara had to agree that she did, in fact, look very, very good, as Dominique had put it. No, she looked better than that. She looked stunning.

The dress was full-length, ending at her ankles. It was cut low in the back, to just above the slope of her buttocks, and the V front, outlined in black sequins, plunged to her waist. The shoulders were wide, padded, and over them were lush, shiny black feathers interspersed with delicate clusters of onyx beads and black sequins. She had curled her hair, and back-combing and spray had done nothing to spoil its full, soft appearance. One side was swept off her face, with a comb inserted to hold the sophisticated style in place. Dominique had loaned her a pair of diamond earrings, mementos, she had said, of her more flush Parisian days. It was all she had left of her jewelry. The rest had been sold or hocked in pawn shops to pay for living expenses since she had been separated and on the run from Charles Moreau.

A staccato rap on the door brought her away from her reflection. "Yes?" she called.

"You wanted to know when Mr. Gautier has arrived."

Mara swung the door open.

"He's here," said the waiter.

"Thanks. Please seat him at the reserved table in front. I'll be right down."

From the upstairs balcony overlooking the main salon, she watched Alex being led to his special table near the stage. He had arrived exactly on time, good-naturedly going along with all her mysterious and emphatic rules for the evening of her opening. She had chosen the intermission, just prior to Dominique's opening set, for him to come. It was important that he have the time to focus on what she had done with Salina's Place since the last, sad debacle he had attended. Also, she wanted him to see her as she had always wanted to appear, as elegantly striking as any of the women who had been at that party they had attended together. She wanted to show him, needed to show him, how far she had come since the simple blue dress.

She waited until he had been served his drink, pre-ordered also. Then she began her practiced, studied descent down the stairs. What she had hoped would happen, occurred. A head turned in her direction, then another and another, and finally Alex's.

She was watching him, waiting, almost breathlessly, for his reaction, and when it came, she was not disappointed.

There was at first total male absorption, as if she were a woman he had never before seen, one who had totally captivated his senses by her beauty. That was not far from the truth, she realized, for it was clear that at first he did not recognize her. She was different. The dress was sophisticated, her hair arranged differently, her makeup flawless and dramatically applied. There was no hint of the simple girl from Ohio who had drooped, tired and uncertain, into his fine quarters a month before.

Mara moved with regal assurance down the stairs, the skirt molded to her body, the kick pleat in front provocatively displaying a length of silky leg.

His expression changed to one of almost shocked recognition that this was her, not some exotic stranger who had entered into his presence. He rose slowly, as if in a trance, his eyes burning over her as she moved through the room.

Alex had dressed in a white tuxedo and pale blue shirt. With his tan, brilliant white smile, dark eyes and raven-colored hair, he was her counterpart in dramatic effect. She could feel eyes shifting from her to Alex and back again. Yet her only real concern was Alex. He was her world, and she was his. Everything else—the people seated at the tables, the striking surroundings of the club—was only a backdrop for their all-consuming attraction for each other.

"Who are you?" he asked when she stood before him.

"I'm yours," she said, meaning it more than he could ever realize.

"You're magnificent," Alex said. They faced each other, standing only inches apart. An electrical charge pulsed through her, rushes of energy seemingly from him, filling the space between them. His black eyes sparkled as they swept over her hungrily, with undiluted, unabashed, undisguised male greed. "You're mine. If you weren't mine, I'd take you. Do you know that?" he asked with absolute seriousness. "I'd possess you no matter what I had to do, no matter what the obstacles, be it another man or any condition on this earth. And no man," he added, his tone dark and certain, "is ever going to touch you as long as I'm alive."

The intensity was almost more than she could bear. She wanted him. She wanted him then, at that moment, physically and emotionally. But then, inanely, they were standing there together in the middle of an enormous room, both of them the focus of countless pairs of eyes.

"Let's go upstairs," Alex said, his thoughts following hers.

Mara smiled. "But there's more," she said. "Entertainment."

Alex took her hand and kissed it. Looking into her eyes, he said, "Mara, what more entertainment could I want than to have you in my arms, in a bed, beneath me?"

"You are a very wicked man."

"You have no possible idea just how wicked," he said, joking, but not joking, as his eyes slipped to her cleavage.

"Oh? Don't I? What makes you think you're the only one with imagination?" Imitating him, she returned her own sultry female variation of the male once-over. Then she became business again. "Alex," she cajoled, "sit, please, there's more."

Reluctantly, he did, with Mara taking her seat beside him.

Now, as the accompanist reappeared, the focus of attention shifted from them to the small platform stage. One of the waiters activated the performance lights. The pianist began.

Alex threw her a suffering look. "I want to make love to you," he said, his voice low enough that only she could hear.

"Not now," she returned, trying hard to remain serious.

"When?"

"Later, after—"

"After what? After we're married?"

Though listening to Alex, Mara had been looking toward the back, to where Dominique would make her entrance. She snapped her head around. "What?"

"I want you to marry me. I want you to be my wife. I want us to live together, to be together. Forever."

She was stunned. She thought he might be joking. But he wasn't. His expression was serious, his whole demeanor tensed for her response.

"I . . ." But her response was muted by Dominique's appearance and the announcement by the pianist into his microphone.

"Ladies and gentlemen, the incomparable Dominique Moreau."

Dominique took the stage, just as they had planned. She

was a golden, burnished goddess beneath the soft lighting. A hush fell over the room. Even Alex seemed momentarily mesmerized by her commanding presence.

Leaning against the piano, as if she were singing alone, for her own pleasure, she began. There was a hypnotic quality to her voice. Smooth and full, textured with infinite shadings of emotions, the magical voice took command of the room.

The night was exactly as Mara had planned. As happy as she had ever been, Mara looked to Alex, certain now that she had proven herself in his eyes. She had proven her worth to herself, as well. She could marry him; she would marry him.

A coldness washed over her, as he, too, turned to her.

Absent from his look was the admiration she had expected. In its place was disbelief laced with anger.

"Alex?"

"Are you crazy?" he asked. His voice cut through the distance separating them, and into her, like a blade of cold steel. "Do you know who she is?"

"I don't understand," Mara said, looking in confusion from Alex to Dominique and then back again.

He seemed about to answer, but either the reply evaded him or the response was futile. With a stiff dignity, Alex rose out of his seat. A few people turned their heads, but forgot about Alex as Dominique slid her voice into a higher register, capturing a new mood.

Alex said nothing more to her. He started off, going toward the front door. Mara hurried after him, frightened and bewildered.

Near the door, and seeing that he wasn't going to stop to offer any explanation, she called after him, her eyes stinging, her voice wavering, "I'd like to forgive you for this, Alex, but you're making it impossible."

He spun around on his heels. His eyes were cold. "You'd like to forgive me?"

"This was my night. It was our night. Everything here was planned for you, and you suddenly just—"

He took a step forward and something in his eyes made her back away.

"If you'd taken a knife, plunged it into my back, and twisted it, you could not have hurt me more than you have tonight," he said.

She was so stunned she could not speak. All she could do was watch helplessly as he walked out on her.

Chapter 9

THE HIRED STAFF WERE FEW IN NUMBER, BUT NEVERTHE-
less capable of running things at Salina's Place the rest of
the evening. They were, in fact, far more accomplished
than Mara, a total novice in the business of catering to the
public. From the start, all she really had in her favor was
her nerve, translated "guts" in more heroic terms, and
now she didn't feel much like she had even that as an
asset.

Feeling psychically whipped, she made it clear to
anyone who needed to know: she was going to her room
and she was not to be disturbed.

"But if Mr. Gautier should return," she revised,
making a valiant attempt to keep her soul's despair from
her voice, "I'll see him."

Of course there was not much chance of that happening.
But regardless, she waited in her room, pacing back and
forth, stood on the outside balcony looking down the
street in vain for the sight of Alex heading back or merely

loitering nearby, as unsure of himself as she was. Her vigil went unrewarded.

She was only dimly cognizant that the club drew in crowds that night. She was equally disinterested when the music below ceased and she heard the doors being locked. How ironic it was that values changed so drastically. For days the goal of filling her club to capacity had obsessed her. Now, finally, when she could savor the fruits of her accomplishment, it didn't matter. The triumph was only an aside in her life, an empty one at that. What was anything without Alex? All else was meaningless, would continue to be meaningless the rest of her life without him. She was not naive or shortsighted; she knew that an obsession over a perceived "Mr. Right" could turn out to be the same as the value she had placed on the club's success—changeable, fluctuating like an emotional Dow Jones. There were a million Mr. Rights, and if you didn't believe it, one had only to pick up the latest issue of any women's magazine. For sure there would be an article by a psychologist proclaiming just that fact of life. Facts of life were definitely in these days. But they were generally other people's views based upon their own tainted perspectives.

At a certain point, one had to stop listening to other people. Other people always had something to say about how to live your life, but in the end, when all was said and done, it was your life. That was Mara's philosophy, as she stared blankly at her reflected image in Salina's oval mirror over the dressing table. It must have been her uncle's philosophy too, and Salina's.

It wasn't even a question of Alex being "Mr. Right." Alex was Alex, right or wrong, or a combination of both. He had left an imprint on her heart that could never be erased. It could not be washed away by the tides created by a billion tears, nor dissipated by the erosion of time or diminished by marriage to another man by whom she might someday bear children. When they buried her, wherever they buried her, he, Alex, would still be a part of her. Let the experts write their articles; they had never truly loved.

When she was sure she was alone, she ventured into the hallway, and still in her black dress, began her second trip down the stairs. The main salon was dark; only a single light remained on by the front entrance. At the bottom of the stairs, Mara stood looking into the vacant room, like a spectator to the past. The night had gone so terribly wrong. There was to have been such happiness, such celebration. And it had all gone so wrong.

An unexpected noise sounded from within the dark, shadowy confines of the room. Mara tensed. The fear expanded as she saw the form coming forward out of the gloom.

"I'm sorry," the shadow said, and Mara relaxed. It was Dominique. "I saw him leave."

She came to just inside the dim pool of light by the front where Mara stood. She was still in the magnificent gold dress, but the ravaged expression she wore diminished its effect.

"I was afraid he would walk out," Dominique said flatly.

For once Dominique did not look so brave. She looked wan and beaten, as exhausted as Mara felt.

"How could you have thought that?" Mara returned. "Even I don't know why, so how could you have expected he might leave?"

"Because I am the reason. If he becomes the district attorney, I will be one of his cases. His link to solving his biggest case," she added, and looking up, she sighed deeply. "He could not have been very happy tonight, seeing me here."

Alex's face flashed before Mara. Now she could understand his cold fury, the disbelief in his eyes as he looked at her. ·

"Now I am being prosecuted by the current district attorney. Withholding evidence, they call it. I am a material witness in the *State versus Charles Moreau*. At first I thought you had to know that. You bailed me out. I thought it was some kind of a trick. Some kind of deal he was working through you. He arranges for work for me and I return the favor when he takes office. I talk to him about Charles. But of course I was wrong. He did not know anything about it, did he?"

"You were my secret."

"He could not have been pleased to see me here."

"An understatement," Mara said weakly. "He must have thought—"

"That you betrayed him." Dominique's voice was dull, lifeless. No one seeing her would have believed she was the same woman who had radiated so much emotion hours before.

"Why didn't you tell me this? How could you have let me—"

"Because I didn't care at first!" Dominique flared, her voice at last rising out of its monotone. "You wanted me to sing. You took me out of jail. I never asked for any of this. So I thought, what the hell, I would take something for myself. I'd have been a fool to pass up the chance to make some money in a decent place. And I was tired of running from Charles."

"But you knew how much I loved Alex. You knew that everything I was doing was for him, because of him. And I thought we were friends." Mara faced Dominique, her arms loosely dropped at her sides, no strength left to her body.

"Oh, please," Dominique said, moving jerkily a few

steps in one direction, then another, like an animal looking for a way out of a trap.

"Look," Dominique said defiantly, "at first it didn't matter. And then I saw how much you were counting on me for this club. Without me, you would have had nothing. So how could I have walked away from you then? I maybe should have told you how serious what you were doing might be. But I couldn't, I just couldn't do that. I thought, I prayed even—believe me, I actually prayed—that some miracle would happen. That he would understand or forgive or . . ." She broke off. "You should forget him," Dominique said suddenly.

"Forget him?" Mara stared at Dominique, incredulous that she could have heard right. "How do I do that, Dominique? How do I forget a part of myself, because that's exactly what he is. I will never, never, not ever be the same again without him or even with him. He's touched me . . . in here." Mara brought her hand up, laying it upon her heart.

"Look," Dominique said, her voice calm, tinged with that timeless, eternal quality of wisdom that came through in her singing, "I am your friend. Now, I am—truly. I should have told you what would happen before, but I didn't. Now I am going to tell you this—the truth. You are never going to be with this man. You may love him, he may love you, but this man has a job to do, a place in this city that is as much a part of him as his eyes are and his arms are and the legs he needs to be a complete human being are. This work he does is like another piece of him. As a friend, Mara, I tell you the truth . . . you must be realistic."

"Thanks, but I don't like your kind of realism."

"You don't have to like it. It's there anyway, like it or not."

"He loves me."

Dominique didn't say anything.

"He'll understand, Dominique."

"I'll see you tomorrow night," Dominique said, going slowly past Mara to the door. "Your club's a success," she said.

Somehow that fact was no consolation.

Consoling or not, Dominique was right. Salina's Place was a smash hit with the public. Within two weeks' time, the crowds inside had expanded to overflow in lines of people waiting outside for the next show time.

With Dominique and the accompanist's guidance, Mara hired new and better talent. Two hours of every morning were spent auditioning singers and musicians. But it was Dominique herself who was the drawing card.

In a way, Mara was, too.

In an effort to forget her break with Alex, which she still hoped was only temporary, and while she waited for him to call her, to come to her, she threw herself into her work. She purchased new gowns for herself and Dominique from Morrie Baby, and in her finery and with her newly acquired aura of sophistication, she was becoming a minor celebrity in her own right, noted as much for her business acumen as for her beauty.

Dominique's court date was postponed again, and her life proceeded hassle-free, at least for the time being. The current D.A. was apparently happy to know the whereabouts of his star witness.

"This is the best time of my life, at least in a long time," Dominique would say again and again. "It is peaceful."

Charles Moreau, it appeared, had clever lawyers who were able to fight his extradition from another state.

"Maybe it will all fade away," Mara said whenever Dominique's tenuous good spirits turned to gloom.

"Maybe the moon will not shine at night," was the singer's reply.

Giving credit where it was due, Dominique had a track record of usually being right when it came to her assessment of how things were.

For one thing, just as predicted, Alex had made no attempt to get in touch with Mara. On two separate occasions she had tried to call him herself. Both times she had worked herself into such a state of physical and emotional turmoil, she had become nauseous. And both times her efforts were for naught. Anna had answered on each attempt to reach Alex, once saying, "Mr. Gautier is out of town," and the second time taking a message that Mara had called. Mara never heard from him, and although she rationalized the cause as being Anna's refusal to transmit her message, she couldn't be certain. A combination of pride and fear and hope that he would soon, of his own accord, contact her, gave her the strength to endure the ongoing silence.

She wondered if he were aware of the club's meteoric rise to success. She wondered if he hurt as badly as she did. Did he lie awake at night, unable to sleep, remembering the feel of her body in his arms? Did he remember his proposal to her? "Marry me." Those words burned into her whenever she was not vigilant enough to stifle them from her consciousness. "Marry me."

She saw his picture in the paper. He looked wonderful, the dark eyes fervent, the smile so achingly reminiscent of good moments they had shared together. Zealously she studied the stories written about him, following his campaign as closely as she tabulated each night's cash take at Salina's Place. From her assessment, Alex was giving LaPierre's candidate a fine run for his money. She was so proud of Alex, so proud of him.

But still, the pain of their ongoing separation was

sometimes close to unbearable. Love was no longer kind. Love was a monster whose claws ripped at her night and day. What terrible torture.

Of course this was all on the outside. To all but Dominique, she was the image of a woman with everything, and a woman with everything was naturally good copy. A feature was run in the paper on her. The day the article came out, she hung by the telephone, hoping Alex would respond. Surely he would have to see her picture. Memories would take him over, and then projections of the future that could be . . . if only he would dial her number.

The phone did ring, many times. People called in to book reservations for that night and for days in advance. A television channel's talent-booking director called to ask if she would appear on their morning show. It was a local show, having a good audience. She was certain Mara would get excellent coverage for her club, and they could use "a beautiful, clever woman and new face."

Mara agreed to appear. The opportunity meant little to her, though. The telephone with its illusory promise of a call from Alex meant the world.

"Forget him," Dominique said with uncommon kindness after watching Mara drop the phone into its hook. The familiar expression of disappointment flooded her face after a momentary surge of hope had revitalized her briefly. "Think only of this," Dominique advised. "Here is where your true future lies." She nodded to the club's main room, already filling up by eight o'clock.

For Mara's television date, Morrie Baby selected a white suit from his shop. At his suggestion, she wore her hair down, Morrie claiming that the suit was too tailored to withstand the severity of an upsweep. He even showed up at Salina's at five in the morning to make certain she "had it all together."

"Morrie, you didn't have to—"

"You're representing me. My honor is at stake," he clucked, but she knew he was concerned for her own good. When she left for her shot at "show biz," she both felt and looked like a proper movie star.

She was put in the green room to wait her turn before the cameras. The green room was actually a pale shade of peach. It, Mara learned, was a term universal to the entertainment business, a room in which all performers assembled before their appearances. There were two televisions on either side of the room, a table with coffee and tea and various rolls, a silver bowl containing a thoughtful offering of some over-the-counter stomach-calming tablets, and several chairs and sofas in which to have comfortable mini nervous breakdowns before being called to appear.

Alone in the room, the other guests having already been called for their turns, Mara stared at one of the television monitors. She was not nervous. In fact, she was barely thinking about what she would say and do on camera, her thoughts instead being on the club, her mind as usual waging a losing battle against entertaining thoughts of Alex.

At the edge of her vision, a body entered the door. Expecting the man who had made several other recent appearances to whisk people to the studio, Mara automatically rose, and turning to him, said, "My turn at bat . . ."

But the words trailed away, becoming lost in the space between her and Alex, who was looking at her with as much evidence of shock as she herself was currently experiencing.

"I had no idea," she said at last.

He nodded. The gesture carried no discernible meaning

with it. Just a movement of the body. Neither of them knew what to say. Too much time had passed in painful silence between them to pretend lightness. *Long time no see, huh?*

It was Alex who regained his composure first. "So," he said, "you've become a celebrity."

"I called you, twice," Mara said, not able to pretend.

"Yes. I was told."

"I see." But she didn't. She didn't see at all, dammit. What was he really saying? That he despised her? That he was ashamed of himself and had too much pride to apologize? What did he mean?

"I didn't return your call because there wasn't any point to it."

"No point? Alex, we were—"

"Were, Mara. We were."

"I still love you," she said, finding it impossible to believe she was hearing right. Had she dreamed up the moments they had shared together? Had she hallucinated the passion, only imagined the words he had said to her in the dark while they lay together after making love for half the night? Had she lost her marbles?

He couldn't look at her. His eyes moved to one of the television screens. "It's a matter of dealing with the—"

"Dealing? Dealing with the what, Alex? With the present? With reality? Fine. Then here it is. I will always love you, and nothing, nothing is ever going to change that." Bottled within her for so many lonely days and nights, the words spilled out one on top of the other. She was caught between love and anger and futility.

"Listen to me," Alex said, his eyes at last connecting fully with hers. He reached for her, jerked her roughly to him. He held her there, close against him. His hand squeezed her captured wrist, and coming from him in succeeding waves of emotion, she felt his passion and his anger at being trapped—like her—in the passion. But as much as anything, she understood his frustration at having been unexpectedly cornered into what was clearly to him an untenable situation.

"We've got to let it go," he said finally.

And while he was proposing their ending, she could think only that she was in his arms again, that this was how it should be, forever. It was right and good. She never wanted to leave.

"It's not possible," she whispered, listening to his heartbeat, knowing the satisfaction of his body's warmth mingling with her own. She could feel him relaxing against her. He loved her, he did love her.

"I didn't want this to happen," he said, still not allowing her to look at him. "I didn't ever want to see you again."

He was emphatic. A small pocket of fear began to expand in her.

"You and I are an impossibility." He dropped her wrist then, as if having lost his strength in making the assertion.

"Because of Dominique," she said accusingly.

Alex moved away, careful to keep his face averted from her. "Would you let Dominique go?" he said in retort.

"I couldn't."

"No, you couldn't," he repeated, facing her again. "And that, Mara, is why we are an impossibility."

"But you love me," she said without any doubt that she was right.

"What you and I feel for each other has no bearing on our situation," he snapped back, as if the truth could be quashed if he responded quickly and forcefully enough.

But he had not denied his feelings, and from that she took heart.

"Dominique will testify for the state," Mara said, snatching at a solution.

"Mara, I cannot afford to be linked to a woman who is the employer of the ex-wife of a known criminal. I will lose my bid for district attorney. There are some things a person can work around, but this isn't one of them. I'm sorry."

"Sorry?"

"Look, I don't like it that life is this way. No more than you do, Mara. In my own inept way, maybe I even try to change the things I think are unfair and wrong. The point is, if I become D.A., then I have a better opportunity to whittle away at injustice."

"You don't think asking me to fire Dominique is an injustice?"

"Yes!" he shouted, then, calming down, went on. "Of course it is. It stinks. It makes me sick, quite frankly. But it's a case of sacrificing one woman's welfare for the good of many other people I could potentially help in my capacity as D.A."

"She's my friend, Alex."

"And you're the woman I love," he said sorrowfully. It was a fact, stated in a tone that convinced her more than a million words ever might, that that love made no difference in their situation.

They stood apart from each other, the feeling between them almost overwhelming, drawing them closer into each other's hearts and souls, and at the same time the barrier of Reality keeping them separated.

"You see, it isn't possible to slice honor into different pieces. Honor must be served whole, or it isn't honor. I have a job to do. You have a friend you won't betray by casting her out to the wolves. And a business to run for your own welfare, too. I respect that," Alex said. "But I can't change what is, not for myself, not for Dominique Moreau, and not for you. No matter how much I want to," he said.

"We could see each other quietly," Mara proposed.

The slightest light appeared in his eyes, then went out. "No, that's tawdry. You deserve better than that."

"Well, now it's the only way, isn't it? And I wouldn't mind. Being a back-street woman has a certain kind of glamour. All those old movies—Hayward, Bergman . . ." She was trying to be light, but in fact she could have been pleading for her very life. Alex knew it, too. He understood, and the risk was weighing heavily on him.

But the shuffling of footsteps severed their conversation. "Mr. Gautier," said the man with the clipboard, "you're next up. Then you." He nodded to Mara.

The man made no move to leave without Alex, and Alex stepped forward to be escorted. When he was halfway out the door, he turned back and said quietly, and not with enthusiasm, "Come tonight. Late . . . eleven . . . whenever you can break away. I wanted something better for you, for us." He shook his head. "I must be crazy." Then he left her.

She watched him on the monitor. He was brilliant. He was her love. She would be with him tonight, his back-street woman. It didn't matter.

Her interview went smoothly, except at the end. The host went from the subject of Dominique Moreau to hint at Mara's relationship with Alex Gautier. It was supposed to be left that way, and Mara knew it. It was supposed to be an insidious aside, a planting of dark suspicions in the public's imagination, without risking a forum in which the truth could be discussed.

But something in Mara clicked at that moment. From

deep within, a wise voice rose up, and taking control, said, "Alex Gautier and I were once very close, but we never see each other anymore. Of course our relationship ended at the time Dominique came to work for me. Mr. Gautier is the most honest and honorable man I've ever known. In a conflict of interest, he would always choose what is good for the people, over his own personal interests."

An amused, cold light caught briefly in her host's eyes, and Mara knew her intuition was not based upon paranoia. Now, upon reflection, this visit of hers also bore the discreet markings of the LaPierres on it. This time, though, their machinations had worked against them.

The interview was concluded, the show was over. Mara smiled when she said good-bye to the host. "It was a pleasure," she said enthusiastically.

He nodded halfheartedly, seeming distracted. He was probably expecting a call, Mara mused, watching him scurry off.

"I'm taking off from here early," Mara told Dominique that evening before they opened. She was behind the bar, taking inventory of the liquor supply. "Keep an eye on things?"

Dominique looked up from opening a packet of cocktail napkins inscribed with "Salina's Place." She stared a moment, then nodded. "Your face is flushed, your eyes are bright. You look like you're alive. You're seeing him again."

"Yeah, well, don't sound so happy about it."

"It's none of my business," Dominique said with an accompanying shrug.

"Oh, great." Mara put down her list and fixed Dominique with a stare. "Like don't wish me well."

"Some people go out of their way to get trouble. Me, I try like the devil to avoid it. It comes to me naturally, like a magnet."

"Maybe if you changed your attitude," Mara snapped.

"Maybe," Dominique snapped back, "my attitude has nothing to do with it. Maybe certain facts do. Like the fact that there is a crazy man in my life who makes nothing but misery for me."

"Charles isn't bothering you now."

Dominique said nothing. Her silence bothered Mara.

"Charles isn't bothering you now, is he?" Mara pressed, suddenly concerned.

"No," the singer said. "I'm going upstairs to change. Have a good time tonight. I'll watch everything."

The uneasy feeling remained with Mara for a while, and then she pushed it out of her mind. Alex. She would be seeing Alex again. Then desire filled her, obliterating all else.

Alex met her at the door. It was only ten o'clock. She was early; neither of them had to ask why.

Closing the door after her, he brought her up against him. His mouth came down upon hers with a savage need that made her respond unabashedly with her own. Kissing his neck, kissing his mouth, his face, her hands moving over him with as much demand as his moved over her, she moaned softly, now and then calling out his name.

"Oh God," Alex said, throwing back his head with his eyes closed. "I have needed you." He looked down at her, and then to give credence to his next statement, he brought his hand over her breast. "I have wanted you."

"I'm here," she whispered. "I'm always going to be here." She looked past him to the stairs. "Let's go up."

"There's wine in the other room."

"I don't want wine, Alex."

"Neither do I."

They laughed, but the shared look was serious. It was not just she who had lain awake, her body a desert without the touch of his hands, her life barren.

Alex undressed her and let his clothes fall where they were. Maybe because it was so difficult, the time with each other seemed even more precious, holy almost, as they came together lying on the bed.

They did not wait this time. There was no ritualistic, pleasurable foreplay. Both of them were ready, and neither of them was able or willing to wait.

Tremors shook them as their bodies moved in tandem. The rhythm of love took over their separate identities, so that as her fingers raked along his back and his lips found pressure points along the hidden folds of her body, they lost all consciousness of the world beyond themselves.

The heat built until they were wild; both of them gave themselves over to it completely. Running his hands down the smooth incline of her legs, he guided her up, lifting her, until she surrounded him as he wanted her to.

"Tightly," he said, breathless, "don't let me go, not ever, let it be like this always. Keep us together."

He took control, took her sense of her own body away, so that all she could feel was him, and as he cried out, so did she. For a moment she felt his ecstasy before the force of her own crashed through her body, sweeping her into that other world only reached with Alex.

They joined with each other again, barely waiting. It was slower the second time. There was passion, but of a different nature. There was an intelligence added to each caress, there was an awareness to the feel of his hand on her breast, and to her fingers encircling him. There was a new love to their union that had not been there before.

When it was over, she lay in the crook of his arm.

"Are you asleep?" she asked.

"No, are you?"

She punched him lightly in the gut. "I begged you today, you know. I begged for this."

"No," Alex said, "you just read my mind and said what I was too big an ass to say for myself."

"That's how I felt. Otherwise I would have felt humiliated."

"Mara . . ." Alex turned onto his elbow. His eyes glistened in the dark. "What I said today was true, though."

"I know," she said, and sighed as she turned to her other side in an effort to dismiss what was unpleasant.

"No," Alex said, guiding her back around so that she lay on her back again.

"Not now, Alex . . . not now. Let's not spoil this."

"It's got to be now. Because we don't have the daylight anymore. You've got to realize that."

"Why must we be so desperate?" she lashed out.

"Because things are desperate."

"You and Dominique. You look for trouble."

"Dominique's made her own misfortune. And I've seen enough twists and turns of life to recognize the breeding grounds for future misery."

"There won't be any trouble," Mara said. "There won't . . . there won't. . . ." Covering his mouth with kisses, she shifted her body to lie atop him.

It was four-thirty in the morning when Alex turned the Mercedes down her street. She was half-asleep, but happy by his side, listening to him talk about his recent edge over LaPierre's man. Neither of them were prepared for the blaze of lights at the end of the block.

Mara gripped Alex's arm. "Alex . . . what is it? What is it!"

Parked in front of Salina's Place were two ambulances,

five squad cars and a fire engine. The lights on the squad cars were still going around. Neighbors had appeared in robes and hastily thrown on clothes to view the curious spectacle.

A patrolman blocked their way to continue farther down the street. Alex stopped the Mercedes and before he could get out, Mara had thrown open the door and was running down the sidewalk.

She heard him call to her, but didn't stop. There, ahead of her, Dominique was being led out the door to one of the squad cars.

"Dominique!" she screamed, arriving just as Dominique was being maneuvered into the vehicle.

"So," she said, "you see now. Trouble follows me."

That was all. The door slammed shut. She exchanged one long, dark, inscrutable look with Mara, then stared ahead. The engine started up and with flashing lights the car pulled out from the curb.

When she turned around, Alex was speaking earnestly to a stocky, middle-aged man. Mara approached, and the man said to her, "I want to talk to you."

"No," Alex said.

"Look, this is police business," the man started to argue.

"Later, okay?" Alex said, the tone of his voice a threat. "You can talk to her later."

The man pointed a finger at Mara. "Tomorrow," he said, and started to back off just as a covered stretcher was borne out the front door.

"Come on," Alex said, ushering Mara into her place. "You go upstairs. I'll handle whatever's left to be done."

It was forty-five minutes before he rejoined her in her room.

She rushed into his arms. They enfolded her, only there was a reserve to his embrace. But of course, there would be; he knew things she did not. "What is it, Alex? What's happened?"

"Why, out of all the singers in this city, did you have to pick Dominique Moreau to sing for you?"

"What's happened?" Mara repeated, starting to give in to the hysteria she had thus far managed to keep under control.

"She's been picked up for the murder of a man connected with the underworld."

Mara separated herself from Alex. Facing him like an adversary, she said, "No. She didn't, Dominique couldn't have."

"Funny, that's what she says, too."

"She's telling the truth, Alex."

"How do you know that, Mara? How do you know anything about the kind of life she's led, the things a woman with Dominique's background might be led to do?"

"I know because she's my friend."

"Excellent. That's really an excellent, thoroughly reasonable reply."

"It's enough of one for me, Alex."

He raised his hands. "Don't get angry with me, Mara. I'm not the one responsible for your friend's arrest."

"I've got to help her. Imagine how she must be feeling."

"Mara, please, this doesn't concern you. This mess is Dominique's affair. Stay out of it. I wouldn't have wanted it to happen this way, for her sake, but I'm relieved she's gone." Then, obviously recognizing the horror on her face, Alex amended, "Look, don't think I don't have sympathy for your friend. I appreciate that she's had some hard knocks in life, and I'm sorry. I'm not a coldhearted bastard. But I'm more concerned over your safety in fraternizing with—"

"She's my friend, Alex. I knew where she came from when I hired her. Dominique doesn't have anyone else. I can't turn my back on her now."

She threw him a look of apology, and taking her purse with her, started for the door. "Thanks for caring about me, but I've got to do this."

Alex went with her, followed her down the stairs, all the time cajoling her to listen to reason, but careful to keep their conversation private. There were still men on the ground floor taking pictures and measurements.

"Would you please listen to reason?" he called as she went out the front door.

"Reason has nothing to do with this."

"No kidding."

But as he came through the door after her, she cried, "Alex!" and fell against him.

They were caught in an explosion of white light and the staccato burst of many voices calling to them.

"Back it up, back off, you guys!" The police fought to maintain their tenuous control over the mob of news reporters gathered with cameras and microphones at the ready.

"Hell," Alex said, protectively turning Mara's face into his chest. Under his breath he said, "This is just the beginning of it."

Chapter 10

THERE WAS NO PROVISION GRANTED FOR DOMINIQUE'S bail, and it was another three days before Mara was given the opportunity to talk to Dominique in person. That accommodation was due only to special arrangements made by Alex through the current D.A.'s office.

Seated at a long counter separated by a glass partition, the two women spoke quietly to each other.

"I'm going to get you out of here," Mara said with a conviction meant to be uplifting. As if to demonstrate her sincerity, she leaned forward as close as she could come to the glass.

On the other side, Dominique sat quietly detached. "Forget it," she said blandly.

Mara ignored her. "I'm going to ask Alex to defend you. He's the best. He'll handle everything. All of this trouble you've had for so long will be handled once and for all. You'll be free, Dominique. I promise."

Dominique responded with a look of disdain. Except for the fleeting show of contempt, to Mara she had never looked more emotionally removed, more in control. For that reason alone, Mara was able to gauge the true degree of her friend's fear. Dominique was frightened, extremely so.

"You don't have to like it or not like it. All I need from you is your promise that you'll at least cooperate."

Dominique eyed her coolly. "I would like you to keep your nose out of my business."

"Tough. Because I'm not going to."

They stared at each other until finally it was not Mara who gave way, but Dominique. Extraordinarily, a tear traced down her cheek, then another, and another, until she had to resort to using a tissue. Being soft, being weak, was the severest kind of humiliation to a woman of Dominique's pride. On the other side of the glass, Mara waited out the storm, more determined than ever not to abandon her crusade.

"Did you kill him?" Mara asked bluntly.

Dominique's eyes drifted off to the side, became momentarily unfocused, as if recalling the event. Her eyes became clear again as she looked back to Mara. "No," she said.

"Who, then?"

"What difference does it make?"

"Cut it out, Dominique. If you want to play the martyr, fine. But do it on your own time. I don't have all day."

Across from her, Dominique sighed and looked to see she wasn't being overheard. She pressed herself closer to the aperture through which their voices traveled, and said, "It was someone who did not like Charles. A real enemy. Charles had cheated his group. That man came to tell me to talk to the government. If I did, I'd get money and a guarantee of protection. If they could put Charles out of business, they would have their revenge and there would be more profit for them."

"And?"

"Someone working for Charles must have seen him come to me. They always watch each other. Nobody trusts anybody else. So one of Charles's friends must have taken care of the guy. I didn't even see it happen. After he made his speech, I told him to leave me alone, to just go. I was going into the kitchen when it happened."

"Then we can prove you're innocent."

"Innocent, guilty, it makes no difference. What I must do is what I have been doing. I must keep my mouth shut. If I do, I go to prison, but I'll be safe there. Afterward Charles won't bother me anymore. I will have paid. My freedom in return for my loyalty. I know how Charles thinks. It's the only way."

"But you're innocent."

"Oh, Mara. You are so naive."

It was all the time they had then. Dominique was called away.

Alex was waiting for her outside. He drew his arm protectively about her as they walked to his car. "It was bad?"

"Yeah, bad. She's so fragile, Alex. So fragile. She actually cried, do you know?"

"I'm sorry. Really," he said, squeezing her against him. "If only I could change things."

"Maybe you can," she said, but that was all. It wasn't the time or place to have a discussion which would, in all probability, make or break their relationship for good.

Their plan to return to Salina's Place had to be aborted. A group of reporters hovered outside the locked front entrance and another group hung around the back door. All of them were fidgeting, all of them were anxious, even desperate to take their crack at Mara, and with extreme luck, Alex, too.

"I can't face them, Alex. I just can't take it now."

"Neither can I," he said, his eyes hard.

Instead they went to his place. Anna must have called the police to remove another group of reporters from Alex's premises. As Alex pulled the Mercedes into the drive, a few of the more diehard stragglers were being supervised by uniformed patrolmen into their parked cars.

"Stay here today. Tonight, too," Alex suggested when they were safely inside the house.

"So you can keep your eye on me?" Mara joked, but only partially. There was too much truth in her question. Her association with him could cost him dearly.

"Because I love you," Alex said, opening the door to his office, the room in which they had first met. He followed her inside. Standing behind his desk, he went through the ritual of checking for messages.

A pink slip of paper evoked a scowl, as did several others he read in turn. He glanced briefly at Mara, and then, sinking into his chair, sat back with his eyes closed tightly.

"It's serious?" she asked, rising and coming around to where he sat. She caressed his forehead, and bending to kiss his shut eyelids, said, "Is it?" Her gaze strayed to the messages on the desk.

But Alex leaned forward, blocking the messages from her vision. One hand drove open his desk drawer, and the other gathered together the pink slips of paper. Before he could put them away, Mara interfered. Taking his hand, she stayed it, and holding firm, said, "No. I want to see."

Alex remained gravely silent, appraising her reaction as she riffled through the small square pieces of paper. "Yeah," she said, putting them down. Her eyes pierced the distance between them. "They're serious, all right."

She walked into the center of the room, an unconscious reflex to separate herself from Alex's sphere.

Each call was from one of Alex's major supporters. Each call warned him to keep his nose out of the "Moreau Situation," as it seemed to be almost universally labeled by the interested parties. Through association, Mara was included, if not mentioned directly.

"They're right, of course," Alex said.

"Are they?"

"You know they are."

"No," Mara returned. "I don't know that."

"Or maybe you refuse to? Well, it doesn't matter, anyway. Since I haven't any direct involvement in the Moreau case, the issue isn't applicable."

"But it is," Mara said emphatically, the three words taking on the mournful weight of a death knell. "I want you to help her."

Alex looked at her for a long moment. Nodding, he said, "I was afraid of that."

"And?"

He looked down at the slips of paper scattered on his desk. "And I can't. Not if I'm going to realistically entertain plans to become D.A." He shrugged in a gesture of hopeless resignation. "I can't, Mara."

It wasn't that she hadn't considered a negative response. She had. She just hadn't gone any further with her projections. Somehow it was all to have worked out, and worked out to her liking. But now, hearing the "no" as really "no," as in "end of story," she was stunned by the reality of defeat. Dominique was right, she was naive. She had harbored the obviously erroneous impression that the concepts of fairness and loyalty would triumph over personal aggrandizement at the expense of another's basic rights.

Never had she thought she could be angry at Alex, he who had represented everything idealistic. But she was. And when she said, "I must have been mistaken—I thought you supported what was noble and right,'' she threw an inclusive look to the gleaming leather-bound law books on his shelves.

"I'm not going to have the opportunity to support anything if I defend a woman who has connections to the underworld. LaPierre could just as well retire his efforts to see me defeated. I'd be slinging mud at myself.''

"But she's innocent! And if she doesn't get someone good to get her out of this, she'll probably just get railroaded through the system. That's pretty plain, isn't it, Alex?''

He took in a sharp breath. "Dammit, Mara. You know my situation. I'm caught between a rock and a hard place.''

"Sure, I know it. If you defend her, then you lose your chance of making great sweeping changes in our legal system. If you don't defend her, you lose your self-respect.''

"Yes, that's it. Precisely what I've got to face.''

"But there's something else, Alex, one other thing you'll lose . . . correction, that we'll lose.'' Trembling, she broke off, not wanting to go on with what she had to say, any more than Alex wanted her to say it. But he knew; she could see it in his eyes.

Then he said, "Mara, don't. This doesn't have to tear us apart.'' A torrent of anguish poured from his eyes, sweeping over her, dissolving her recent anger to sorrow.

But she couldn't go to him for the same reasons he could not agree to her wishes. Speaking softly, she said, "I don't understand, Alex. In the moonlight you make beautiful speeches to me, all about how it is better that one innocent person go free than a hundred guilty people are convicted. But I guess in the daylight justice looks different. Maybe that's the way our relationship looks to you too? It only counts when it's convenient.''

She saw the hurt in his eyes and wanted to go to him. But couldn't.

"That's not the way it is," he responded.

"I've given my friendship to Dominique. I won't go back on that, no matter what."

"Have you thought that you could lose Salina's Place? Bad publicity could draw in public protest."

"I'd rather lose a building than lose myself," Mara said. "How about you?"

"I love you," Alex said passionately, coming around to her. Taking her into his arms swiftly, before she could protest, he squeezed her so tightly her breath was shortened. Then he kissed her, his mouth bruising in its need to express his desire and, in a way, she sensed, his control over her.

At first she remained rigid, pitting her conscious will against the power inherent in her body that would rise up and overwhelm her senses.

Her resolve was short-lived, however. Within seconds she was lost to the familiar sensations he could always bring forth in her. Like a wizard familiar with secret spells, he knew every erogenous pressure point on her body.

"Stop," she moaned softly, "I can't think this way."

His hand caressed the small of her back. Instinctively she pressed into him. He shivered as if a jolt of electricity had passed from her to him, and immediately quickened against her. With his other hand he explored lower, feeling her thigh through the material of her suit's straight skirt. Palm down, he brushed over her stomach, rousing familiar bursts of fire through her abdomen, each new caress a promise of ecstasy. Feeling herself drowning in a hazy, satisfying pool of sensation, she gave up her fight and responded with a yearning whimper to the insinuating rhythm of his body against hers.

"Don't think," Alex said, softly biting her lower lip, then moving quickly on to her ear, her neck, and nuzzling her collarbone. "Just feel," he said. "Mara . . . Mara . . . don't ruin it all. Don't let the world ruin us. Just let us be together and feel what we feel. Don't complicate things now when we have the chance to win at last."

Her eyes opened then, just for that moment, and she saw the tortured look on his face. As if pulled there, her eyes fell upon the picture of Alex's father on his desk. He had sacrificed so much for what he believed in. Alex was right; they didn't have to let the world tear them apart. It would take only one word, either way, to seal their fate.

"Let's win," Alex said, his mouth covering hers, the heat spreading through her body further dulling her convictions of what was honest and true, and what was dishonest and false. Being with him mattered and nothing else mattered at all.

Alex's fingers had bunched up the material of her skirt. One finger was hooked into her panties, when Anna knocked lightly against the door. "Umm-hmmm," she coughed from the other side. "I'll be leaving now, Mr. Gautier. Might I speak with you?"

Alex's hand went slack, and he moved his fingers away. "That woman has a talent for bad timing," he said, and slowly disengaged himself from their embrace.

His face was flushed. Mara smiled. Unless Anna was blind and dumb, she'd take one look at him and have to know they weren't behind locked doors reviewing legal briefs together. Smiling sheepishly, as if he was also thinking the same thing, he winked at Mara and excused himself to confer briefly with his housekeeper before she left for the day.

With Alex gone, the room was suddenly cooler. Her mind was again clear.

Mara's heart beat in frantic leaps as she wrote hurriedly on a lined piece of paper torn from a legal pad.

"Darling Alex, I love you. And I know you love me. But we both know nothing will work unless we do what we believe is right. I told you once I would not see you dragged down at my expense, and I meant it. But I can't abandon my friend, either. How can I win at the expense of her loss?" She scribbled her name and "I love you" again at the bottom. Leaving it where he would see it upon returning to the study, she slipped out the back door.

Even before Alex entered the room, he sensed it would be empty. When it was, a series of conflicting emotions raged like separate violent storms coming at him from different directions. He was free to realize his dream of becoming district attorney, but at a price to himself, because while what he was doing was sensible, it was counter to his sense of decency. Surely life could not be lived in black and white; the marbling stain of gray on all areas of life could not be denied as nonexistent.

He sank into his chair, holding tightly to the message Mara had left him. It was all he had of her—that piece of paper, that hastily scribbled explanation. Tenderly he traced his fingers lightly across the words, trying to feel her through them. Mara, he thought, sensing her anguish of a few moments ago, still feeling her body against him. If they had made love, then perhaps . . . But, no, he couldn't think of that, nor of all the what-ifs and could-have-beens, because what he had was this reality; he had his power intact, he had retained his platform to do great amounts of good for great masses of strangers.

Only, the price was losing the woman he loved. There would not be another Mara in his life. There could be other women, perhaps one woman, a wife someday, a woman who would be "satisfactory." But she would never be this one woman whom he loved.

His father had had other women after Alex's mother had died. It was never a matter to be discussed openly, but Alex had known. The women were biological necessities. They were temporary fillings in the empty chambers of his father's heart. And then there was Tad Engle. Alex doubted that after Salina's death, Tad had ever been with another woman. For years, although Alex had respected Tad's deep feelings, he had not understood them. Now he did. There were degrees of love, he considered as he clutched the yellow paper, and a love like that experienced between the merchant seaman and the beautiful Cajun woman burns so hot that when extinguished, nothing remains but a wasteland of feeling. Tad must have wandered over that desolate, charred terrain for years, a man alone, a man remembering, imagining, in the bleak territory left to him, the way it had been before.

All the inner storms converged at once in the apex of Alex's soul. Angrily, with the one hand still clinging to Mara's message, he snatched up the picture of his father, the man from whom he had inherited an unresolved past. Strangely then, the fury he had been feeling altered; it became a realization that it was not just the situation he had received as his difficult legacy. He had also received teachings. His father's teachings. . . . With his eyes open, memories flew by, conversations of his father overheard, direct advice received, observations made while a child of five and when a boy of twelve and when a young man.

Slowly Alex replaced the frame on the desk.

The inner storms had quieted now. He knew that somewhere in those memories, somewhere locked in that hazy, phantom-populated past, was the answer he needed to win.

There was no animosity. Mara loved him as much as she ever had, but for both their sakes she stuck to her resolution to handle Dominique's situation without even so much as Alex's indirect intervention. It was only fair. Their relationship, flaunted in the faces of the media, could only hurt his chances to win the election.

So after her parting note left on his desk, she made no attempt to contact him, nor did he phone or visit her. It was what she had wanted, of course. She knew he understood that, and that he was making an effort to honor her own sense of integrity. Yet she missed him, missed him terribly, with an ache that was always present, day or night, no matter how busy she became.

But there also existed in her a strange joy, a happy sense of fulfillment.

She was on her own and doing well.

Besides seeming to have become a focal point of the city's media, thrilled with the palette of "local color" she provided, Salina's Place continued to draw the public for evening performances. Undoubtedly some of her establishment's allure was due to Mara's notoriety as Dominique Moreau's champion. But also, Mara was now providing a higher standard of entertainment than when she had first opened her doors with her rag-taggle band of questionably talented performers. That had been three months ago. Anytime before that seemed to have belonged to someone else's life, certainly not hers.

Except for the letters she received from her mother, Ohio was more and more becoming a dim memory. New Orleans was her town. Each morning when she rose, she took time to step onto the balcony and survey her kingdom. She belonged there in its changeable, exotic climate. She took pride in each step she made over earth that was always under siege by the river held in check by levees. It was a city that gave moment-by-moment testimony to man's ingenuity and his indomitable will to survive. Leaning against her balcony, she would breathe deeply, holding in the remnants of tradewinds that now slapped gently against the silk of her cobalt-blue dressing gown, just as it had played in the canvas sails of frigates and schooners two hundred years before. She felt sensuously feminine, but she also felt determined and alive.

Once Alex had told her the city held the past in every brick, that history existed as a time-rider on each breeze, but now she would object. There was another New Orleans emerging slowly, the one which she and others like her would represent. The past could be honored for the beauty it contained, but it would no longer have the power to insist that the present duplicate the contours of an outmoded past. Creoles, Cajuns, pirates, and slaves— labels to separate any groups of human beings as being better or worse, higher or lower, were anachronistic.

Grant Forbes was a man of the twentieth century. His law office was in a glass high-rise overlooking the harbor. Educated in one of America's finest law schools, he had a solid history of winning both criminal and civil suits for his defendants. He was totally behind Mara's efforts to see Dominique receive justice.

The appearance of Grant Forbes in Mara's life had, in fact, seemed guided by Providence.

One night, upon leaving Salina's Place as a customer, he had stopped her. Shaking her hand, he had expressed his admiration for her establishment, as well as for her staunch loyalty to Dominique Moreau. He had read a recent article in the paper in which Mara had been quoted as saying, "You don't desert people when they are no longer convenient to your life."

"Here's my card," Forbes had said. "I'd be happy to help you in any way I can. I believe in fighting the good fight myself."

Mara talked to Dominique about him the next day. Dominique did not care for her public defender. Still, she deliberated for a period way past reason, until, when under additional pressure from Mara, she reluctantly agreed to take Forbes as her attorney. "For your sake," she had told Mara, who had insisted she needed Dominique at Salina's Place. The crowds were thinning, Mara lamented, and she didn't know how much longer she could hold out before the doors would close. It was, of course, untrue. But the game they were both playing served its purpose. Dominique was able to save face while she received Mara's help.

"It's important that she get out on bail," Mara emphasized to Grant Forbes during their first meeting in his office. "She puts up a good front, but she's been through way too much already. Years of cumulative pressure. I think she's at her breaking point."

Grant had nodded sympathetically. "Of course. I'm totally with you."

"Then you can arrange it?" she asked, leaning forward in her anxiousness to believe fully in the miracle of this wonderful angel seated across from her, yet still half-afraid to hope.

"There won't be any problem," the attorney had assured her. He rose out of his chair, the matter appearing concluded in his mind.

But the hearing to have the court grant bail for Dominique was postponed three times. Each time, Grant apologized profusely. "I'm feeling like hell about this," he said, calling Mara early on the morning of the third scheduled attempt to make a plea before the court on

Dominique's behalf. "But I can't make it. There's a serious matter—a life-or-death case. Has to be handled today."

"Of course," Mara murmured, "I understand." But she didn't. She didn't understand at all. That afternoon, without an appointment, she paid Forbes an unexpected visit.

He did not mask his displeasure.

A tall man with salt-and-pepper hair, he wore impeccably tailored suits. Never had she seen him appear ruffled. But as she began to speak, the usual pleasant line of his mouth became a tight, ugly slash, and the warm hazel eyes narrowed, hiding what she glimpsed as a deceitful cleverness.

"I don't understand all these unexpected delays," she said. "I can't leave Dominique to mold in there. I explained the situation to you in the beginning. You said you understood. You said you would do something about it."

"And I will," he said, peevishness edging his reply.

"Then why haven't you?"

"The wheels of justice grind slowly—" he began in his smooth rhetorical style, but standing, she cut him off.

"Thank you, Mr. Forbes. But, see, I don't need a speech. I need action. I'll see myself out, and you can consider your services terminated as of this meeting."

She hadn't gone five steps toward the door when he stopped her, coming quickly around his desk, saying, "We'll go to court in three days."

Mara appraised him. "Three days?"

"I promise," he said, and to Mara he appeared strangely, unaccountably shaken that she was considering taking her business elsewhere.

"What about the packed court calendar?" she asked, referring to one of his previous excuses.

"Yes, well, I have some favors owed me. Perhaps I can arrange—"

"Three days," Mara said firmly. They exchanged long looks of what she took as mutually held resentment of the other, and then she turned to leave.

The experience had shaken her. She felt alone. She was alone.

That night she had broken down and called Alex.

"Hi," she said.

"Mara?" His voice sounded alert. It was late, almost midnight, and she had taken a chance that he might not be asleep. Now she imagined him sitting in his office, papers spread out on his large desk, the picture of his father a subliminal reminder of all he had to accomplish in life.

"I miss you," she said.

"Mara, don't—"

"But I do. I feel alone and miserable, Alex."

"Same here."

"And we both know why," she stated. "And we both know there isn't any other way."

"What's happening with Dominique?" he asked then.

"Nothing."

"I read you had an attorney . . . Grant Forbes."

"Grant Forbes, yes. In three days we go to court to ask for bail for Dominique."

"It's taken a while," Alex commented, but a shade too casually to be just an idle observation.

"Yes, a while. But in three days it'll be handled. Then we can go from there." She didn't like the subject. It put Alex in an awkward situation, which wasn't the purpose of her call. She didn't want to embarrass him for not being there to help her. She had only wanted to talk to him. No, she thought, what she really wanted was to sleep with him, to lie in his bed, to be in his arms, to feel his warmth. "I shouldn't have called," Mara said.

"No, maybe not."

It wasn't a rebuke, but the truth as they both knew it.

"Forgive me?" she asked, trying to put some lightness in her voice. "I'll try to keep my itchy fingers off the phone."

There was a pause on the other end of the line. "Good luck with the hearing," Alex said.

But that wasn't what he had been going to say. She knew that. In that pregnant pause he had been saying silently: *I love you.* But aloud he couldn't, just as she also could not. It would make everything hurt even more than it already did. Unleashed passion would create a danger for them. Look what it had done to Tad and Salina.

When she put the phone down, it was as if her arm had been severed.

Grant Forbes was finally true to his word. In three days they met inside the halls of justice. Mara noted how his manner toward her had changed since their first meeting. Gone was the warmth, the display of fatherly concern, the courtly solicitous air that had characterized their earlier association.

While Grant Forbes pleaded his case before the judge, Mara sat on the wooden bench resembling a church pew. Otherwise they were alone. Dominique's presence was not required at the proceedings.

It was over quickly, in less than five minutes.

When the judge issued his decision, he looked quizzically toward Mara, as if he half-expected her to protest his pronouncement.

He gave a short summary of his reasoning, but the only words she heard were, "Bail denied."

After that, everything else seemed to pass in dreamlike

sequence: the judge leaving for his chambers, Grant Forbes slowly returning to the table where he had laid his closed briefcase, she rising from her seat, she intercepting the attorney as he was making his way to the hall.

"I want to talk to you," she said, catching hold of the cuff of his jacket.

Forbes allowed himself time to deliver a demeaning glance her way, then jerked his arm free. He continued on, his full strides quickening purposefully.

She went after him, almost having to run to keep up.

"You didn't do a thing in there," she said, not making any attempt to mask her anger. "Any bum off the street could have presented a better argument than you did."

"What can I tell you? We bombed. A roll of the dice, that's what the system's become."

But Mara kept pace, and when they were in the hall, she blocked his way. He was forced to stop. "But you didn't even try."

He stared down at her, and then he did an extraordinary thing. Grant Forbes laughed. It wasn't a laugh to release tension. Not a laugh of irony that things had unexpectedly turned so sour. It was a mean and sniggling laugh, a hoot of contempt, carrying with it treachery and duplicity and, at last for Mara, the truth.

"You . . .." Mara said, stepping back, as if to avoid a foul odor. "You work for them."

He looked at her blankly. "Now I have things to do," he said. "So you'd best step aside. You keep your accusations to yourself." He brushed past her. Then, pausing, with only a quarter of his face to her, he said, "Life's a river, young woman. Let it run its natural course."

"If we all did that, Mr. Grant, then you'd be underwater at this very moment. But don't worry. So far, New

Orleans is safe. Thanks to the people who stand against the current.''

He stiffened, then said, ''Be careful.''

She let him go, watching him walk jauntily down the hall, his hand rising to greet a deputy sheriff, then saluting another expensively dressed man with a briefcase in tote.

She would have gone after him. She would have made a scene, at least that, a rip-roaring scene that he would never, never forget. But she couldn't. Instead, she turned on her heel and went the other way down the hall, moving quickly into the ladies' room, where she locked herself in a stall and vomited.

Chapter 11

SHE HADN'T BEEN HOME TEN MINUTES WHEN HER PER-
sonal line rang. She was in her office, which was until
recently an unused bedroom on the second floor.

The Yellow Pages of the telephone directory were
spread open before her. The phone rang again. One finger
continued to trace down the listing "Attorneys at Law."
Once again the phone shrilled. Annoyed, she looked up
and let it ring a third time before reaching for it.

"Yes?" she answered abruptly.

"How'd it go today?" Alex asked on the other end.
"Or should I take a clue from the way you greeted me just
now?"

At the sound of his voice, a warmth invaded the
coldness she had been feeling. She almost, but not quite,
managed a smile.

"Thanks for caring," she said, meaning it more than he
could ever know. "It went lousy."

"I'm sorry." There was that awful silence again, the one that made demands on them both, that provided a dangerous open forum in which they could easily change the existing situation. "Do you want to talk about it?" he asked finally.

Yes, yes! She would love to talk about it. She would love to scream about it, to stand on her balcony and screech out invectives denouncing Grant Forbes and all the other walking, talking bums on the planet who cleverly masqueraded as decent human beings.

"No, not really," she said, trying to keep her voice moderate. "How's the campaign going?"

"I think I've got a chance. No, strike that from the record. I know I've got a chance."

"You're going to win," Mara said. "How could you not?"

"I miss you, dammit. That wonderful stubbornness of yours, which most of the time I want to shake out of you so you'll be a nice pliable rag doll for me to manipulate to my own pleasure."

"Ah, the eternal male fantasy."

"Quite right." Then he paused, and more seriously said, "Winning. Sometimes I wonder if it's worth it. What good can any one person do? It's a ridiculous conceit, when you think of it."

"Well, at least it's a good conceit. An honorable one." She thought of Grant Forbes. She thought of King LaPierre. They loomed large in her mind as commanders of evil, beings overblown to gargantuan proportions. Behind them she saw their legions, smaller men with less expansive appetites for power, who compromised with right, who were content to trek dutifully along in the easy footsteps of their ignoble leaders. But every once in a great while, a brilliant supernova would ignite the sky and give hope to those who, looking up, previously had seen only blackness. But there were so few Kennedys, so few Churchills.

Why could she not have fallen in love with just a man, a nice ordinary man? Why had she been so unlucky as to have fallen in love with a supernova?

"What are you going to do now about Dominique?" he was asking her.

Closing her eyes was easy; lying took more effort. "I've got a new lawyer," she said.

"You weren't pleased with Forbes?" Alex asked.

The understatement of the century, maybe of the millennium. "I need someone with more time to devote to Dominique's case."

"What happened today?" Alex asked. It was a pointed, direct question, one that clearly demanded a clear answer.

Mara pretended to be distracted. "Uh, Alex . . . look, I've got to run. Just got called to go downstairs. Crisis behind the bar. Something about branch water."

"I see," he said. "One of those nasty branch-water affairs. They're always cropping up when you least expect them or need them."

He didn't believe her. Well, she couldn't help it that she was lousy at lying. She couldn't help a lot of things.

"Thanks again," she said, a fat tear of self-pity easing its way out and beginning its slow course down her left cheek. "Thanks for caring."

She quickly put the phone down, disallowing him the opportunity to grill her further.

Out of a list of ten attorneys—four names given to her by customers with whom she had developed more than a passing acquaintance—Mara made five appointments.

The appointments took place over a period of three

days. On the third day, upon conclusion of the final interview, Mara had reached a point that, in psychological degrees, made the term "low" appear high by comparison.

She could not exactly say she was paranoid, but she was well on her way. Each interview was a variation on the same theme:

"You had retained other counsel?"

"Yes."

"And?"

"And I found other counsel unsatisfactory."

She found it easier to begin with euphemisms. But eventually the name was named, and the tone of each interchange would dramatically alter. There was a clear pattern.

"I see," was the universal comment, followed by a pause, perhaps a slight downward stroking of the chin. "He has a very good reputation." The eyes across from her would suddenly flick off, attaching their interest almost anywhere else than on her.

She would know, of course, that they were aware of more than her previous counsel's legal reputation.

It was only the last man who finally leveled with her. On her way out, after declining the case, he suddenly stopped before opening the door. He made clear what she had up to that point only strongly suspected.

"I'd like to help you," he said, looking as if he meant it. "I honestly would. But I think we're both aware of the real reasons. I've got a family, and things can get nasty sometimes if you take on a case in which the wrong people have an interest at stake. That's the way it sounds to me, knowing the little I do about Dominique Moreau's situation."

There it was, the "situation" again. But at least he was

honest with her. She thanked him for being candid, and left, wondering as she rode home in the backseat of a cab, what she was going to say to Dominique now.

Suspended on a rubber string tied around the cab's rearview mirror, a protective voodoo doll danced a jig to ward off catastrophe. Mara contemplated buying a gross of them and setting them all in motion on her own behalf.

She had a feeling that within a day she would be needing them on her side. Along with that thought, she remembered how once, when she had first come to New Orleans, she had wished upon one. She had wished for Alex.

Alex could not work. He sat at his desk staring down at a legal brief with about as much interest as he'd find in a mound of spaghetti after a full meal.

Earlier that afternoon he had participated in a public debate against his opposition—LaPierre's "boy," so to speak.

He told himself to forget any damage meted out by his adversary. He still stung from his own self-inflicted venom. He had not been laid flat by the deadly verbal jousting of his foe; instead he had embarrassed himself before an elite gathering at a distinguished men's club. He, who was excellent at extemporaneous speaking, he, who had carried his school's forensic team to first place in a national competition waged among twenty-eight American universities, on this afternoon lost his concentration, found himself rambling like a dull-witted neophyte to public speaking, and (the gravest crime of all) replying explosively to various insinuations from the opposition that he did not have the morally pristine background necessary to uphold the flawless banner of justice. In short, he had that afternoon distinguished himself mainly for his unprofessional and undignified assault in what was by long tradition a gentleman's arena.

Mara. Mara. The four letters came together and separated. He sat back in his chair, eyes closed. Hypnotically the letters forming her name danced in his mind like the fabled sirens, leading him against his will into dangerous regions.

He had spoken that name—Mara—today before all of them. He had said the name of Dominique Moreau as well. Oh, LaPierre was a clever scoundrel, a rat with keen instincts to lead him through the most complicated maze ever constructed by man. LaPierre had seen his weakness —his love for Mara—and had exploited it by setting him up.

No, Alex thought, suddenly sitting upright. No, he could have kept his mouth shut, but had chosen not to. Thinking back to those moments earlier in the day when he had stood before the audience, he realized it had been his own conscious decision to make their relationship public record.

He was on her side, and he wanted everyone to know it. He wanted most of all for her to know it.

Earlier that day, when he had defended her support of Dominique Moreau, a feeling of intense pride had mixed with relief; a crazy kind of joy had overcome him.

Alex reached for the telephone. He dragged it closer to him, thought for a while longer, and then, having become comfortable with the decision, dialed.

"Judge Paine's office," he said.

A moment later, when his old classmate from law school came on the line, he said, "Off the record, what happened in Dominique Moreau's case the other day?"

"Don't ask," Paine replied.

"I'm asking, Jack."

"It's a can of worms. I saw what was going down at the hearing, but I couldn't do anything about it. Legally, he was in his rights. He was just a sloppy lawyer. Intentionally sloppy."

Mara did not know if her picture would be taken, but in the event it might be, she had prepared herself.

From the time she had stepped off the streetcar four months before, she had revamped not only the house she had inherited but also herself. Inside and out.

Within, she was no longer a passive spectator, content to stand on the sidelines watching life being played around her; she was a part of it. For better or worse.

She had also made sweeping changes in her appearance. Her hair had been lightened and cut in layers to just above her shoulders by a cosmetologist knowing every trick in the beauty business. Mara's new look was feminine and natural, but her grooming was precise. Whereas she did not look plastic, she did appear deliberately and intelligently "put together." In one article, a reporter wrote that Mara gave the impression of a woman clever enough to be able to pamper herself if no one else was there to see to it for her.

For the occasion at hand, she wore minimal makeup. But what she had on accentuated the width and depth and the exotic shape of her blue eyes. Her mouth was slick with a medium shade of coral lipstick, nothing overbearing, its color blending well with the loose weave of the rust-and-beige suit she had chosen from her expanding wardrobe.

It was the end of September, the suit appropriate to the season and the meeting alike. Even Morrie Baby would have approved, she thought, but then reconsidered. Smiling, she remembered how his motto was to make fashion statements, not political statements.

A few minutes later, she led the reporter to the inside patio. There had been one frost already, and even in the late afternoon there was a marked edge to the air. Lots of things were changing, Mara thought as she invited her guest to be seated at a round glass cocktail table.

The reporter was a veteran, a colorless man, probably in his fifties, with wisps of beige-colored hair overlapping in an effort to feign abundance on an almost bald dome. Mara knew his work. He was a fair man, a reasonable man. No longer the wide-eyed innocent, she did not count on getting a fair hearing, but by giving him the exclusive interview, she felt she was at least giving herself a sporting chance to be presented objectively.

It took her less than fifteen minutes to say her piece. He listened attentively, every now and then interrupting to ask a question, but mostly listening in silence and taking rapid shorthand as she spoke. She spoke candidly, first of her admiration for Dominique's talent, and declared flatly that they had become friends in spite of Dominique's debatable checkered past. Then she reviewed her attempts to provide legal help for her friend.

"Those are serious allegations," he said when she had finished. "Possibly libelous."

"You can quote me, can't you? That lets your paper off the hook. I want Grant Forbes's name in there."

"If you're right—"

"I am right," she shot back.

"Okay," he said evenly. "So, saying you are right, have you considered the danger to yourself? If not libelous, your statements are certainly inflammatory. Retaliation might not be ruled out."

Mara stood. "I appreciate the concern, but that's my business. Yours is to publish the truth. That still *is* your business, isn't it?" she asked, fixing him with eyes she knew were no longer naive, no longer trusting.

"It is," he said, and she smiled. He had looked her in the eyes squarely, unflinchingly.

The story hit the next day in the morning edition. There was a picture of Grant Forbes and a picture of her, both of them apparently taken from the paper's morgue. Mara read through the three-column article appearing on the front page while having a cup of coffee in her office. Scandal concerning leading citizens and beautiful women always sold newsprint. The reporter had done a solid job. He had even reached Grant Forbes, allowing him opportunity to rebut her remarks. Forbes denounced her as a liar, but did not elaborate on her comments.

Mara smiled at that. Alex had once told her that when an incumbent was running for reelection, the worst thing he could do was to respond to the accusations hurled against him by the opposition. It only called attention to the unfavorable claims and promoted his competition's name.

The telephone calls began shortly after eight o'clock that morning. Some of them were from zealous freedom fighters rallying to her cause, some from detractors, and some of the calls were even obscene. All the calls came over the publicly listed phone number of Salina's Place. At ten o'clock she told her staff to take messages, she herself being busy with the financial ledgers in her upstairs office.

So it was without trepidation that she reached across her desk to answer her own private telephone.

"Hello . . ." Her attention was on the accounting for the previous week's liquor bill.

There was a beat; then a familiar voice said, "You've got until tonight to make a retraction of that story."

Mara stiffened. The voice brought a chill to the room. "No," she said. "No, but why don't you prove me wrong, Grant? Why don't you take me to court and sue me?'' she challenged.

So, she had him. She was smoking him out. Or almost, anyway. If he would just go one step further and give her the real public platform she wanted to totally expose him and the low-lifes for whom he worked.

''Are you stupid? Or just plain reckless?''

''I'm honest,'' she said.

''By this evening's edition . . .'' The click on the other end was strangely final.

Mara went back to her ledgers, but it was hard to concentrate. In the back of her mind she kept hearing the click. Again and again, it repeated. Angrily she pushed herself away from the desk, determined to put away the fear he had meant to plant in her mind with his call.

Alex slapped the newspaper down on Grant Forbes's desk.

''Don't bother with the denials, Grant. I've already checked out her story with someone who confirmed everything she said. Someone who knows,'' he added pointedly. He had gotten his information from his friend in confidence. It was unnecessary to name names to Forbes. His word would be enough. ''You messed up, Grant, when you did zip for Dominique Moreau. But worse, you did nothing purposely.''

Forbes tilted back his Leatherette executive's chair, relaxing his body into its soft folds. He would have put his feet up on his desk and chewed a piece of straw, and it wouldn't have been out of keeping with his air of composure.

Standing and looking down at Forbes, Alex could not affect the same easy air of well-being. He had gotten out of bed with a tight knot in his gut. Then, as he read the morning's edition of the paper, his anger inflamed. As he waited for Forbes to say his piece, he realized something bordering on the profound. He suddenly understood that his real anger was at himself. Forbes was just an outlet for his own self-condemnation, for not coming to Mara's aid in a forthright manner. Even as he stood before Forbes, ostensibly in the role of her benefactor, he was still only championing Mara from behind the scenes.

After a moment during which he rocked gently in his chair, Forbes said, "All right, Alex. You know I respect you. Professionally. Personally, too." Then, sitting forward so suddenly that the springs of the chair twanged, he abandoned all pretence of being just a jovial country gentleman chewing the fat with a like-minded compatriot. His jaw hardened. His eyes leveled with Alex's. "I did a bad thing. You know it, I know it. There was some pressure put on me." His eyes dived to his desk. "But no excuses. I'm ashamed," he said. Then, looking Alex in the face again, he said, "I'd like to gain back my self-respect. I'm going to arrange to have a public interview with the young woman. A fine young lady, too. A real fighter," he said, pausing reflectively. "We're going to put the issue to rest for good."

Alex nodded. "I've your word?"

Forbes rose. His arm reached out across the desk. Alex took the proffered hand. The clasp was firm and dry. "My word," Forbes returned.

It was four in the morning before Mara got to bed. There was too much to do to retire any earlier. The evening had been long, the crowds never-ending. She could only guess that the newspaper article had whetted the public's curiosity. It was probably like taking one of those tours of the stars' homes in Hollywood. People craved a closer look of a public person's private life.

She drew a bath, quickly washed, slipped into a long

nightgown, and flopped into bed exhausted. Too exhausted to sleep.

So she lay there, her mind chattering like a demented magpie, subjects coming and going, fears expanding, worries spiraling off, then returning a few moments later.

Click. Mara turned over, bunching up her pillow. *Click*. She lay still. *Click*. There it was again. Her breath stopped and her body grew rigid, as if to increase her concentration. *Click*.

Fear stiffened her spine, and the breathing process which had halted came now in rapid, shallow bursts.

Someone else was in Salina's Place.

Click.

With an annoyed tug, Alex drew the tie of his dressing robe tighter around his waist. Leaving his bedroom suite, he switched on the lights of the hall and started down the stairs. In the family room, he helped himself to a strong dose of brandy from the bar, downed it in several deep swallows and poured another to take back with him.

The feeling of unease had not abated. He had thought by confronting Grant Forbes he could rid himself of his own guilt. But it hadn't worked, had it?

He started to leave, then, eyeing the bottle, took it along with him. It would save him a trip later on.

Looking down at the burnished gold circling in the glass, he faced another fact. Booze wasn't going to help either. He stopped where he was, halfway up the stairs. From the corner of his eye he caught his shadow. It slanted long and dark, off to the side, seeming to waver slightly in the diffused light from the chandelier high above. His shadow, his companion, a constant self he could not escape no matter how clever his ploys or how fast his maneuvers.

Then his gaze swept to his opposite side.

Below, the double doors to his office were open, waiting to be entered.

"All right," he said aloud. "I accept the invitation."

He crossed the portal and went straight to his desk. Putting down the glass and the bottle, he placed his father's picture squarely before him. Then, lifting his brandy glass, he said, "Father, I honor your history. But now I must make my own." When he had emptied the glass, he lifted the telephone and dialed.

"Oh God," Mara whispered, "help me. Someone help me."

She slipped out from under the covers, her body feeling separate from her mind.

Across the room was the telephone. She could see it in the dark, its form outlined in the mirror of the dressing table on which it sat.

Below, she could hear the sounds of movement, muffled, indistinct. But they were sounds that did not belong. Living sounds. The click again. What was it? That click, that terrible clicking. . . .

Her feet were numb of all feeling as she crossed the room. The dark was terrible. It was a nightmare fog through which she had to push her way or perish.

Then suddenly she doubled over, a pain shooting through her lower legs. She almost fell. Hysterical, for a moment she could not make out the attacker. Then she did. It was the small stool slightly out of place in front of the dressing table.

Her knuckles ground against her teeth as she forced herself not to scream. All she had to do was call for help. Another few feet and she would have the telephone in her hand.

A shrilling filled the silence.

The phone. The phone, Mara told herself. It's the phone!

But she couldn't move. Every instinct she had was directed toward survival and she continued to stand there immobile. She was afraid of the dark, afraid to move.

It rang again, sharply, in a short burst. This time she went for it, aiming her entire body at it, grabbing it off its hook and sobbing into its mouthpiece, "Help me. Help. The police . . . call the . . ."

But she stopped. There was no one there. There was no one on the other end of the phone. There was nothing but hollowness against her ear. Something had happened to her phone.

She held on to it, its weight dead in her hand.

And soon, she thought, staring at the door . . . soon she could be dead, too . . . .

Alex let the phone ring ten times before he hung up and redialed, thinking he might have made a mistake.

He was careful the second time. This time he let the phone ring another ten times before putting down the receiver.

For a moment he puzzled over the situation. Surely she had a right to be out. She was young and beautiful and a celebrity, and it would stand to reason that some man would want to take her out.

But he abandoned that train of thought, partly because the idea of another man being with her would make him wild. Also he knew, dammit, that she loved him.

So where the hell was she?

Then he thought that the phone was out of order.

Quickly he punched "operator" and waited while the phone rang. Between the second and third rings, a dark thought crossed his mind.

Mara was in danger.

Chapter 12

His heart did a turn. The worst had already happened. Ahead of him the entrance to Salina's Place was obscured from view by two units of firefighting equipment and an ambulance.

Alex left the Mercedes in the center of the street, not bothering to park it even when the police yelled at him. They could have fired a round of shots his way, the sky could have fallen, and he still would have gone on. Nothing mattered, only Mara.

"Hey! Hey, you!" an officer shouted. Alex kept going. Another uniformed man made a grab for his arm. Alex pushed him away and adroitly dodged another man who also tried to stop him as he went through the front door. "You can't go in there . . ." he heard, but he was already in, the voice trailing impotently behind him.

There she was. Someone had wrapped her in a gray blanket. To Alex, the bold strawberry color of her silken nightgown, its folds edging out from the drab utilitarian coverlet, took on the property of a silent scream of alarm. Her head was tilted slightly down and to the side. The thick mass of hair looked flaxen, its color washed by an overhead globe of light. He could feel it, even now, that luxuriant, erotic softness as it tumbled upon his chest as they made love. But the sweetness of the memory suddenly contorted. The realization that there would be only a past, never again a future, was like a violent assault. In the remembered moonlight of the past, his mind twisted in agony. Her hair, now a veil as it hung heavily before her face, had once lain spread upon a pillow as he had bent to kiss her mouth.

With each step he took toward her he was aware that what he found might not contain a future. If she were . . . But he couldn't even think it.

He still could not see her face.

No one was paying attention to him. Kneeling beside Mara, the men in white were fully concentrated on her motionless form.

His heart wrenched again for her graceful frailty. Her slender body was like that of a defenseless bird's whose life and beauty had been taken for granted by those who equated the joy of living with an absolute strength it did not in actuality possess. Now he saw that and much more.

An eruption of power surged through him. Raw male instinct, primal and true, swept aside a lifetime of social patterns. Driven by this wellspring of passion, he knew he could—and would—with his bare hands, tear out the heart of any man who would cause the slightest harm to the woman lying before him.

His journey ended; he had reached her.

Her mouth was covered by an oxygen mask. She was slightly propped up now, cradled against the chest of one of the attendants. He saw now that there was a square of bandage over her temple. *What the hell has happened?* Alex's mind screamed. Her eyes were closed, but she took a deep breath, then another and another. She was alive. Mara was alive.

Tears flooded his eyes, and as he stooped down beside her, her face swam before him like a beautiful mirage. The men in uniform who had followed him in had sensitively drawn back.

"Mara . . . Mara . . ." he choked, taking her limp hand and clasping it against his chest. "I love you. I love you so," he repeated, this time with a frightening violence he could not contain. Then, more softly, for her sake, he said, "I am never, never going to leave you." Her eyes remained closed. He looked helplessly to the man administering first aid.

"She'll be all right," the medic said, and added, "Luckily."

"Damn right she'll be all right." Alex looked down at her. She was so small, so incredibly vulnerable.

"What happened here? What went on here?" he barked, not taking his eyes from Mara's all-but-lifeless form.

"Some sonofagun set fire to the place. Emptied a gasoline can."

Another spasm of rage shook Alex. He smelled the spilled fuel. It was not an accident, but deliberate. Who could have done it? And how the hell could he have been such a selfish bastard to have let it happen?

"Her head," Alex said, "what happened to her head? Was she attacked? Did the bastard—?"

"Looks like she fell trying to get down the stairs. She was out like a light when we got there. Man oh man, she's one lucky lady. Whole place could have gone up in flames if one of the neighbors hadn't of seen whoever the bum was who did it, runnin' out the door.''

''She could have been . . .'' Alex couldn't say it.

''Sure could have met her maker this night. Lucky, lucky lady. . . .''

''Stop looking at me that way,'' Mara said.

''What way?'' Alex replied, with too much innocence to be believed.

''Like you expect me to go up in smoke—'' Mara stopped, looking shocked. ''Oh,'' she said. ''That wasn't exactly a good turn of phrase.''

''It was accurate,'' Alex replied, not smiling. ''Have some more juice.'' He poured it for her. Even if she hadn't wanted it, he would have insisted. Vitamin C for her welfare. Rest for her welfare. If he could have insulated her in a pink cloud surrounded by an electrified wall, he would have.

Any reminder of having almost lost her drove him wild. As he looked across the table, he realized that he wanted it always to be like this: secure and safe and ordinary, the two of them seated in his breakfast room, the smell of Anna's bacon still pungent in the air, each of them within touching distance of the other.

He hadn't let her out of his sight since the night of the fire three days before. Thank God, he had repeated to himself a million times, someone had been suspicious. Thank God, he repeated another million times, that there were good souls in New Orleans who kept the city going round the clock, who were awake to notice the ugly and unusual along with the alluring beauty of the Vieux Carré.

Mara had told the police what she had heard, and with the fire department's investigator there, they pieced together the source of the mysterious ''click.'' It must have been a special can filled with gasoline, the suction of its sides indenting and expanding as its contents were spilled. Whoever had done it was a professional, that much was sure. He had attempted to make it look like an accident, the source being in the kitchen, and the gas only spilled in strategic places elsewhere. Starting the fire in the kitchen had saved Mara's life and the fire department had come before it had done much damage to the main room.

Of course there was no way to prove Grant Forbes had been responsible, as a professional had been used to set the blaze, and there were no clues leading to his identity. However, both Alex and Mara knew the fire had been in response to her story.

Salina's Place was closed. "Temporarily," Mara continuously asserted to Alex, who was waging a campaign for her early retirement from the entertainment business.

The paint in the club was being freshened in the few places darkened by smoke, and it was even necessary to replace a couple of pieces of furniture scarred by the short-lived blaze. The kitchen was a mess, and whatever couldn't be salvaged was being replaced.

Also since the fire, Alex had not let her spend a night away from him. He insisted she stay at his place during the day. When it was necessary for her to tend to business details at Salina's, he went with her.

"Alex!" Mara had complained. "You're being obsessive about this."

"I'm being safe," he had argued. "All right, obsessive. I'll get over it. Just give me time." That was yesterday. He didn't know how much time he would need to get over worrying about her; it could take several lifetimes.

Now, with downcast eyes, Mara sipped thoughtfully on her juice. When she looked up, she shook her head disparagingly again. "Alex, please. Stop this. You're making me feel like a specimen under glass. I'm not an invalid. I took in some smoke and I got scared out of my wits, but I'm alive and well." She stood, stretching her arms wide and turning around like a mannequin to demonstrate her fitness. "I'd like to get on with my life."

"Good," he said, and gave the tabletop a resounding slap with the flat of his palm. "I'm glad you're fit. You're right, it is time to get on with our lives." He emphasized the "our." Standing, he said, "It so happens we've got work to do."

A minute later they were in his office. Casually, as if it could have been just any scrap of paper, he handed her the legal brief to look over.

Quickly her eyes skimmed over the print. She looked up at him. "Alex, no."

"Yes," he said, and almost imperceptibly his eyes skated over to the picture of his father before returning to her. "I'm going to defend Dominique."

"But—"

"If it costs me being D.A., then so be it."

Mara was silent. "I know you've thought this out."

"I have."

"And I suppose I couldn't stop you," she said.

"You suppose right."

"If it's because of the fire, if it's because you feel guilty somehow for—"

"No, I'd made up my mind before that. In fact, it's why I came over. I'd been trying to reach you. I had wanted to tell you that night, when everything finally came clear to me." He walked around the desk. Removing the brief from her hands, he laid it down. "It suddenly became obvious how a man's own good opinion of himself has a higher ultimate value than whatever opinions a thousand other men hold of him. If a man doesn't value himself, if he doesn't understand the true worth of a human being, then how can he defend the values of others?''

Mara reached up. Tenderly, with the pads of her fingers she caressed his face. He caught her hand. Reverently he brought her fingertips to his lips. ''I was on my soapbox making loud noises about being brave, about defending the good of the people. Only I wasn't. You were, though. You weren't just talking, you were doing.''

''You couldn't. You'd have had to gamble on losing a job you wanted since you were a child. It was different.''

''No,'' he objected. ''Don't give me that. What I had was important to me. But Salina's Place was the chance you'd been waiting for all your life, too.'' He lifted her chin, forcing her to look him in the eye. ''Even if you didn't know you were waiting, you were. You were looking for your opening to get out, to escape into who and what you really are, not what your parents were and their friends were. I saw it in you that first time. It was a hunger almost, a desperation. I guess it was partly what excited me about you, that edge. That sharp edge combined with all the softness.

''And I,'' Alex continued, ''have discovered something very interesting about my own self. I thought to be D.A. was my whole reason for existence. The other night, I found out I was wrong. The only thing that matters . . .''

But he couldn't say any more. All he could do was feel, and feeling was more than enough. It was everything.

Almost with a sob, he grabbed her to him. They held each other with a quiet, intense passion going beyond the scope of words.

''There's only one thing,'' Alex said. ''Before this

thing with Dominique is over, we might be seeing some desperate times." He held her even closer to him.

The first proof of what Alex had projected as their stormy future came from Anna.

"May I talk to you, Mr. Gautier?" she said one afternoon shortly after the papers had carried the news that he would be acting as defense counsel in Dominique Moreau's case.

Mara was seated at Alex's desk, using a corner to go over some figures relating to supplies for Salina's Place. She continued to work, but Alex looked up and said, "Yes, of course."

"If I might speak to you alone?"

Mara felt Anna's eyes slide to her. The glance was cold, even reproachful. Alex must have noted it too. "No, we're all friends. You can speak freely here."

"I see." Anna hesitated slightly, as if reevaluating her situation in this new light. "The newspapers and television have been filled with stories about your trial—the Moreau trial. The publicity is very bad and people are saying things." Her voice trailed off, as if she hoped he might conclude the message for her.

"Yes, Anna, I'm certainly aware of that. How could I not be?" He smiled at Mara. She smiled back warmly. Their eyes touched and held; an unspoken intimacy was exchanged. Mara had not expected this sweetness to come as a by-product of adversity. They were there together, two soldiers in the same battle, two lovers whose hearts beat to the same rhythm.

"It's unpleasant," Anna said.

Alex arched his eyebrows. "Yes, unpleasant. But really that's my concern, isn't it?"

"Unpleasant for me," Anna clarified stiffly.

Mara saw Alex's face darken, but he was controlled when he said, "I'm sorry you're finding your employ disagreeable, Anna. Every attorney takes an unpopular case now and then."

"It isn't just the case."

The room was quiet. Mara did not dare move. Her very breath seemed frozen in her lungs.

"Then what is it?" Alex asked quietly.

Anna said nothing. Then she looked to Mara.

"Yes?" Alex challenged. "Please continue, Anna."

"All right," the housekeeper said finally. Once begun, the words spilled out one upon the other. "It's her."

The "her" was Mara, although now Anna would no longer look Mara's way, relegating "her" status to that of an absent entity.

"To the eye of the public, it is one thing to defend a client, but to"—she hesitated, searching for the right word—"live with someone who is personally involved in supporting a person connected to crime is another matter. You have a certain station in this city. It should be respected. Lowering your standards makes you look foolish."

"You mean it makes you look foolish," Alex said.

He rose from his chair. From the black look on his face, Mara thought he might actually be angry enough to strike the woman on whose face suddenly appeared red splotches set in a paling skin.

"Well?" Alex said, walking around the desk.

Mara rose, now truly afraid of what he might do, and mentally prepared herself to step between them.

Anna must have also feared the same, for she took a few steps back, angling herself out of his reach.

"Yes," she said. "I take pride in my employment. But I can't anymore. People look at me. They ask things. I know they're laughing behind my back. If you were smart, if you cared about your future, you'd end things with her and continue your life the way it was before."

While Anna spoke, Alex had walked to the door of the office. "You can leave now, Anna. There will be a check in the mail for you tomorrow. No more painful laughter to endure," Alex added without a hint of sarcasm.

Anna looked shocked. For a moment she only stared; then she once again acknowledged Mara's existence by turning her way. Anna's expression seemed to convey total bewilderment, as if it had never occurred to her that Alex would not take her side against the upstart Northerner who had so royally messed things up. "You don't belong here," Anna said coldly. "You have ruined his life."

With that, she turned and without a look to Alex, who stood by the door, passed out of the room. Her heels clicked angrily over the hardwood floors as she went down the hall to the back of the house. A moment later the front door slammed shut.

"So," Alex said, "that's over with."

"I'm sorry," Mara said.

"Don't be. She's a jerk, a foolish woman with unfounded snobbish tendencies."

"No," Mara said, "she was right. We both know it. I have caused you trouble."

"But you've brought me joy, Mara. You're my life, dammit, not those fat cigar-smoking icons with their petty-minded wives who can think of nothing else but what sort of canapés they should serve at their next brunch."

"That was partly your life before I came into the scene. And you were satisfied then."

"I was living my father's life. Or so I thought," he said. Walking to his desk, he lifted the framed print of his father to look once again at the face that had shaped his destiny. "But I was wrong. I really didn't understand my father at all. I didn't understand a lot of things," Alex said quietly and put down the photograph.

"Like what?" Mara asked, intrigued.

"I'll tell you someday. When the time's right," Alex said.

There were, or so it seemed, no right times after that day.

A few days after the episode, Mara announced to Alex over dinner that she was reopening Salina's Place.

"Don't," Alex said. He had said it as an order. He had meant it as an order.

"Alex, I must! You knew I was going to."

"Mara, no. At least wait until after the trial."

"I don't care what they print about me in the—" She stopped mid-sentence. "Oh," she said. "You mean I'll be bad publicity for you. Like waving a red flag in the face of a bull, the bull being the press."

"I'm thinking of you," he said.

"Take a look. I'm a tough guy, Alex. Give me some credit. I'm still here. I haven't been run out of town yet, have I?" She laughed, but he didn't join in. Undaunted, she continued. "I've withstood crooked lawyers, hot flames, bad press, an angry ex-girlfriend of yours, and one powerfully snobbish maid."

Alex's dark eyes continued to hold their troubled expression.

She reached over, closing her hand over his. "Don't you see? Salina's Place is part of me. You were right when you said it was something I had been waiting for all my life. I don't want to take the course of least resistance like my family and stay in safe quarters."

"The quarters I offer you can hardly be called safe."

"But they're your quarters, not my own."

"No matter what I say, you're going to open, aren't you?"

"It's what you said to me, remember? You had something to prove to yourself by taking on Dominique's case. I couldn't have changed your mind because we were arguing emotion, not realistically evaluating facts."

So Mara reopened Salina's Place to packed audiences.

She called Alex from her office. He had remained at home to work on a campaign speech to be made the next day. "Total sellout," she crowed triumphantly. "Maybe the public likes to rub elbows with a low-life like me. Maybe it gives them a thrilling sense of danger," she joked.

"Just don't let them rub anything other than elbows," Alex cautioned, but she could hear the pleasure in his voice. He was glad for her.

He was in bed, but awake, when she returned early that morning. His arms went around her as she crawled beneath the covers and took her place beside him.

There was no need for conversation. They were ready for each other, Mara's desire seeming partially borne of a heady excitement at her victory, with Alex's passion containing elements of a darker nature. In his lovemaking Mara sensed a need for an affirmation that was beyond her ability to give.

"What's wrong, tell me, Alex?" she whispered.

"Nothing," he said, and kissing her fiercely, silenced any further questions.

He made love to her in the same manner, with a male force that was possessive and demanding. By covering her with the hardness of his form, by filling her so completely with his love, it seemed there would be no space left over for the demons of reality to take residence in the daylight.

Afterward, Alex did not sleep. Nor did she, although

she tried, and then pretended for his sake to have drifted off.

He tossed from side to side several times, and then rose and left the room wearing his dressing gown.

She found him downstairs at his desk, not doing anything, just sitting, staring at nothing.

"Now will you tell me?" she asked softly.

He looked up, worried, not happy to see her. "I guess I have to. You'll find out anyway."

"Go on," Mara said, feeling that somehow this was going to be the worst.

"Dominique tried to take her own life this evening."

Mara felt her legs folding beneath her. Alex was up, his arms supporting her as he lowered her into a chair. He bent down on one leg, putting his face in her lap and holding his hands tightly in his own. "But she's alive, thank God. She's going to make it, at least physically."

"It's my fault," Mara said. "I was so stupid to go to Grant Forbes. It's taken too long. She wasn't strong enough. I saw that, Alex. I saw that."

But Alex was shaking his head, denying her words. His face, always so handsome, was now ravaged with concern. Mara reached forward, forgetting her own miseries, and stroked his face, his hair, kissed the lines of care from his forehead, then brushed her mouth against his, saying, "I love you, love you. Don't hurt, Alex. Please don't hurt."

"I saw her this afternoon. She was very upset then. She told me the word was out that she wouldn't get a fair break. That politically I was a pariah—her meaning, not her words—and that there was no way I could help her. I'd only be dragging her life up to public scrutiny for nothing. When she finally went to prison, either Charles Moreau or his enemies would take their revenge for what she might say in the trial."

"Is that possible?" Mara asked, her eyes burning from the thought of such horrible injustice.

"Anything's possible," Alex replied.

"Then so is winning."

It wasn't, of course, a case of backing down or backing out anymore. The truth was, they didn't have those options left open to them. They had committed themselves publicly to Dominique's defense. If Alex abandoned her at this point, he would look like a coward, a man of inconstant resolve.

There came a point when their lives seemed to have dipped into a deep trough between two enormous cresting waves.

The same papers carrying stories glorifying LaPierre's "boy" ran other accounts of Alex's involvement in the defense of Dominique Moreau. Nothing untrue was said about him, yet the slanted truth cast a shadow on Alex's integrity. It was all very subtle, and therefore lethal.

For days the October sky had hung low overhead, its color an ominous gunmetal gray. It was only three weeks before the election day for district attorney, and one week before Dominique's trial would commence. The mood between Alex and Mara and Dominique was oppressive as they met to go over final pretrial briefings. Silent rebuke rode on each exchanged glance.

"You aren't cooperating," Alex said. "This is your trial. Don't you care about it?"

"No," Dominique answered sulkily. "I don't."

"Well, I damn well do. My reputation just happens to ride on it."

"Tell him to get off my back," Dominique snapped, turning to Mara.

"He has to ask you questions like that. It's what the prosecution is going to do. You've got to be ready," Mara explained for what seemed to her the millionth time. Understandably, Dominique did not like to hear about her past life with Charles. But it was necessary to cool her out now, before she went on the stand, where a display of emotional pyrotechnics would not be well-received.

"I didn't ask for his help. I just want to be left alone."

"Fine," Alex said. Abruptly he rose from his chair, and snatching up his legal notes and briefcase, strode from the room.

Mara looked across the table to Dominique. "Great," Mara said. "That was really great. You can't see that the guy is hurting? You can't see he's tired? You can't see his life is falling apart? I want to know one thing," Mara said, leaning forward. "I want to know just how long you're going to continue this big drama of yours, in which you play the poor victim of life. I want to know when you're going to get up and fight. Because, Dominique, there is only so much that people who care about you can do. You've got to care too. Got that?"

Mara didn't bother to wait around for a reply. She picked up her purse and left Dominique. The only answer that counted would come at the trial.

Alex was looking grim. He stood in the outside waiting room, staring at nothing but the yellowing plaster wall.

A clap of thunder shook the heavens as they exited the building together and entered into a solid sheet of water. "Here," Alex said, and lifted his briefcase over her head to protect her. Near them, a brightness filled the gloom. For the briefest of moments, Mara thought it was lightning, but then another burst of white light came from the other side and two men rushed forward with microphones extended.

"Alex Gautier," said one, "what's it like being counsel to a member of the underworld?"

Alex looked into the man's face, smiled, and stepping slightly back, brought his fist back and then forward in one smooth movement.

The man staggered and fell to the ground, holding the side of his jaw.

There was another flash off to the side.

"Far-out," the other photojournalist said as he scampered away to safety with his camera equipment in tow. "Hey, guy, you just hit the wrong dude. We're talking national media here."

And so they were.

The next day the picture appeared in syndicated editions throughout the country. Still clips of the picture were carried on national television.

Alex turned off the news show after they had viewed three separate coverages of him hitting a member of the press. He left the house then, walking in the rain that had stopped only intermittently since the day before. There was nothing Mara could do but love him. She watched from the window as he disappeared down the walk in the gloom. The rain pounded relentlessly, sounding to Mara like a billion judges' gavels. She was still standing there when he returned, a lone figure in a raincoat; but now he was walking with more purpose. Her heart felt lighter. He'd given himself a pep talk. He hadn't lost heart.

She threw open the door, a smile already set on her face.

But it faded immediately. "No," she said as the man in the trench coat stepped forward with his hand outstretched in greeting. "No. There's nothing here for you vultures. You've already picked all the bones you're going to. Get the hell out of—"

"I'm on your side," the man said evenly.

He was, too. It took him ten minutes to convince Mara,

who made him stand on the porch until she was satisfied he was being truthful.

"Okay, come in," she said.

"He's not here, I take it?" He didn't slide curious eyes around, but spoke to her politely.

"No, he's not. He's out walking. I'm sure he's feeling like he'd like to drown out there."

"Well, maybe we can throw him a life raft."

Mara nodded.

"Shall we begin?" the man asked, nodding toward the living room.

"Not in there," she said. "In his office."

He followed her down the hall and through the double doors. The rain whipped against the windowpanes, causing the glass to chatter where it was not wedged against the wood tightly enough. It was an old house, Mara thought lovingly, an old house with a lot of history and loose joints, too.

"Where do you want to start?" the reporter asked, staring down at the picture of Alex's father on the desk.

"Right there," Mara replied softly, and nodded to the picture. "At the beginning."

When she had finished with the whole story, her eyes were moist. The man remained silent for a long moment, as if he too could not trust himself to speak. Then he cleared his throat, and with some effort said, "Thank you. For trusting me." He stood up and slipped his notes and the miniature tape recorder into a deep side pocket of his drying coat. Throwing the coat over his arm, he said, "I can see myself out."

When Alex returned, it was after dark.

They didn't talk much. He was wet and cold and lost in his own thoughts. It was all coming down the wire—his life, his father's life, Dominique's life, their future together. Mara just hoped to hell there wasn't going to be an explosion at the end.

The trial opened on another rainy day.

Mara accompanied Alex to the courthouse. Walking through the halls, he looked handsome and self-assured. Mara tried to match his manner, smiling easily at his side, as if between them they had not a care in the world. It was a tough act.

Reporters were everywhere, including inside the courtroom, filled to capacity with the curious. Mara inventoried the odd assortment of people in attendance. A motley group, the audience partly comprised society matrons in expensive French raincoats—out for a day of slumming, Mara supposed. They'd probably retreat for lunch at Arnaud's, where over *pompano en croute* and *crème brûlée* they'd exclaim over Alex's handsomeness and "wasn't it all a shame, wasting his life like that." Interspersed among the expensive Parisian fragrances were scents of strong cheeses and pungently spiced meats, carried in the oversized bags of women wearing plastic rain slickers. There were elderly men whose main entertainment was to follow the fortunes of others in trial after trial, just as other, more affluent men followed the fluctuations of the Dow Jones averages. Clustered together in a front row, a gathering of eager-faced students— probably from a law school—followed Alex's every movement as he arranged his notes and legal papers on the long table before the judge's bench.

Even she found herself fascinated. No wonder Alex had drawn a full house. He cut what would have at one time been called "a dashing figure" in a pin-striped gray suit and white shirt, the tie a muted wine with a subtle pattern of black shapes. His dark hair glistened beneath the overhead lights, with his eyes matching the sparkle as he spoke briefly to the bailiff and court reporter who had just arrived. Looking at him now, Mara saw no traces of the angst visible that morning as he dressed quietly, almost resolutely.

"You'll win," she had told him, straightening his tie.

"I'll fight anyway," he had told her.

It had frightened her to hear him say that. Even a month before, his response would have been, "Damn right I'll win." But since that time so much had happened. He had been a glowing golden figure, a three-dimensional model of what man should be in his finest form. But relentlessly, that image had been hammered upon by outside forces. His substance had been flattened and thinned to a dangerous transparency. Yet, she told herself, watching him move toward Dominique, who was being escorted from a side door into the courtroom, the substance itself remained the same in essence. Alex was still the same fine man he had always been.

Mara watched Dominique carefully, trying to detect signs of her emotional state. If anything, Dominique appeared disinterested. She nodded to Alex, who spoke a few words to her. Then the judge entered.

"All rise," the bailiff ordered.

Then the trial to convict Dominique Moreau for murder began.

Opening statements were made to the jury by both Alex and the state's prosecuting attorney.

Alex had consistently claimed the trial was a political maneuver backed by LaPierre's interests. There was just enough evidence to bring Dominique to trial, which is what LaPierre wanted. With Alex acting as defense, he would be in the public eye and, as such, a target for LaPierre, who could control elements of the media to his own best interests. But, Alex said, LaPierre's power ended inside the courtroom. He had a jury of people chosen for their impartiality, if such a thing were truly possible in this case, he added.

It was also in the current district attorney's best interests to pound away at Dominique. If frightened enough, Dominique might have broken, given the information he sought.

The judge gave a stern speech about unnecessary histrionics and orations. "Save the taxpayers' money," he droned. "Stick to the facts. We're all smart people," he said, his eyes traveling to the jurists. "We don't need a full-scale opera. Just the main melody, gentlemen."

And so it went. To do otherwise, Alex confided in Mara during lunch, would antagonize the judge. "The case will be won or lost on the basis of one thing."

"What?" Mara asked.

"The testimony of your friend Dominique."

Dominique was called to the stand by Alex. The female voice that could easily fill an enormous room was low and flat, almost inaudible as she answered Alex's questions.

Mara watched, her fingers itching to slap Dominique silly. At one point Alex turned back to the table and his eyes met Mara's. She read defeat in that look, as clearly as if six-foot letters were arranged on a billboard.

Then it was the prosecution's turn. The attorney almost bounded up to the witness stand. And why shouldn't he? Mara had to ask. Dominique had been a hostile witness to her own defense. It was as if she had decided not only to lose, but to lose by her own hand.

"Did you dislike the deceased?" the prosecutor asked.

"Yes. I hated him."

Mara saw Alex's head dip down. The case was lost.

"Did you hate him enough to kill him?" the prosecutor continued with barely restrained glee.

"Yes, of course. He was scum."

238   MAIN CHANCE

That was when Mara rose from her seat and started
down the aisle toward the door. She felt sick. She had to
get out of there. Her purse clattered to the floor, and the
catch opened, spilling her lipstick and brush along with a
few other objects. There was a moment of frozen silence
as people reacted to the unexpected sound with reflexive
fear. Mara herself was startled. It was, after all, a murder
trial.

Shaking her head by way of apology, she bent to gather
up the scattered items.

"You can continue, Counselor," the judge said with
annoyance.

Cringing, Mara stole a brief glance in Alex's direction.
But she was invisible to him. His head was down as
he reviewed the papers before him on the table. Instead, it was Dominique's eyes who sought and held
hers.

Mara was shocked at what she saw, or rather by what
she didn't see. There was no emotion in the green eyes.
There was no particular sense of shame, no fear. If
anything, there was perhaps a challenge, a look saying:
"So, you see now . . . I was right. I will lose in spite of
all of you."

And then in one sweeping wave of complete and total
understanding, Mara saw how idiotic she had been. She
really hadn't understood at all, even though in a million
ways Dominique had tried to tell her. Dominique saw
herself as a person who could only win by losing. That
was her pattern. That was her game in life. And Mara,
fool that she had been, had drawn Alex into it, right down
to this moment of total humiliation.

Slowly Mara rose, her purse clutched against her chest,
the square of leather like a shield that might protect her
from further debilitating revelations.

The prosecutor for the district attorney's office had

taken a moment to approach the judge's bench with Alex. Alex was raising an objection on a point of law.

Dominique kept her gaze aimed defiantly, even proudly at Mara. Mara merely nodded. It was the slightest of gestures, saying that, "Yes, I see. You've won. You have now shown everyone that you are alone." Then she turned around and walked from the court. The door closed after her quietly.

"Would you give Mr. Gautier this message?" Mara asked of the guard outside the courtroom door. She handed him a square of paper with the information that she would be going home to her own place. He should come there afterward.

It wasn't, she told herself, that she was a rat deserting a sinking ship, but more that she understood he would need the space to be alone with himself after the guilty verdict was pronounced.

When she entered Salina's Place, the day staff was busy preparing for the evening's crowd. Four telephone lines were lit and on hold, while the reservationist quickly wrote down names in blocks of space corresponding to the various show times. No one could merely drift into Salina's Place anymore for a glass of wine or some beer. There was a cover charge and seats were at a premium. Talented new entertainers had been booked to showcase acts good enough to be picked up by booking agents for first-class clubs in New York and Las Vegas.

"We're sold out for next Saturday," the reservationist called out excitedly to Mara as she walked past. "Oh, and there's mail. Telegram, too."

Mara took the stack of envelopes. "Thanks," she said listlessly, and proceeded on her way up the stairs.

Going first to her office, she threw the mail on her desk to be opened later. Then she reconsidered and picked up the telegram, tore it open, and read:

MARA, OLD ROOM WAITING FOR YOUR RETURN. EVERY-
THING CAN BE SAME AS BEFORE. FORGET ALL ELSE. LOVE,
MOTHER AND FATHER.

Mara stared at the words, trying to decide how she felt
about them.

There was another interpretation of the note:

*Mara. Come back home where like us you will live an
uneventful but safe life. There will be no rainbows
because there will be no sudden storms. But, Mara,
remember, there is no pot of gold at the end of the rainbow
because a rainbow is only an illusion. Come home, Mara.
Come home and forget the pain and the pleasure. Let all
passion turn cold.*

They were right. There were no rainbows. Not for her,
anyway. She dropped the telegram on the desk, started
away, then returned and took it with her. No rainbows,
she told herself. Hold on to reality.

She thought of reality again as she closed the bedroom
door behind her and looked around at what she now
recognized as nothing more than a borrowed dream.

With everything else she had borrowed from Salina
over the past few months—the passion for a man, her
destruction of that man through that very passion, her
fight to be accepted in a world to which she did not belong
and never would—she had borrowed this, her ultimate
defeat.

Like Salina, Mara thought, the best thing for her to do
was to check out. In a different way, symbolically, at
least, she would do the same.

She'd done enough to hurt Alex. A tear trickled down
her face and she brushed it away. *No melodrama, thank
you. You thought you could handle things, then handle
this . . . but for once handle things right, Mara. Stick to
the facts, ma'am, stick to the facts.*

She only had one suitcase, the same one that had come with her off the train from Ohio. Throwing it open on the bed, she began to pack. It wouldn't hold much, and really, she didn't care what she took back with her anyway. All the clothes she had bought for her new life would be a joke back in her town in Ohio. The Duchess, they'd call her. They'd laugh; they'd have every right to laugh, because she was a fool to think that she was any different than they were.

She'd leave her new manager in charge of Salina's Place for the time being, until she decided either to sell it as it was or to close it down completely and sell the building as just a building.

Just a building!

To think of Salina's Place as just a building—the idea cut into her with a stabbing pain. Living and loving and fighting and hoping had built these rooms.

No, keep your mind on the present. Let go of everything else but what you must do now.

Then, after the building's sale, she'd take the money.

Mara brushed away another renegade tear and threw a cashmere sweater into the suitcase. She'd take whatever money she got for Salina's Place, and maybe she'd go to cosmetology school. She didn't have to go back to the assembly line. The assembly line. How could she? *Be realistic, Mara, be realistic. You're not some fairy-tale princess, here.* Two more tears splashed down on her hand. *I can open a beauty shop. And then . . .* But she wasn't thinking too clearly because the tears were raining down on the clothes she had just packed. All she could think of was that, like Salina had once felt, there was no reason to want to live anywhere on this earth anymore.

Behind her, there came a brief knock, then the door opened before she could tell whoever it was to go away.

Quickly she swiped at her tears. Careful to keep her back to the intruder, she said, "I'd like to be alone, please."

"Mara . . ."

At the sound of her name, Mara spun around to Alex, who was looking at the suitcase with a dazed expression.

"Alex, don't say anything. I love you. And I'm leaving. I'm going home," she said, and with that closed the suitcase. "That's all you really need to know. Those are the facts."

He strode swiftly across the room.

Taking her by both shoulders, he looked angrily into her face. "I see, a rat deserting a sinking ship. Is that it, Mara?"

She tried to avoid his glance, but he held her chin steady between his fingers, forcing her to look at him.

"No, what I'm doing is really saving your life. You can still swim to shore and be safe. But I can't swim in these waters. I'm not going to hang around here any longer, just to weigh you down, and I don't want to drown either. I'm going home to where I belong."

"You belong here."

"No. I just borrowed someone else's dream for a while. Now I'm seeing the end of it."

"Oh," Alex said, "I get it. Just like Salina, huh?"

"Exactly," Mara said. "Just like Salina."

Alex stepped away. He kept his back to her as he walked to the French doors and looked out. Gravely he said, "I won the trial today. Dominique was acquitted."

It took a moment for the words to unscramble themselves in her head. Mara's breath caught.

"Oh, Alex . . . Alex! You did it! You won!" She started to rush to him, but then checked the impulse.

Something of her previous caution remained. Hadn't

Salina also been acquitted at her trial? The legal victory had come, but at a terrible cost to the man she loved.

Subdued, her emotions under control, Mara said, "Congratulations. When I left this afternoon I thought it was all over. You must have worked a miracle."

"Dominique came through for me. Something changed her mind, I guess. It was like another person had suddenly slipped into her body. She came out fighting. She was reasonable, persuasive and credible."

Mara felt a flush of pride, imagining Dominique captivating the jurists.

"So, if there was any miracle today, that miracle was Dominique's sudden conversion to her own cause. She's even agreed to work with the district attorney on the names he wants. Charles Moreau's going to be put away for good. His friends, too. Dominique's prepared to go all the way with this. She'll never have to run again. She'll be safe."

"She finally woke up," Mara said. "I wonder what did it?"

Alex nodded. "So did I. Of course I'd have liked to say I finally broke her down through my kindness or my legal virtuosity, but that wasn't it. After the verdict was handed down, I had about two minutes with her before the press converged. She was surprisingly subdued over her victory. No, not subdued. More relaxed, I'd say. When she tried to thank me, I told her to forget it. If anything, it was her change in attitude that brought about the acquittal. I asked her what made her change sides at the last minute." He looked at Mara. "She said it suddenly occurred to her there wasn't anybody left on her side. Not even her. So she came over. Yeah," Alex said, remembering the scene, "and she was smiling."

"I wish I had been there."

"Just before the time things were turning around, you lost faith."

"Can you blame me? I saw the way things were going, and that was downhill. Alex, I was the cause of the whole thing! I felt like some rotten limb attached to an otherwise healthy body. I had to be cut off from you. I've been poison all along, Alex. That's what I've been, and today I finally faced that truth."

"You know, whenever I thought back to what my father lived through with Tad and Salina, I saw all the suffering he went through. I saw what he lost, and what they lost. Frankly, I thought he was a fool. But I'd forgotten something about him: I'd forgotten that there wasn't any bitterness or regret in his face afterward. All of that negative stuff was coming out of me because I simply didn't have the perspective to see clearly how things were."

"I know how things are, Alex."

"No, you don't know." He walked over to her. "Do you know why regret never touched my father? It was because his heart was whole. He loved, and that goes beyond mere legal integrity. He did what he did because he loved, and nothing of material value could compare to that sense of love he had found inside himself.

"I didn't really understand all of this until today. It was just when I thought we'd lost, that it finally hit me. When you do anything out of love, you can't ever lose. So I kept going just when I was ready to throw in the towel. Then Dominique came around. It was a pretty spectacular finish. The jury was out for only twelve minutes. The verdict was unanimous—not guilty. I wish you'd been there, Mara."

"So do I." Her hand touched his cheek. But then, quickly, she let it fall to her side. "You won the trial, but your election—"

"Didn't you hear a word I just said?" Alex interrupted, and this time he looked angry.

Mara was quiet. "Something about love, I think."

"You got it. So?" he asked, his eyes moving to the suitcase.

Slowly she turned around, seeing the suitcase, seeing the telegram from her mother.

"I think," Mara said, her eyes filling with tears, "I think after I unpack, I'm going to get rid of that old suitcase. I don't need it anymore."

Chapter 13

IT WAS SEVEN IN THE EVENING AND ON ANY OTHER DAY she would probably have been downstairs at that time, busily supervising the staff of Salina's Place and solving what purported to be that evening's imminent crises. But this was Mardi Gras, and instead, she was luxuriating in bed.

She lay on her back, her hair spilling against the pillow and falling over her shoulders. She felt sensuous, a lazy and pampered woman. It was a good feeling to be devoid for once of her ingrained work-ethic guilt. Her clothes still lay where they had been dropped item by item along a trail leading from her bedroom door over to her bed.

That had been when? she wondered. Two hours ago? Alex had surprised her, arriving early. He had herded her away from her work downstairs, and carrying two large plastic garment bags over his shoulder, had maneuvered her up the stairs. All the while, he laid aside her every argument by muttering low, suggestive phrases of what he would like to do to her.

246

Then, wonderfully, he had done them all.

Mara sighed. Yes, there was something to be said for being in love with a refined Southern gentleman. But there was something else to be said for being in love with a refined Southern gentleman who had the good sense to abandon good manners in private.

Mara squirmed a bit beneath the covers, shifting her position slightly so that her leg brushed against Alex's. He slept beside her, his breathing regular and deep, a man whose physical needs had been happily satiated.

As for her, a full half-hour later, she was still experiencing the aftershocks of her own fulfillment. The merest thought of what they had shared together brought a reminding rush of heat to her pelvic region, and tiny pleasurable tremors coursed through her body.

On the nightstand, the phone rang, spoiling the mood.

Alex mumbled and turned over, burying his face against her bare breast. She shivered slightly from the moist heat of his breath.

The telephone rang again.

"You going to get that, or what?" Alex asked.

No, she didn't want to get the phone. She wanted this to continue. "Ummm . . . I've got it." Mara shifted position. She wanted to make love again, not answer a damned telephone.

"Get rid of them," Alex said, reaching around and cupping her breast.

The phone rang for the fourth time.

Mara crawled over Alex to get the phone, which was on his side. As she did, Alex maneuvered himself up against his pillows, and leaning over, bit her lightly on her bare rump.

"Ow . . ." Mara said while lifting the receiver.

The connection crackled just slightly, Long distance. "Mara?" came the voice on the other end of the phone.

"Domi!"

"What's happening over there? An 'ow'? Not a hello anymore?"

Mara wriggled away from Alex, who was doing his best to get her to hang up. His distractions were of a predominantly lascivious nature. They were also effective.

Trying to stifle her laughter, talk on the phone, and protect her body from Alex, she said, "I stubbed my toe."

"Why don't I believe that? Say hello to Alex for me," Dominique said warmly.

"How was the Paris opening?"

"Thought you'd never ask. Naturally, I was a smash. Papers say I'm the new white Billie Holiday."

"We miss you."

"I'm glad," Dominique said. "Because I'm coming home. In two weeks from now, you will see my famous face at Salina's. I am tired of living in these posh five-star European hotels and being adored by the rich, beautiful international set in Europe. A woman can only tolerate so much luxury. Otherwise, the champagne begins to rust one's soul. I would like some crawfish, *ma chérie*." Dominique paused. In a choked voice she said, "Charles has been convicted. Did you know? For murder. He is in prison for life. They have told me he will never get out. And the others . . . they are in prison, too. I am safe, ah . . . at last."

"I know, we heard. Your job's here, waiting. It's always here for you. I think we can even manage some soul food, too," Mara said, smiling as Alex began to work his tongue down her spine. "Uh, listen, Domi, I've got to run now. That pain in my toe needs fixing."

"What did she say?" Alex asked as she returned the phone to its cradle.

"I think the last thing was something very naughty,

because she said it in French." Laughing, Mara said, "I think I caught the gist of it, though. It's kind of international." Slipping her hands beneath the covers, she caressed him. Pleased with her power over him, she said, "Don't you ever, ever get enough?"

Moaning softly, Alex let his eyes fall closed. "Umm . . . what do you think?"

"That answer requires some research," she replied, and began to inch her body down beneath the covers. "It requires some exploration," she said suggestively. "It's just so very difficult to think of you as virgin territory."

"Then don't think," Alex said. "Don't think." He arched his pelvis, intimating an alternative to thought.

But he was wrong that she should not think. Sometimes, letting one's mind rush off on its own was to be avoided. The mind generally had a habit of seeking dark places better left unvisited. But that wasn't the case here. Mara wanted her mind to escort her on a tour—a grand tour—of a recent past that was all brightness.

Alex's triumph in court had hit the papers that next day. Not just the local papers, but the national papers, too. LaPierre must have gone crazy. The three of them, Alex, Dominique and Mara, had laughed until they were crying thinking of LaPierre and Grant Forbes and all the rest of that nasty little bunch lamenting the sudden change in Alex's fortunes, which brought about a corresponding change in their own. As a countermove, LaPierre must have attempted a rally in his boy's favor, but only managed to plant a few feeble stories about his candidate for D.A. in the center pages of various local newspapers. In the meantime, features on Alex blazed on all the front covers.

The story Mara had given the Washington reporter broke the day following the trial's conclusion. The paper arrived special delivery for her at six in the morning. She brought it in to Alex with a kiss, a cup of coffee and of course the whole confession of her duplicity.

"Thank heaven," she had said, "my instincts were on target."

Alex shook his head. "You play pretty fast and loose with my life, don't you?"

He was only joking and she knew it. She knew he was proud of her for having taken the initiative. "Our life," she corrected. "Our life, Alex."

Before they had even finished their coffee, the telephone began to ring. *Time* and *Newsweek* were vying for exclusives on the rebel attorney from New Orleans.

In November, Alex had taken the election in a clean sweep against LaPierre's candidate. It wasn't even a contest. There was a lot of scurrying around after that. Members of the local ruling class who had snubbed Alex as the dark horse, soon to lose, must have suffered from writer's cramp. Invitations to parties and letters of congratulation on his victory came by bushel baskets. Mara thought some of them made lovely paper airplanes. Lately there had even been talk about something national for Alex.

So, yes, sometimes it was nice to think, and sometimes it became quite impossible, Mara discovered, as Alex trailed his fingers along and up the inside of her thigh. It was possible to do only one thing at a time, and thinking came in a poor second to lovemaking.

Afterward, it was Mara who drifted off to sleep. She awoke to the dark. The digital clock on her nightstand read 9:15 P.M. Beside her, the bed was empty. She could hear the sound of water running in the bathroom where Alex was bathing. Outside, a racket had started up—shouts and what sounded like gunshots.

Alarmed, Mara slipped out of the bed, throwing on a

robe as she ran to a French door to see what the trouble might be.

It was not cold, but she shivered. Directly beneath the balcony, swinging, striding, dancing down the street, came the throngs.

She relaxed, grew warm again.

Mardi Gras. No guns, only fireworks and high spirits. That was all.

Men in clown costumes were pressing against women dressed as riverboat dance-hall queens. A giant chicken collided with a dragon. Mara laughed. She was feeling good, and was about to call out to Alex to watch with her, when the happiness vanished.

There beneath the balcony was a papier-mâché creature holding a club in its hand. Its head was raised, watching her watch it. With bulging eyes and a protruding tongue that curled and uncurled, it waggled its great head at her.

She stepped back into the shadows, and the creature took a lunge forward, its club swinging in her direction.

Suddenly it was not Mardi Gras. It was a dark night many years ago and an ugly crowd was milling below the balcony. They were drinking and waving torches and pieces of wood. All the terror of that long-ago night filled her as if through someone else's memory. Outside, a bottle falling to the pavement took on the impression of panes of glass shattering.

Mara caught the flicker of something bright behind the creature.

A small white ghost appeared. It moved in erratic, quick hops around the monster's ponderous and frightening dignity.

Almost by design, it seemed to have captured the monster's attention, pulling the horrifying eyes away from Mara, who stood frozen in fear.

Twirling and skittering, trying to pass the monster that now blocked its path, the creation in sheets suddenly broke free. Maneuvering itself directly before the fearsome beast, it jumped into the air, waving its hands about.

The monster raised its club as if to strike, but hesitated, as if stunned by the ghost's nerve to challenge its might.

In that second, the ghost scampered gaily away, running with a crazy, freewheeling, energetic joy until Mara could no longer see it.

Smiling, she turned from the balcony, no longer cold.

Alex was in the bedroom, a towel wrapped around his waist. He was brushing his thick black hair in the mirror. She could see his eyes watching her in the reflection.

The plastic garment bags containing the costumes it had been Alex's duty to select for the party that night were empty, and spilled out from the top of the waste can where Alex had stuffed them.

"So what am I going to be tonight? A dancing pickle? A Martian lady, a—"

But she stopped.

There, on the bed, was a wedding gown. On it was a small velvet box, opened to display a diamond.

Mara looked across the room at Alex, who was brushing off the jacket to a groom's suit.

"Hey," Mara said, "costumes like these are taking a big chance, you know." She was smiling through her tears.

"I'm game if you are."

Mara nodded, and then she gave a shout and rushed into his arms to be swung around.

Outside, beyond the balcony, a horn blasted and laughter rose up to fill the room.

WIN

a fabulous $50,000 diamond jewelry collection

ENTER

by filling out the coupon below and mailing it by September 30, 1985

Send entries to:

U.S.
Silhouette Diamond Sweepstakes
P.O. Box 779
Madison Square Station
New York, NY 10159

Canada
Silhouette Diamond Sweepstakes
Suite 191
238 Davenport Road
Toronto, Ontario M5R 1J6

SILHOUETTE DIAMOND SWEEPSTAKES ENTRY FORM

☐ Mrs. ☐ Miss ☐ Ms ☐ Mr.

NAME   (please print)

ADDRESS   APT. #

CITY

STATE/(PROV.)

ZIP/(POSTAL CODE)

RTD-A-1

RULES FOR SILHOUETTE DIAMOND SWEEPSTAKES

OFFICIAL RULES — NO PURCHASE NECESSARY

1. Silhouette Diamond Sweepstakes is open to Canadian (except Quebec) and United States residents 18 years or older at the time of entry. Employees and immediate families of the publishers of Silhouette, their affiliates, retailers, distributors, printers, agencies and RONALD SMILEY INC. are excluded.

2. To enter, print your name and address on the official entry form or on a 3" x 5" slip of paper. You may enter as often as you choose, but each envelope must contain only one entry. Mail entries first class in Canada to Silhouette Diamond Sweepstakes, Suite 191, 238 Davenport Road, Toronto, Ontario M5R 1J6. In the United States, mail to Silhouette Diamond Sweepstakes, P.O. Box 779, Madison Square Station, New York, NY 10159. Entries must be postmarked between February 1 and September 30, 1985. Silhouette is not responsible for lost, late or misdirected mail.

3. First Prize of diamond jewelry, consisting of a necklace, ring, bracelet and earrings will be awarded. Approximate retail value is $50,000 U.S./$62,500 Canadian. Second Prize of 100 Silhouette Home Reader Service Subscriptions will be awarded. Approximate retail value of each is $162.00 U.S./$180.00 Canadian. No substitution, duplication, cash redemption or transfer of prizes will be permitted. Odds of winning depend upon the number of valid entries received. One prize to a family or household. Income taxes, other taxes and insurance on First Prize are the sole responsibility of the winners.

4. Winners will be selected under the supervision of RONALD SMILEY INC., an independent judging organization whose decisions are final, by random drawings from valid entries postmarked by September 30, 1985, and received no later than October 7, 1985. Entry in this sweepstakes indicates your awareness of the Official Rules. Winners who are residents of Canada must answer correctly a time-related arithmetical skill-testing question to qualify. First Prize winner will be notified by certified mail and must submit an Affidavit of Compliance within 10 days of notification. Returned Affidavits or prizes that are refused or undeliverable will result in alternative names being randomly drawn. Winners may be asked for use of their name and photo at no additional compensation.

5. For a First Prize winner list, send a stamped self-addressed envelope postmarked by September 30, 1985. In Canada, mail to Silhouette Diamond Contest Winner, Suite 309, 238 Davenport Road, Toronto, Ontario M5R 1J6. In the United States, mail to Silhouette Diamond Contest Winner, P.O. Box 182, Bowling Green Station, New York, NY 10274. This offer will appear in Silhouette publications and at participating retailers. Offer void in Quebec and subject to all Federal, Provincial, State and Municipal laws and regulations and wherever prohibited or restricted by law.

READERS' COMMENTS ON
SILHOUETTE INTIMATE MOMENTS:

"About a month ago a friend loaned me my first Silhouette. I was thoroughly surprised as well as totally addicted. Last week I read a Silhouette Intimate Moments and I was even more pleased. They are the best romance series novels I have ever read. They give much more depth to the plot, characters, and the story is fundamentally realistic. They incorporate tasteful sex scenes, which is a must, especially in the 1980's. I only hope you can publish them fast enough."

S.B.*, Lees Summit, MO

"After noticing the attractive covers on the new line of Silhouette Intimate Moments, I decided to read the inside and discovered that this new line was more in the line of books that I like to read. I do want to say I enjoyed the books because they are so realistic and a lot more truthful than so many romance books today."

J.C., Onekama, MI

"I would like to compliment you on your new line of books. I will continue to purchase all of the Silhouette Intimate Moments. They are your best line of books that I have had the pleasure of reading."

S.M., Billings, MT

*names available on request